Praise for *N* uthor

MALLERY

"If you want a story that will both tug on your heartstrings and tickle your funny bone, Mallery is the author for you!"
—*RT Book Reviews* on *Only His*

"When it comes to heartfelt contemporary romance, Mallery is in a class by herself."
—*RT Book Reviews* on *Only Yours*

"An adorable, outspoken heroine and an intense hero...set the sparks flying in Mallery's latest lively, comic, and touching family-centered story."
—*Library Journal* on *Only Yours*

"Mallery...excels at creating varied, well-developed characters and an emotion-packed story gently infused with her trademark wit and humor."
One of the Top 10 Romances of 2011!
—*Booklist* on *Only Mine*

"Mallery's prose is luscious and provocative."
—*Publishers Weekly*

"Susan Mallery's gift for writing humor and tenderness make all her books true gems."
—*RT Book Reviews*

"Romance novels don't get much better than Mallery's expert blend of emotional nuance, humor and superb storytelling."
—*Booklist*

Also available from Susan Mallery and HQN Books

Only His
Only Yours
Only Mine
Finding Perfect
Almost Perfect
Chasing Perfect
Hot on Her Heels
Straight from the Hip
Lip Service
Under Her Skin
Sweet Trouble
Sweet Spot
Sweet Talk
Accidentally Yours
Tempting
Sizzling
Irresistible
Delicious
Falling for Gracie
Someone Like You

Watch for more Fool's Gold books, coming soon!

Summer Nights
All Summer Long

SUSAN MALLERY

Summer Days

Recycling programs
for this product may
not exist in your area.

ISBN-13: 978-0-373-77683-2

SUMMER DAYS

This edition published by arrangement with Harlequin Books S.A.

For questions and comments about the quality of this book please contact us at Customer_eCare@Harlequin.ca.

www.Harlequin.com

Printed in U.S.A.

This book is for Kristi.
Here's what she asked that the dedication say:

I'd like to dedicate this to my mother, Doris, for teaching me the fun and value of reading and always having a good book for me. To my dear friend, Ann, who exchanges books with me and can laugh with me for no good reason and then do it again! To my husband, Kevin, you are the love of my life, keep me laughing and never keep me from a good read. Then to my dear daughter, Julie, who inspires me and I am so proud of you. I love you all, thank you for all the fun and laughter and the love of a good hat. oxox Kristi

Summer Days

CHAPTER ONE

ONLY IN FOOL'S GOLD would a Mercedes be brought to a stop by a goat. Rafe Stryker turned off the engine of the powerful sedan and climbed out. The goat in the middle of the road surveyed him with a confident gleam in her dark eyes. If he hadn't known better, he would have sworn she was telling him this was her road and if anyone was going to back down in this battle of wills, it would be him.

"Damn goats," he muttered, looking around for whomever owned the wayward animal. Instead, he saw a few trees, a broken fence line and, beyond all that, mountains soaring up to the heavens. Some would describe this as God's country. Rafe knew that God, being smart and all knowing, would have nothing to do with Fool's Gold.

Hard to believe that a three hour drive west would return Rafe to San Francisco—land of fine dining, high-rise buildings and beautiful women. It was where he belonged. Not here, on the outskirts of some town he'd promised himself he would never set foot in again. And yet he had returned, drawn by the one person he could never turn his back on—his mother.

Swearing under his breath, he eyed the goat. He

would guess she weighed about a hundred and twenty pounds, give or take. While he'd spent the past eighteen years doing his best to forget his time in Fool's Gold, the lessons he'd learned on the Castle Ranch lived on. He figured if he'd been able to wrestle an adult steer as a scrawny fourteen-year-old, he should be able to take a goat now. Or at the very least, pick her up and move her to the side of the road.

He lowered his gaze to her hooves, wondering how sharp they would be and what they would do to his suit. He rested his elbow on the roof of his car and pinched the bridge of his nose. If his mother hadn't sounded so broken on the phone, he would turn around and go back home. In San Francisco he had a staff, minions even. People who would take care of things like goats in the road.

He chuckled, imagining his starchy assistant facing down a goat. Ms. Jennings, a fifty-something powerhouse with an innate ability to make the most successful of executives feel incompetent, would most likely stare the goat into submission.

"You found her!"

Rafe turned toward the voice and saw a woman jogging toward him. She had a rope in one hand and what looked like lettuce in the other.

"I was so worried. Athena lives to get into trouble. I can't find a gate lock that will keep her contained. She's smart. Aren't you, baby girl?"

The woman approached the goat and patted her on the back. The goat moved toward her, like a dog seeking affection. She took the lettuce and the rope around her neck with equal acceptance.

The woman glanced back at him. "Hi. I'm Heidi Simpson."

She was maybe five-nine, with blond hair she wore in braided pigtails. A cotton shirt tucked into jeans showed him she was leggy and curvy, a combination that normally appealed. Just not today. Not when he still had to deal with his mother and a town he despised.

"Rafe Stryker," he said.

The woman—Heidi—stared at him, her green eyes widening as she took a single step back. Her full mouth trembled slightly and she lost her smile.

"Stryker," she whispered and swallowed. "May is your—"

"Mother. How do you know her?"

Heidi took another step back. "She's, ah, at the ranch right now. Talking to my grandfather. There seems to be a mix-up."

"Mix-up?" He used what Ms. Jennings referred to as his scary, serial-killer voice. "Is that how you'd describe what happened? I was thinking more along the lines of fraud and theft. Felony theft."

THIS WAS BAD, HEIDI THOUGHT, wishing she could simply run for it. Not that she wasn't one to face her problems. But in this case, she would feel a lot better facing them around other people, rather than on a deserted road. She eyed Athena, wondering if the goat would protect her, then decided probably not. Athena would be more interested in getting a taste of Rafe Stryker's well-cut, obviously expensive suit.

The man standing in front of her looked seriously pissed. Pissed enough to plow her over with his big car and keep going. He was tall, with dark hair and eyes, and right now he looked angry enough to crush her with his bare hands. She had a feeling he was strong enough to do it, too.

She drew in a breath. Okay, maybe he wouldn't crush her, but he wanted to do something. She could read that in his brown-black eyes.

"I know what you're thinking," she began.

"I doubt that."

His voice was low, silky and made her feel unsettled. As though she couldn't predict what was going to happen next and, whatever it was, it was going to be bad.

"My grandfather overstepped his bounds," she began, thinking it wasn't the first time Glen had given in to his "ask forgiveness rather than permission" philosophy of life. "He didn't mean to hurt anyone."

"He stole from my mother."

Heidi winced. "You're close to her?" She shook her head. "Never mind. Stupid question." If Rafe didn't take care of his mother, he wouldn't be here now. Not that she was surprised. From what she could tell, May was a lovely woman who had been very understanding about the mistake. Although not understanding enough to keep her son out of it.

"Glen, my grandfather, has a close friend who was diagnosed with cancer. Harvey needed treatment, didn't have insurance, and Glen wanted to help." Heidi did her best to smile, but her lips didn't feel as if they were cooperating. "So, um, he got the idea of selling part of the ranch. To your mother."

"The ranch that belongs to you."

"Technically." Her name was the one on the bank loan. She hadn't done the math, but she would guess she had in the neighborhood of seventy thousand dollars in equity. The rest of the ranch was tied up in her mortgage.

"He took two hundred and fifty thousand dollars from my mother, and in return she owns nothing."

"Kind of."

"Your grandfather has no way to pay her back."

"He gets social security and we have some savings."

Rafe's gaze moved from her to Athena and back. "How much in savings?"

Defeat made her shoulders sag. "Twenty-five hundred dollars."

"Please move the goat. I'm going to the ranch."

Heidi stiffened her spine. "What are you going to do?"

"Have your grandfather arrested."

"You can't!" Glen was the only family she had. "He's an old man."

"I'm sure the judge will take that into account when setting bail."

"He didn't mean to hurt anyone."

Rafe was unmoved by her plea. "My family grew up here, Ms. Simpson. My mother was the housekeeper. The old man who owned the ranch paid her next to nothing. At times there wasn't enough money for her to feed her four children. But she hung on because he promised to leave her the ranch when he died."

Heidi didn't like this story. She just knew it had a bad ending.

"Like your grandfather, he lied. When he finally died, the ranch went to distant relatives back east." His dark eyes turned into lasers that seemed to bore into her, promising untold punishment. "No one is going to screw my mother out of this ranch twice."

Oh, no! It was worse than she'd imagined. Much worse. "You have to understand. My grandfather would never hurt anyone. He's a great guy."

"He's the man who stole two hundred and fifty thousand dollars from my mother, Ms. Simpson. The rest is simply window dressing. Now, move your… goat."

Unable to think of what else to say, Heidi stepped to the side of the road. Athena trotted along with her. Rafe got in his car and drove away. The only thing missing from his angry departure was a cloud of dust. However, the road was paved and well maintained by the city. One of the advantages of living in Fool's Gold.

She waited until he'd gone past, then turned toward

the ranch and started to run. Athena kept up easily, for once not insisting on extending her time of freedom.

"Did you hear that?" Heidi asked, her athletic shoes pounding on the pavement. "That man is really mad at us."

Athena trotted along, apparently unconcerned about Glen's fate.

"You'll be sorry if we have to sell you to pay back May Stryker," Heidi muttered, then wished she hadn't.

All her life she'd only wanted one thing. A home. A real home with a roof and a foundation, hooked up to sewer and water and electricity. Something most people took for granted. But she'd grown up moving from town to town, the rhythm of her days defined by the carnival where her grandfather worked.

When she'd found the Castle Ranch, she'd fallen instantly and madly in love. With the land, the old house and especially the nearby town of Fool's Gold. She had a herd of eight goats, uncounted feral cows and nearly a thousand acres of land. She'd started a business making goat cheese and goat-milk soap. She sold goat milk and goat fertilizer. There were natural caves where she could age her cheese. This was her home and she wasn't giving it up for anything.

But she might have to give it up for somebody. Glen. Who'd sold a part of what he didn't own to a woman with a very angry son.

RAFE PULLED IN NEXT TO HIS mother's car and parked. The ranch looked worse than he'd remembered—the fence lines more theory than substance, the house sagging and in need of paint. He could think of a thousand places he would rather be than here. Leaving wasn't an option. Not until he got this mess cleaned up.

He climbed out of his car and looked around. The sky was blue—typical for California. That impossible color movie makers loved and songwriters sang about. In the distance, the Sierra Nevada mountains rose toward heaven. When he was a kid, he'd stared at those mountains, willing himself to be on the other side. Anywhere that wasn't here would have been better. At fifteen, he'd been trapped. Funny how all these years later he was back and just as stuck.

The front door to the house opened and his mother stepped out. May Stryker might have been in her mid-fifties, but she was still beautiful, with shiny black hair that fell to her shoulders and a tall, lithe build. Rafe had inherited his height and coloring from her, although, according to his mother, his personality came from his father. May was a softhearted nurturer who wanted to take care of the world. Rafe would rest a lot easier when he'd conquered it.

"You came," May said, crossing to him and smiling. "I knew you would. Oh, Rafe, isn't it wonderful to be back?"

Sure, he thought grimly. Maybe later they could stop by hell for a marshmallow roast. "Mom, what's going on? You weren't very clear in your message." What he meant was she hadn't explained how she'd gotten in this situation in the first place.

All she'd said was that she'd bought a ranch, and that the man was now telling her she couldn't have it. Mostly because he didn't own it. Fraud before noon. Or grand theft. Either way, it was going to be a long day.

"Everything is fine," his mother said, moving toward him. "Glen and I have been talking and..."

"Glen?"

The smile widened. "The man who sold me the ranch." She gave a little laugh. "Apparently he had a friend who was sick and—"

"I've heard this part," he said, interrupting.

"From who?"

"Heidi."

"Oh, you met her. Isn't she wonderful? She raises goats here on the ranch. They've been here nearly a year, and they're just wonderful people. Glen is Heidi's grandfather. She lost her parents when she was little and he raised her." May sighed. "They're a wonderful family."

He didn't like the sound of that. "Mother," he began.

She shook her head. "I'm not one of your unruly clients, Rafe. You can't intimidate me. I'm sorry I called you and asked you to come all the way out here, but I have everything under control."

"I doubt that."

Both eyebrows rose. "Excuse me?"

"You're not the only one involved. I signed the paperwork, too. Remember?"

"You can unsign it. I'll take care of this. Now, go back to San Francisco."

Before he could explain there was no "unsigning" a legal document, the front door opened again and an older man stepped out. He was taller than May, with white hair and sparkling blue eyes. He winked at May, gave Rafe a charming smile and hurried forward.

"There you are," the man said, holding out his hand as he approached. "Glen Simpson. Nice to meet you. I understand there's been a mix-up with your lovely mother here, but I want to assure you, we're going to work it all out."

Rafe doubted that. "You have the two hundred and fifty thousand dollars you stole from her?"

"Rafe!"

He ignored his mother and continued to stare at Glen.

"Ah, not exactly," the older man admitted. "But we'll get it. Or work out something with May. There's no reason for any of this to be difficult, don't you agree?"

"No." Rafe drew his phone out of his shirt pocket and turned away from his mother and Glen. Before pushing the number, he loosened his tie. Then he hit speed dial.

"I told you not to go there," a familiar voice said by way of greeting.

"I pay you for legal counsel," Rafe muttered. "Not to say, 'I told you so.'"

Dante Jefferson, his lawyer and business partner, chuckled. "You get the 'I told you so' for free."

"Lucky me."

"How bad is it?"

Rafe looked around at the familiar acres of land. He'd grown up here, at least until he was fifteen. He'd worked his ass off here, had gone hungry here.

"It's bad. I need you to drive over," Rafe said. He'd filled Dante in on what he knew before he'd left town that morning. "There's no money to pay her back and, from what I can tell, the old man isn't the owner of the ranch."

Dante snorted. "Did he think she wouldn't notice she wasn't getting a ranch after paying two hundred and fifty thousand dollars and agreeing to a schedule to pay the rest?"

"Apparently."

"I've never been to Fool's Gold," Dante said.

"Everyone's luck goes bad eventually."

Dante chuckled. "Your mother loves the town."

"My mother also believes there are space aliens in Area 51."

"That's why I like her so much. Did I tell you signing documents without reading them would get you into trouble? Did you listen?"

Rafe tightened his grip on the phone. "This is you helping?"

"In my own way. I'll call the local police and have..." There was the sound of rustling papers. "...Glen Simpson picked up. He'll be in custody before I hit town. I should be there by six. Between now and then, don't do anything I'll regret."

Not a promise Rafe was willing to make, he thought as he hung up. He turned, only to find his mother rushing toward him.

"Rafe! You're not arresting Glen."

The old guy looked less charming and more pale. As Rafe watched, he swallowed and started backing toward the house.

"Mom, this guy took money from you by making you think you were buying a ranch. He doesn't own the ranch, so he stole your money and he has no way to pay it back."

May's mouth twisted. "If you're going to make it sound like that—"

He cut her off. "It is like that."

"I don't understand why you have to be this way."

He glanced back at the house, expecting to see Glen slinking inside. But the old guy had only made it as far as the porch. Maybe he was going to try and bluff his way out. Rafe didn't mind a good fight, but he preferred a more formidable opponent.

His gaze moved from the building to the yard. There were flowers—different from the ones his mother had planted, but just as colorful. A big sign offered goat milk, goat cheese and goat manure for sale. He fleetingly hoped they were kept in separate containers and on different parts of the property.

Speaking of goats, he could see a couple beyond the fence by the house. There was a big horse by the barn. No steers, he thought, remembering having to deal with them when he was a kid.

There had been good times here, he admitted to himself. Moments when he'd had fun with his brothers and sister. While his father had taught him and Shane to ride, Rafe had been the one to teach Clay and later Evangeline. Rafe had stepped into his father's shoes after the man had died. Or he'd tried—after all, he'd been only eight. He could still remember how long it had taken to realize his daddy was never coming home again and that it was now all up to him.

The woman—Heidi—jogged up to the house, the goat trotting at her side like a well-trained dog.

"Glen, are you all right?" she asked, slightly out of breath. "What's going on?"

"It's going to be fine," Glen told her, looking calm for a man about to go to jail.

"It's not fine," May said firmly. "My son is being difficult."

"Not much of a surprise," Heidi muttered, turning to him. "I know you're angry, but we can come to terms. If you'd just listen and be reasonable."

"Good luck," May said with a sigh. "Rafe doesn't believe in being reasonable."

He shrugged. "Everyone has a flaw."

"You think this is funny?" Heidi demanded, her green eyes snapping with outrage and fear. "We're talking about my family."

"And mine."

A car pulled in behind his. Rafe saw the city seal for Fool's Gold and a sign, Fool's Gold Police.

A woman in her forties got out. She wore a uniform and sunglasses. The name tag read Police Chief Barns. Rafe was impressed. Dante hadn't just made calls, he'd gone to the top.

Still clutching the goat, Heidi moved toward the woman. Heidi smiled, although her lips trembled, and despite his annoyance at her and the situation, he acknowledged she looked as innocent as a milkmaid. He glanced at the goat. Make that a goat maid.

"Police Chief Barns, I'm Heidi Simpson."

"I know who you are." The police chief pulled a smartphone out of her pocket and scrolled through the screen. "I'm looking for Rafe Stryker."

"That's me." Rafe moved toward her. "Thank you for coming out here personally."

"Your lawyer insisted." The police chief didn't sound pleased about the fact. "So, what's going on?"

"Glen Simpson claimed to be selling the Castle Ranch to my mother for two hundred and fifty thousand dollars. He took her money and gave her fraudulent documents to sign. He doesn't have ownership of the land, never opened escrow and has spent the money. Despite his claims of wanting to work things out, he has no way of paying her back."

May made a soft, distressed sound in the back of her throat. "My son is clear on the facts, but he's leaving out an important point."

"Which is?" Chief Barns asked.

"That there's no need for this to involve you and the law."

"I'd like to agree with you, ma'am, but your son here has filed an official complaint. I don't suppose you can tell me that he has no legal claim on any of this? Am I getting my hopes up here for nothing?"

"I signed the documents, as well," Rafe told her. Which was his own damn fault. "My mother may believe in Mr. Simpson's innate goodness, but I do not."

"He's not a bad man," Heidi insisted.

The police chief turned to Glen. "You have anything to say about this?"

Glen looked up at the sky for a moment and back at Chief Barns. "Nope."

"Then I'm going to have to take you in."

"You can't." Heidi physically moved between the chief and her grandfather, the goat still at her side. "Please don't. My grandfather isn't a young man. It's jail. He could die in there."

"It's not Alcatraz," Rafe told her. "It's a city jail in a small town. Not exactly hard time."

"You know this from personal experience?" Heidi asked.

"No."

"Then stay out of it." Heidi's eyes filled with tears as she returned her attention to the police chief. "There has to be something you can do."

"You'll need to talk to the judge," Chief Barns said, her voice surprisingly kind. "Your friend here is right. It's not a bad jail. He'll be fine."

"I'm not her friend."

"He's not my friend."

Heidi and Rafe looked at each other.

"Can I kick him?" Heidi asked the police chief. "Just once, but really hard?"

"Maybe later."

Rafe knew better than to protest. The way the two women were glaring at him, getting off with a single kick would be a light sentence.

He wanted to point out that he hadn't done anything wrong here, that Glen was the bad guy. But this wasn't a time for logic. He knew his mother well enough to guess that, and he doubted Heidi was all that much different.

Glen didn't put up a fight. He was quickly handcuffed and put in the back of the car.

"I'll be there as soon as I can," Heidi said. "To bail you out."

"We won't be able to set bail until the morning," Chief Barns told her. "But you're welcome to visit. Don't worry. He'll be fine."

The chief got in her car and drove away. Heidi led the goat away, and May turned on her son.

"How could you arrest him?"

Rafe thought about pointing out that he hadn't arrested Glen—he'd only arranged to have it done. A detail she wouldn't appreciate.

"He stole from you, Mom. You lost this ranch once. I'm not going to watch you lose it again."

Her anger visibly faded. “Oh, Rafe. You’ve always been so good to me. But I can take care of myself.”

“You just got swindled out of two hundred and fifty thousand dollars.”

May crossed to him. “If you’re going to bring that up.”

He put his arm around her and kissed the top of her head. Despite her height, he was still a good half foot taller.

“You know you make me crazy, right?” he asked.

She hugged him back. “Yes, but I don’t do it on purpose.”

“I know.”

She looked up at him. “Now what?”

“Now we get your ranch.”

CHAPTER TWO

HEIDI STOOD IN THE MIDDLE of Fool's Gold, not sure what to do first. Glen needed her help, and she needed a lawyer. Not that she had any money to pay one, but that was a problem for another time. Right now, the pressing issue was getting her grandfather out of jail.

She turned in a slow circle, seeing the sign for Morgan's Books and the Starbucks where she hung out with her friends. There was Jo's Bar, but no large banner proclaiming "excellent and free legal advice here!"

Pulling out her phone, she scrolled until she found Charlie's number, then sent a quick text: *Urgent. Can we talk?*

Seconds later, came the reply: *Sure. At the station.*

"The station" being the city fire station. Heidi left her truck where it was and walked the short three blocks to the firehouse.

The firehouse was in the oldest part of town. It was a two-story brick-and-wood structure with big garage doors facing the street. They stood open in the warm April afternoon. Charlie Dixon was waiting by the red fire engine she drove.

"What's up?" she asked as Heidi hurried forward.

"There's a problem with Glen."

Charlie, a tall, competent woman who had never met a man she couldn't beat at anything, put her strong hands on her narrow hips and raised her eyebrows.

"He's your grandfather. How much trouble could he be in?"

"You have no idea."

Heidi quickly brought her friend up to date on Glen, the perky widow he'd swindled, the mysterious and ruthless Rafe Stryker, and the fact that Glen was now sitting in the Fool's Gold jail.

Charlie swore. "It's so like a man to make all this mess," she grumbled. "Glen seriously sold someone your ranch?"

Heidi sighed. "There was paperwork and everything."

This wasn't the first time her grandfather had flirted with the wrong side of the law, but generally he kept his scams smaller and avoided the felony category. For the past few years, all she'd had to worry about was his propensity to have a woman in every city. For a guy in his seventies, he got a lot of action.

"I need to get him out of there," Heidi said. "He's the only family I have."

"I know. Okay, stay calm. I mean that. Fool's Gold jail isn't exactly grim. He'll be fine there. As to getting him out—" She looked at Heidi. "Don't take this wrong, but do you have any money?"

Heidi winced as she thought about the sad little balance in her checking account. "I've put everything I have into my goats."

"There's a mortgage on the ranch?"

"A big one."

Charlie gave her a quick hug. "Living the American dream."

"I was," Heidi told her, appreciating the physical support. "Until this happened."

She didn't mind making the monthly payments to the bank. They were a sign of stability, proof she had a home, something she would one day own outright.

"I know a lawyer," Charlie said. "She takes on pro bono cases from time to time. Let me call and talk to her, then I'll send you over."

"You think she'll help me?"

Charlie grinned. "She adores me. I used to date her son. When we broke up, he got involved with some bimbo, got her pregnant and had to get married. While he's wildly in love with his new bride and family, Trisha thinks of me as the one who got away."

Charlie was the least feminine woman Heidi knew. She wore her hair short, dressed for comfort rather than fashion and would deck anyone who came at her with mascara. But that didn't mean she wasn't attractive, in a low-maintenance kind of way. Heidi had seen guys around town watching Charlie. As if they suspected she was the kind of woman who was hard to tame, but once loyal, would be a wild ride for life.

"His loss," Heidi told her.

"You're a good friend."

"So are you. I didn't know who else to talk to about Glen."

She had other friends, but she'd known instinctively that Charlie would cut to the heart of the problem, help sort it out and then move on without making a fuss.

"We'll get this fixed."

Heidi hung on to that promise. Her parents had died when she was a toddler. She didn't remember them. Glen had stepped in to raise her. From that moment on, they'd been a team. No matter what he'd done, Heidi would stand by her grandfather. Even if that meant taking on the likes of Rafe Stryker.

According to Charlie, Trisha Wynn should be in her sixties, but she looked forty and dressed as if she were twenty-five. Her dress—a pink-and-gold wrap with a plunging neckline—clung to impressive curves. Her heels were high, her makeup heavy and her earrings jangled.

"Any friend of Charlie's," Trisha said by way of greeting, waving Heidi into her small but comfortable office. "So Glen got himself into some trouble. I can't say I'm surprised."

Heidi sank into the comfortable leather visitor's chair. "You know my grandfather?"

Trisha winked. "We had a long weekend together last fall up at the resort. A suite with a fireplace, plenty of room service. I generally avoid older men, but for Glen I made an exception. It was worth it."

Heidi did her best to smile and nod, when she really wanted to stick her fingers into her ears and start humming. She never wanted to hear the details about her grandfather's personal life, and right now it was especially unwelcome.

"Yes, well, I'm glad you were, ah, pleased," she began.

Trisha's smile widened. "That's one way to describe it. So, what has Glen done now?"

For the second time in an hour, Heidi explained about Glen, May Stryker and her son. Trisha listened, taking notes as Heidi spoke.

"You don't have the money to pay May back."

Trisha made a statement rather than asking a question, but Heidi answered it, anyway. "I don't have any money, to speak of. I have twenty-five hundred dollars in my savings account, and that's it."

Trisha flinched. "Word to the wise. Don't ever tell a lawyer that."

"Oh. Charlie said—well, implied—that you might take this on pro bono."

Trisha steepled her bright fuchsia fingernails. "I do take on a few cases like that. Mostly because they interest me or because I'm guilted into it. My fourth husband, may he rest in peace, left me very well off. So it's not like I need the money. Still, it's nice to be paid."

Heidi wasn't sure what to say to that, so she kept her mouth shut.

Trisha leaned back in her chair. "Here are the major problems as I see them. First, taking two hundred and fifty thousand dollars isn't something any judge is going to find amusing. We're so far into felony territory that Glen could be put away for years. If you're as broke as you say, paying back the money right away isn't going to happen."

Heidi nodded. "If I could make payments..."

"That's going to be one part of our defense. That you want to make good on the money. Come up with a payment plan. What is it you do?"

"I raise goats. I use their milk for cheese and soap. Two of my goats are pregnant. I'll be able to sell the kids."

Trisha raised her eyes to the ceiling. "Just once I'd like to work with someone doing an internet start-up. But do you bring me that?" She returned her attention to Heidi. "Goats. Okay, well that ties you to the community. This Harvey guy—the source of the trouble. Get him here. The judge needs to see the reason Glen took the money. How's Harvey doing?"

"He's great. His cancer treatments worked, and the doctors expect him to die in his sleep in about twenty years."

"Good. Have Harvey bring medical records."

Trisha continued to detail their strategy. When she was done, she said, "What was the son's name?"

"Rafe Stryker."

Trisha typed the information into her laptop. Her perfect lips twisted. "You picked the wrong man to mess with, missy. He would scare a shark." There was more typing, followed by a groan. "Is he good-looking?"

Heidi thought about the tall, slightly frightening stranger who wanted to destroy her world. "Yes."

"If I were you, I'd think about getting him into bed. Sex might be the only way to win this one."

Heidi felt her mouth drop open. She consciously closed it. "Is there a plan B?"

RAFE DROVE SLOWLY THROUGH Fool's Gold, his mother's car a half block behind his. He hadn't been in the town in years and he could easily, not to mention happily, go a lifetime without returning again.

It wasn't that the town wasn't attractive—if one was into pretty, small towns and local color. Storefronts were clean, sidewalks wide. Windows advertised sales and festivals. Despite the fact that it was a weekday, plenty of people were out walking around. From a business perspective, Fool's Gold seemed to be thriving. But for him, this would always be the place he'd been trapped as a kid, taking on more than he could manage.

Everything was smaller than he remembered. Probably the perspective of being an adult, he told himself. He recognized the park where he'd met his friends on a rare afternoon away from chores and family. The road up to the school was the same, and he saw three boys on bikes riding in that direction.

He'd had a bike, he recalled. A bike one of the women in town had given to him. He'd been ten or eleven and desperate to be like his friends. But the bike was charity and his pride had battled with practicality.

He couldn't complain—the town had been plenty

kind. Every August there had been new clothes for school, new shoes and backpacks filled with the necessary supplies. On the holidays, baskets of food had appeared. At Christmas, toys had been left. His lunch at school had been free, something that had humiliated him, even though the cafeteria workers never drew attention to the fact. Once when he was walking home from school, a woman had pulled over, opened her car door and handed him a jacket. Just like that.

The jacket had been new and thick and warm. In the pockets, he'd found gloves and five dollars. Back then, it was all the money in the world. He'd been grateful and furious at the same time.

While he'd appreciated the gestures and the care, he'd hated that either had been necessary. Several nights a week, he'd been forced to lie to his mother and say he wasn't hungry for dinner so his brothers and sister could have enough to eat. He'd gone to bed, determined to ignore the burning emptiness gnawing at him.

He'd never understood the vicious old man his mother had worked for—a man who had made sure there was plenty for himself, but not enough for a hardworking housekeeper to feed her children. The only bright spot in coming back was that, while the old caretaker's house still stood, the place where the old man had lived was gone.

None of which was the town's fault, he told himself. Still, the memories were there. Things he'd tried to forget, to grow past. He was a powerful man, wealthy. He could pick up the phone and be put through to a senator or diplomat. He knew the CEOs of nearly half the Fortune 500 companies. But, driving through Fool's Gold, he was once again the too-thin kid who'd longed to know what it would be like to feel safe and secure. To have a full belly and toys and a mother who didn't hide worry behind a loving smile.

He turned into the courtyard in front of Ronan's Lodge, the main hotel in town. The Gold Rush Ski Resort was too far out of town to be practical, so the lodge would do.

Ronan's Lodge, or as the locals called it, Ronan's Folly, had been built during the gold rush. The large, three-story building was a testament to fine craftsmanship from a time when detail work was done by hand. As a valet hurried toward his car, Rafe took in the carved double doors that led to the lobby.

Years ago, when he'd been small, he'd never imagined he would ever be able to stay in a place like this. Now he got out of his car and took the ticket the valet offered, as if he showed up at places like this every day. Which he did—but it never got old.

He collected the small leather duffel he'd packed and went back to help his mother. May was staring at the hotel and smiling.

"I remember this place," she told him, her eyes bright with delight. "It's so beautiful. Are we really going to stay here?"

"It's convenient."

"You need a little more romance in your soul."

"Now you have a project."

She laughed and touched his cheek. "Oh, Rafe, isn't it wonderful to be back? Driving through town like that, I didn't know where to look first. Don't you love everything about this town? I'm sorry we had to leave. We were so happy here."

He supposed in some ways they had been, but getting out of Fool's Gold had been a goal that consumed him. Which wasn't a conversation he was going to have with his mother, he reminded himself.

"You can be happy again, once you have your ranch," he told her, taking her suitcase and escorting her into the hotel.

The lobby was large and three stories tall. There were carved panels on the wall and a chandelier made of imported Irish crystal. He wasn't sure where that small fact had come from or why he'd remembered it, but there it was.

Even as May paused to press both hands to her chest and gaze around in wonder, Rafe walked to the reception desk and gave his last name.

"There should be two rooms," he said, knowing his ever-efficient assistant would have handled things.

"Yes, Mr. Stryker. Of course. We have you and your mother each in a suite on our third floor." The young woman in a blue suit gave him paperwork to sign, then told him about the restaurant hours and that room service was available around the clock.

He was more interested in getting a drink. Make that several. After glancing briefly toward the bar, he collected his mother and herded her toward the elevator.

"I only need a very small room," she said as they rode to the third floor.

"Uh-huh."

"I'm sure we'll be able to work something out with Glen and Heidi, and then I won't be in the hotel at all."

He stopped in front of the first door and inserted a key card. "Mom, even when you own the ranch, do you really think you'll want to live there? You'll be out in the middle of nowhere." While his mother was only in her fifties, he wasn't sure he was comfortable with her being alone on a ranch. "The house is old and I doubt it's been updated." He thought about the roof and the fading paint, and felt the beginnings of a headache.

May patted his arm. "You're sweet to worry, Rafe, but I'll be fine. I've wanted to return to the ranch ever since we lost it nearly twenty years ago. I belong there. Seeing it was magical. I want to make it into a home. Everything is going to work out. You'll see."

He didn't doubt he would win in court. Dante would see to that. But there was a long, dusty road between winning and everything working out. His mother had a way of complicating a situation.

"I want to go visit Glen in jail," she announced as he took her suitcase into the suite's bedroom.

"Exhibit A," he murmured, watching the first of the complications manifest.

"I feel badly that he's there." Her warm gaze cooled. "You didn't have to call the police."

"He was breaking the law."

"I know and I appreciate that you were also looking out for me, but I think we should find another way."

With luck, his room would have a minibar, he thought grimly. Then he wouldn't even have to go downstairs.

"Glen is fine."

"You don't know that. I'm going to see him."

He recognized stubborn, mostly because he'd inherited it from her. "Give me a half hour to check in with the office and I'll come get you. We'll go together."

The smile returned. "Thank you."

Sure, now that she was getting her way she smiled. He promised to be back in thirty minutes, then escaped to his own room at the end of the hall.

He used the card key and stepped into the quiet, mother-free space. The room faced the mountains, and the drapes were parted enough for him to see the Sierra Nevada peaks aiming for the heavens.

He walked into the bedroom, tossed his duffel on the king-size bed, then returned to the living room of the suite and removed his tie. Instead of searching for the minibar, he grabbed his cell phone and called his office.

"Mr. Stryker's office," his businesslike assistant answered on the first ring.

"Hello, Ms. Jennings."

"Mr. Stryker. You're in Fool's Gold with your mother?"

"Yes, and it looks like I'm going to be here awhile."

"I gathered that when Mr. Jefferson mentioned he would be joining you. It's a lovely town."

Rafe felt his eyebrows rise. Ms. Jennings never mentioned anything personal. He wasn't sure if the woman was married, a grandmother or living with a rock band.

"You've visited?"

"Several times. They have wonderful festivals."

There was no accounting for taste, he thought. "I'll have to check them out."

"I can send you a schedule. It's on the city's website, www.FoolsGoldCA.com."

"Uh, not right now, but thanks for the offer. I'm going to need you to rearrange my calendar. Cancel what isn't important and reschedule everything else."

There was a pause when Rafe knew she was taking notes.

"Not a problem," she told him. "I'm checking the next two weeks now, and it's all things I can handle. Except for your meeting with Nina Blanchard."

Rafe sank onto the sofa and held in a curse. "I'll call her myself."

"Of course."

They finished the rest of their business, then hung up. Rafe returned to the bedroom, quickly changed out of his suit, into jeans and a long-sleeved shirt, then shrugged on his leather jacket.

He couldn't avoid Nina Blanchard forever, he thought. After all, he was the one who had hired her. But there was no way he could take advantage of her services while he was in Fool's Gold. She was going to have to wait until he'd solved the problem that was his mother.

AFTER LEAVING FOOL'S GOLD, Rafe had been determined to experience what the world had to offer. He'd gone to Harvard on a scholarship, had toured Europe and made friends with the rich and powerful. But he'd never been to jail before.

While he was sure they all looked somewhat similar, he had a feeling the Fool's Gold jail was considered one of the better places to be incarcerated.

For one thing, instead of industrial colors, the walls were a warm yellow, trimmed in cream. Bright posters advertised the festivals his assistant so adored. Rather than inhaling the scent of cleaning supplies or something less pleasant, Rafe smelled chili and fresh-baked bread. The woman who signed them in to visit Glen was young and friendly, not the grim-faced officer usually found in the movies.

"We've been busy tonight," Officer Rodriguez said. Her shiny, dark hair was pulled back into a bouncy ponytail.

Rafe studied the hairstyle. Weren't ponytails a bad idea in law enforcement? Didn't they give criminals something to grab on to, thereby giving them physical control of the situation? Or was Fool's Gold so close to nirvana that they didn't deal with serious crime here?

"Glen Simpson is a very popular man." Officer Rodriquez grinned. "The town's averages are getting better, but there's still a shortage for our ladies of a certain age, and Glen's a charmer."

May signed the clipboard. "What averages?"

"We had a man shortage. The news about that all came out last year, and it was a mess. The media came crawling in, and there was a reality show here and everything."

"I think I remember that," his mother said thoughtfully. "*True Love or Fool's Gold.* It went off the air before it was finished."

"No one was watching, which is too bad. I thought it was good. Anyway, since word got out about our man shortage, we've been getting plenty of them moving in. Which has made my life more interesting." Her brown eyes sparkled. "But most of them have been younger. So when Glen came, he was considered hot stuff. He's only been in jail a few hours, and we've already had six..." She glanced at the clipboard. "...make that seven visitors for him."

May looked uneasy. "I assure you, I'm not here on any romantic mission. I wanted to make sure Glen, ah, Mr. Simpson, was all right." She leaned toward the officer and lowered her voice. "My son's the one who put him in jail."

"Way to be supportive, Mom."

"We could have worked things out."

"Not if you planned to get your money back."

May's expression tightened, a sure sign she was getting her stubborn on. He held up both hands. "You're right. We'll check on him. It's the right thing to do."

He resisted glancing at his watch, confident they would be back at the hotel long before the bar closed.

Officer Rodriguez led them down a long, brightly lit hallway, then through a set of double doors. The delicious smells grew more intense, reminding Rafe he hadn't had lunch and it was closing in on dinner time.

"Here we are," the officer said, pulling open another door and motioning for them to enter. "Glen, you have more visitors."

Rafe's only experience with jail came from what he'd seen on TV and in the movies. So he wasn't sure where Fool's Gold stood on the "grim" spectrum. But nothing had prepared him for Glen's current living conditions.

The old man lay stretched out in his cell. There was the requisite cot, although this one was covered with a beautiful quilt, and there were at least a dozen pillows propped up on the bed. A brightly colored rug covered most of the floor. Flowers spilled from vases, and TV trays served as tables.

Just outside the barred front, a large, flat-screen TV sat on a stand. The sound of an action movie spilled into the space. A long shelf to the side of the television served as a kind of buffet. Nearly a dozen covered dishes and Crock-Pots stood waiting to serve. There were pies, cakes and cookies.

"You!"

Rafe turned and saw the police chief marching toward him. "Ma'am?"

"Don't you 'ma'am' me," she growled, grabbing his arm in a steely grip and dragging him back into the hallway.

"This is your fault," she snapped, when they were alone. "Don't think you're not in trouble."

Police Chief Barns might only come up to his shoulder, but there was something about her stance that warned him she wasn't going to take any lip.

"What are you talking about?"

"That man." She pointed back at the door leading to the jail cells.

"If he's a problem," he began, only to have her glare at him. It was a good glare—better than his assistant's.

"Oh, there's a problem, but it's not coming from him. It's those women. Do you know how many have visited here?"

"Six?" he asked, remembering there had been seven according to Officer Rodriguez, and he assumed his mother was in that count.

"Six," the police chief confirmed. "They're showing up here with their food and blankets. One brought that damn television. Another dragged in a foam mattress cover. We wouldn't want our detainees to feel uncomfortable while they sleep, would we?"

"I'm not sure how this is my fault."

"You made me arrest him." She poked him in the

chest. "Make it go away, or I swear I'll make your life a living hell."

"We're going to court in the morning."

"Good. The last thing I want is a bunch of civilians treating my jail like a church social. When the judge asks if you mind if Glen is released on his own recognizance, you better say no. You hear me?"

Rafe thought about pointing out that she was breaking more than a few laws with this conversation. That he had the right to request Glen be held until trial. But where was the win? Until the situation was resolved, he was stuck in town. His mother wanted to make her home here, on that damned ranch. Having the police chief as an enemy wouldn't help either of their causes.

"I'll have a word with my attorney," he told her.

"That's all I ask." She drew in a breath, then released it slowly. "I swear, if someone else shows up with a Crock-Pot, there's going to be blood."

CHAPTER THREE

HEIDI SAT UNEASILY in the courtroom, Glen's friend Harvey next to her. She'd never been to court before—had never even received a parking ticket. She found herself wanting to fidget or run. The judge, a tall, thin woman draped in black robes, intimidated her more than she wanted to admit. The bailiff was equally authoritarian in her uniform. There was an air of hushed expectation, with excited murmurs from those watching.

Her gaze slid from where Glen and Trisha Wynn were having a quiet conversation to the other table. Rafe Stryker sat next to an equally powerful-looking man. They were both dressed in navy suits, with white shirts and red ties, but the similarities ended there. Rafe was all dark—dark hair, dark eyes and a dark scowl. He surveyed the room unhappily, as if annoyed he had to be bothered with something as insignificant as this. Although, according to Glen's lawyer, May Stryker had "bought" the ranch with her son, which meant Rafe was an equal party in the complaint.

The other man had blond hair and killer blue eyes. He was pretty enough to make even Heidi notice, despite her distraction over the proceedings. When she looked at Rafe, she felt a clenching in the pit of her stomach—something that didn't happen when she glanced at his lawyer.

Trisha turned and motioned for Heidi to lean forward.

"Dante Jefferson," she whispered, pointing to Rafe's friend. "I know him by reputation, although I wouldn't mind getting to know him in other ways."

Heidi blinked in surprise. Dante was young enough to be Trisha's son. Not that she was going to judge, she told herself. Trisha was working the case for free.

"Is he good?"

Trisha's amused expression tightened. "The best. He's not just Rafe's lawyer. They're also business partners. Successful business partners. Between them, they've made enough money to rival the GDP of a midsize country."

Heidi pressed her hand to her churning stomach. "Is Glen going to prison?"

"Not if I can help it. It will depend on the judge." She turned her attention to Harvey. "You ready?"

The old man nodded. "I'm here for Glen, just like he was there for me." He gave a wink.

"Good. The judge will want to speak to you," Trisha told him. "Be honest. Just say what happened."

"I will."

Heidi could only hope it was enough.

She glanced around the court as Trisha returned her attention to Glen. May Stryker caught Heidi's eye. Rafe's mother gave her a little wave and a smile. Heidi wasn't sure what to make of that. May was the reason Glen was in trouble.

No, Heidi reminded herself. Glen was the reason he was in trouble. He'd knowingly swindled May out of a lot of money. Only he'd done it to help Harvey, which complicated everything.

She wanted to be furious with her grandfather, but she couldn't get past the fear pressing down on her. In the next few minutes, they could lose everything. The home she'd been so desperate to have, her precious goats and every cent they had. Then what? Where would they go? She'd only ever wanted to belong somewhere, and now that might be taken from her.

Judge Loomis took off her reading glasses. "I've reviewed the material. Ms. Wynn, you're representing Mr. Simpson pro bono?"

Glen's lawyer rose. "Yes, Your Honor. I was so moved by his case, I had to help."

"So noted."

The fear of losing everything forced Heidi to her feet. "Your Honor?"

The judge looked at her disapprovingly. Trisha groaned.

"I'm Heidi Simpson," Heidi said quickly. "May I speak?"

The judge glanced at the paperwork in front of her, then turned back to Heidi. "As this is your ranch we're talking about, all right. What do you have to say, Ms. Simpson?"

Heidi looked at Trisha, who rolled her eyes. Heidi was aware of everyone looking at her.

She was used to drawing a crowd. She'd grown up with her grandfather traveling with the carnival, working various games and helping out with the animals. She knew how to entice people to play the ring toss or gather around while she performed various card tricks. But that was expected attention. She planned for it, knew what to say. This was different—mostly because so much was at stake.

Heidi ignored the shaking that began in her thighs and radiated out. She willed herself to be strong, to rise to the occasion and find the words to impress the judge.

"I'm not happy to be here," Heidi admitted, meeting the judge's neutral gaze. "But I'm glad Harvey is alive." She glanced at her grandfather's friend and smiled. "I've known Harvey since I was a little girl. He's a part of my extended family. When he came to Glen, he was dying. Now he's healthy, and my grandfather made that possible. As much as I love my home, I can't value it above a person's life."

Rafe snorted. His lawyer hushed him.

Heidi found herself staring at the ruthless businessman. "Not everything can be reduced to a dollar value," she said. "My grandfather was wrong to try to sell Mrs. Stryker the ranch and wrong to take the money. But he didn't do it lightly or without a really good reason. He was helping someone who is like a brother to him."

Heidi shifted her gaze back to the judge, but was unable to figure out what she was thinking.

Heidi continued. "The ranch is everything I've ever wanted in a home. I raise goats, Your Honor. I have a small herd of eight. I use the milk to produce cheese and soap. I also sell the goat milk to a few people in town. It's not a big business. It supports me and my grandfather. He took me in when my parents died. He took care of me and loved me, and now I want to be here for him. I'm taking responsibility for what my grandfather did. We're willing to work out some kind of payment plan with Mrs. Stryker."

"You'll put everything on the line for your grandfather," the judge said slowly. "I see. But you don't have the two hundred and fifty thousand dollars."

"No."

"The property is mortgaged?"

Trisha rose. "Permission to approach the bench, Your Honor. I have the paperwork for the mortgage right here."

The judge nodded.

Trisha took the folder to her, then returned to her seat next to Glen. Heidi waited anxiously while the judge flipped through the pages, scanning them quickly. When she was done, she looked up, over her reading glasses.

"In today's financial climate, it's unlikely you could get much of a second mortgage. By my calculations, it would cover less than twenty percent of what your grandfather took from Mrs. Stryker."

Heidi stared at the judge, not knowing what to say. Another mortgage? Where was she supposed to come up with the money for that?

"How much of the two hundred and fifty thousand dollars do you have now?" the judge asked. "In cash?"

Heidi thought of her savings account and swallowed. "Two thousand, five hundred dollars."

Several people watching whispered. Heidi felt herself flush.

Rafe's lawyer stood. "Your Honor, we're all clear on how wonderfully virtuous it is that Ms. Simpson loves her grandfather, and of course she wants to pay back the money. But Glen Simpson stole from my clients. He took advantage of May Stryker's advanced years and business inexperience to swindle her out of a significant amount of money."

"Advanced years?" May said, loud enough for several people to hear. "I'm not in my dotage."

"Sit down, Mr. Jefferson," the judge told him. "You'll get your turn."

"Yes, Your Honor." The lawyer returned to his seat, but he looked more pleased than offended by the request.

Heidi wished Rafe and his friend were a lot more worried.

The judge glanced down at her notes, then back at Heidi. "You may be seated, Ms. Simpson. Am I correct in assuming the man next to you is Harvey, your grandfather's friend?"

She nodded.

The judge asked Harvey to stand and listened while he detailed how he'd learned of his cancer and the fairly straightforward treatment that would give him many more years of life. But as he wasn't old enough to qualify for Medicare and had never made enough to afford insurance, he was helpless to pay for the cure. Glen had been the one to come through with the money, and now Harvey was cancer-free.

Glen was questioned next. He spoke a little about his history and his intentions. To Heidi, he sounded like an itinerant gambler with a heart of gold. Which wasn't far from the truth. Her grandfather had always made decisions without thinking about the consequences—he'd just as easily invited Heidi into his life, and his love had certainly outweighed his occasional irresponsibility. Finally, Rafe's lawyer rose.

He turned to Harvey. "I'm glad you're better," he said. "Good health is a blessing."

Harvey nodded.

Dante faced the judge. "Your Honor, it appears much of this case is about what *home* means. For Ms. Simpson and her grandfather, the ranch is a dream come true. But it's also that for Mrs. Stryker. Thirty years ago, she and her husband came to Fool's Gold to work at the Castle Ranch. Her husband was to manage the ranch, while May took care of Mr. Castle and raised their children. A few years later, May's husband was killed, leaving her alone with three small boys."

Heidi knew what was coming and realized it was

nearly as sympathy-inducing as Harvey's recovery. Not good news for her.

"May continued to work as the housekeeper, but, without her husband's salary, money was tight. Mr. Castle was not a generous man, and the working conditions were difficult, but May hung on. You see, Mr. Castle had promised to will her the ranch when he died. But he lied, and when he passed, the ranch went to distant relatives back east. Crushed, May took her young family to Los Angeles and found work there. But she never forgot the Castle Ranch. When she learned it was for sale, she was finally going to reclaim what had been denied her. But once again, the ranch was snatched from her. This time by a thief."

Dante paused to point to Glen. Heidi was more concerned by his words than his theatrical gestures. Even though she had no part in the past or Glen's actions, she still felt horrible and guilty, as if she'd done something wrong.

"Dante, stop it!" May rose. "Your Honor, can I say something?"

The judge threw up her hands. "Well, everyone else has had a chance to speak today. Go ahead, Mrs. Stryker."

Rafe stood. "Mom, this isn't the time."

"It is exactly the time. I know you're a successful businessman and winning is everything to you, but I don't like any of this. Yes, of course, there's the money, but I don't want Heidi and her grandfather turned out. I know exactly what it feels like to lose a home. We need to work something out. All of us. A compromise."

May turned to Heidi. "We could share it. I'm not sure exactly how, but you seem reasonable, and I want this to work."

"Me, too," Heidi murmured.

"Good." May faced the judge. "Heidi has the most lovely goats. She needs a place to run her business."

"You do realize Glen Simpson stole two hundred and fifty thousand dollars from you," the judge said.

"Of course, but Heidi mentioned a payment plan. I'm open to that."

"She doesn't have the means," Dante said. "Your Honor, she admitted she has twenty-five hundred dollars. My client isn't interested in a payment plan that takes us into the next millennium. As he signed the documents, as well, he should have an equal say in what happens."

The judge nodded slowly. "Yes, I see, Mr. Jefferson. But I'm surprised that a successful businessman such as your client didn't realize the deal was a sham before he signed."

Dante muttered something under his breath. "He was busy, Your Honor."

Her eyebrows rose. "Are you saying your client didn't read the documents in question?"

"No, he did not."

"Caveat emptor, Mr. Jefferson," the judge said.

Trisha turned and whispered, "Let the buyer beware. It's Latin."

Heidi wanted to believe that the judge was on their side, but she had a feeling that she was reading too much into the exchange. With so much on the line, hope seemed painfully naive.

Judge Loomis leaned back in her large leather chair and removed her reading glasses.

"Mr. Stryker, despite your legal claim, am I correct in assuming this is truly your mother's property?"

"Yes, Your Honor."

The judge nodded slowly. She glanced at May, who stood with her hands clasped.

"You've given me a lot to think about," the judge said at last. "While Mr. Simpson took a significantly large sum of money, I believe it was with good intentions. Not an excuse, Mr. Simpson," she added sternly.

Glen lowered his chin. "You are so right, ma'am."

"Ms. Simpson, your willingness to help your grandfather is admirable but, twenty-five hundred dollars isn't going to cut it."

Heidi swallowed. "Yes, Your Honor."

"Mr. Stryker, you're a businessman who signed a contract without reading it. You deserve what you get."

Heidi saw Rafe's jaw muscle clench, but he didn't speak.

"Mrs. Stryker, you seem the most injured party here, yet you're the one who counsels forgiveness and compromise. You have given my somewhat cynical spirit a good dose of hope. I admire you and will therefore consider the merits of this case from your point of view."

Heidi wasn't sure what that meant, but wondered if it was possible they weren't going to lose everything.

"The easiest answer is to put Mr. Simpson in jail, order him to stand trial, or plead out and be done with it. For you, Mrs. Stryker, I'm willing to consider other options. I would like to do some research on precedence for a case like this. Unfortunately, my schedule is fully booked right now, and my law clerk is getting married next week and then going on her honeymoon. So she isn't available, either."

The judge considered for a moment. "There is also the matter of the bank loan. Would they be willing to transfer the note to Mrs. Stryker and her son? While I doubt that would be a problem, they do need to be consulted. As you are all aware, banks can be notoriously slow in responding to this kind of thing."

She paused, then smiled slightly. "All right, Mrs. Stryker, you shall have your compromise. You and your son will share the property with Ms. Simpson and her grandfather. You will in essence co-own it, at least for now. We will continue to work from our end, speaking with the bank and researching the case. In the meantime, Ms. Simpson, I suggest you do all you can to raise the money owed Mrs. Stryker. Legally, of course."

Heidi felt as if she'd just fallen through a rabbit hole. Share the ranch? The four of them? It was better than losing everything, but how was it supposed to work?

She was aware of May beaming at Glen, and of Rafe, who whispered furiously to his attorney.

"Your Honor?" May raised her hand.

"Yes?"

"If Heidi and I agree, is it all right to make improvements to the property? The barn needs fixing and the fences are in terrible shape."

"I remind you, I have not reached a final decision. It is possible you could lose the ranch completely, Mrs. Stryker. Please remember that. But if you and Ms. Simpson agree to the improvement, and you accept there will be no compensation should you lose this proceeding, then go ahead. I will call the concerned parties back when I'm ready to rule. Brace yourself, people. It could be a while."

Heidi was still reeling from the sudden, if temporary, reprieve. She stood, as instructed, then swayed slightly, feeling as if she'd just avoided being smashed by a speeding train.

"This is good, right?" she asked Trisha.

"It's better than Glen standing trial." She smiled at the older man. "Not that I don't adore you, hon, but your bony ass would so be going to prison. Two hundred and fifty grand is miles into felony territory." She turned to Heidi. "Make it work with May. Figure out a compromise, be nice and, for heaven's sake, start putting away money. If you can't come up with a solution on your own, then showing you've made significant progress in paying back the money will help."

"Okay," Heidi murmured, aware that Rafe continued to have a heated conversation with his lawyer. He shot several angry glances in her general direction. May, she decided, wasn't going to be a problem. If only the same could said about her son.

Trisha leaned close. "Remember what I told you yesterday," she whispered. "Sex can fix a lot of sticky situations."

Heidi took in Rafe's well-tailored suit and expensive shoes. Even if she ignored them, there was still the man himself. Everything about him screamed stubborn and arrogant. Sure he was handsome, and it would be easy to get lost in his dark eyes, but she had a feeling falling under his spell would be a lot like a rabbit getting mesmerized by a cobra. It all seemed like great fun until the fangs sank in.

"Rafe Stryker isn't the type to be seduced into anything."

"All men are the type. Trust me."

"Then I'm not the type," Heidi admitted. "I wouldn't know where to begin."

Sex wasn't supposed to be about power; it was supposed to be about love. Or at least caring and attraction.

"Just think about it," Trisha advised her. "The right woman can bring down an empire."

Which sounded great, but wasn't what Heidi was interested in doing. She only wanted to keep her grandfather out of jail while hanging on to her home and her goats. Modest dreams that wouldn't impress anyone but were the world to her.

Still, desperate times and all that. She looked at Rafe, taking in the broad shoulders and surprisingly sensual mouth. Could she do it? Could she seduce a man like him? Make him forget that he was supposed to destroy her?

She imagined herself in something slinky, with heels, and her hair loose and curly, blowing back from the wind of an invisible fan. Like in the movies, she thought. Only instead of making a smooth entrance, she would probably get her feet tangled up in the hem of her outfit and sprawl face first onto the floor. Oh, yeah. Talk about impressive.

The picture was so clear that she grinned, then happened to look toward the man in question. Only he didn't look amused. There was determination in his dark gaze. A steely set to his body, which warned her that he wasn't playing and if she really thought she could get between him and what he wanted, she was going to regret it. The room seemed to get a little chilly and she folded her arms across her chest.

"Heidi?"

May had approached. "I meant what I said," the other woman told her. "About us working it out. I know Glen wasn't trying to hurt me. He wanted to help a friend."

Heidi wondered if she had it in her to be as generous, were their situations reversed.

"I appreciate that. He's not a bad man. A little impulsive sometimes."

May smiled, her dark eyes bright with humor. "Sometimes an excellent quality."

"As long as you don't need a lawyer at the end of the day."

"Exactly."

May was a pretty woman with lines around her eyes. She was about Heidi's height, rounder and with quality clothes that flattered her curves. Heidi tugged at the sleeves of the only "nice" dress she owned. A sedate knee-length, three-quarter-sleeved navy knit that could be worn to business meetings or a funeral with equal ease. She'd found it in a thrift store in Albuquerque about five years ago, along with matching conservative pumps.

"We'll set up a meeting," May said, pulling out her cell phone. "Let me get your number and I'll be in touch."

"THAT WAS NICE," MAY SAID as Rafe escorted her to her hotel room.

Nice? They'd spent the morning in front of a judge, who'd put their case on hold indefinitely. They were in limbo, neither winning nor losing. Rafe had been chastised for not reading a contract, which had been humiliating. All he wanted was to get out of Fool's Gold and never come back. Nothing good ever happened here.

He opened his mother's suite door and followed her inside. As much as he wanted to drive back to

San Francisco that second, he couldn't. Not until he knew her plans.

"You know nothing has been resolved," he told his mother.

She set down her purse on the table by the front door and led the way into the bright, well-decorated living room.

"I know, and I'm fine with that. I thought the judge was very fair. I have so many plans for the ranch."

"You don't own the ranch. Not yet."

"But the judge said I can make improvements if Heidi agrees."

"Wouldn't it be better to wait until this is settled? We could go back to—"

"I'm not leaving." His mother sat on the sofa, her spine straight, her expression defiant. "This is where we were happy as a family. You saw the state of the house and the land. I want to fix it. Even if I don't get to keep the ranch, I want to leave a part of myself there. I want it to be better for what I've done."

He dropped into the club chair on the other side of the large coffee table and held in a groan. "Which means what?"

Determination softened as her gaze seemed to shift to something beyond him.

"I want to make a home here. Oh, Rafe, we had so many wonderful years here in Fool's Gold. I know money was tight and we didn't always have the newest of everything, but we were a family."

He ignored the fact that his memories of the past

and hers had very little in common. "Buying the ranch isn't going to give you a do-over, Mom. Your children aren't going to be small again."

"I know, but I've been dreaming about the Castle Ranch since we had to leave, all those years ago." She shifted her gaze to him and tears filled her eyes. "I know things were difficult for you here. I let you take care of me and of everyone else. You were just a little boy and you never got a chance to be a child."

"I was fine. You were a great parent."

"I hope so, but I'm not blind to my faults. You worried for me and about me. Maybe that's why you can't be happy today."

He thought longingly of a good legal battle with another corporation, or winning a contract against impossible odds. All things he enjoyed. Nearly anything would be better than talking about his feelings with his mother.

"I'm plenty happy."

"No, you're not. All you do is work. You don't have anyone in your life."

"I have lots of people."

"Not someone special. You need to fall in love."

"I've been in love." It wasn't all it was cracked up to be.

He'd made what seemed like the intelligent choice—fallen for a young woman who should have been perfect. She'd been pretty, smart, caring and supportive. He'd been more interested in her than in anyone he'd ever met, and had been able to imagine growing old with her. If that wasn't love, then what was?

Their brief, two-year marriage had ended when she'd suggested a divorce, and he'd felt little more than a vague sense of dissatisfaction and failure.

"You weren't in love," his mother told him. "Love is powerful. Love sweeps you away. You were never swept away."

"Fine. But I'm going to find someone now. So I'm happy."

May wrinkled her nose. "You're going to a matchmaker, Rafe. Who does that? What does this Nina person know about you, anyway? When the time is right, you'll find the one. Just like I found your father."

"Mom," he began.

"No. You have to listen. I'm right about this. You need to find someone who you're willing to risk it all for."

As if that was going to happen. "I'll find the right woman," he promised. "We'll get married and have children."

If he hadn't been so set on having kids, he would have never considered marrying again. But he was conventional enough to want a traditional family. Mother and father. He'd been unable to get it right himself, so he was hiring a professional. For him, hiring a matchmaker was no different than hiring a good travel agent or successful sales rep. When he wasn't the best at something, he found someone who was. Nina had a nearly perfect track record.

"I would love grandchildren," his mother told him, her smile returning. "Just think, I'll have the ranch and you can bring your family to visit."

There was a particular vision of hell, he thought grimly. "Ah, sure, Mom. That'll be great." He guided her back on topic. "You're sure about the ranch? You want it?"

"Yes. I want to live there permanently. Maybe have a few animals and a garden. I could grow my own fruits and vegetables."

"Not with the goats around."

"Heidi and I will work something out."

Rafe didn't bother telling her that Heidi and her grandfather weren't going to be an issue. Like Nina, Dante was the best at what he did. There was only going to be one winner at the end of the day, and it wasn't going to be Heidi and her goats.

"Isn't the ranch close to nearly a thousand acres?"

May shrugged. "I'm not sure. I know there's a fair amount of land."

Maybe he could figure out something to do with it, so his time here wasn't a complete loss. Because the bottom line was—he wasn't leaving. Not until May had what she'd come for.

He stood and pulled his mother to her feet, then hugged her and kissed her temple.

"Okay, then," he said. "You want the ranch, I'll get it for you." No matter what it cost.

CHAPTER FOUR

HEIDI WAS PLEASED THAT her hand was steady as she poured coffee into four mugs on the table. May had made good on her promise of setting up a meeting. Now, barely twenty hours after the judge had dismissed them, they were in Heidi's kitchen, about to make decisions that could potentially change her life forever. She wanted to tell herself not to be dramatic, but she had been unable to chase away the lingering sense of panic. Sure, the judge had given her a reprieve, but she could still lose the ranch, and then what? Where would she and Glen go?

Worries for another time, she reminded herself as she took her seat at the rickety table. For now, she was going to cooperate with May and figure out how to come up with two hundred and fifty thousand dollars in, say, the next three weeks.

"Thank you so much for having us," May said, smiling at Heidi.

"You're more than welcome." Heidi tried to smile back, all the while ignoring the challenging expression on Rafe's face.

This was the first time she'd been in a relatively small room with the man, and she was annoyed to discover he took up too much space. He had broad shoulders that spilled past the back of the chair. She couldn't seem to focus on anyone but him, which frustrated her and made her want to pretend he wasn't there. An impossible task, with his dark eyes holding her captive.

"I've decided to stay in town," May continued, apparently unaware of the undercurrents swirling.

That could have been because they were only swirling on Heidi's end of things. Maybe Rafe was naturally surly and barely knew she was alive. Maybe—

Get a grip, she commanded herself, deliberately focusing on May.

"There's so much I remember about the ranch," the older woman continued. "I have so many happy memories here."

"It's a real family place," Glen told her. "We appreciate your willingness to work things out."

"Of course. Neither of us has to be disappointed by what happened. There's a solution."

Rafe muttered something Heidi couldn't hear, but she knew it wasn't friendly agreement.

May shot her son a warning look, then turned back to Heidi. "Do you think you could take us on a tour? I'd love to see the changes and understand a little about your business."

"Um, sure." Heidi would have preferred giving them directions back to San Francisco, but that wasn't likely to be an option. "When were you thinking?"

"How about now?" May asked.

Glen popped to his feet. "There's nothing I like better than spending time with a beautiful woman."

Rafe rolled his eyes, but May only smiled.

"You're a charmer," she murmured.

Heidi found herself on Rafe's side this time. Glen flirting with May wasn't going to help their cause. She would have to talk to him later. After the tour.

She rose. "There's not a whole lot to see," she began. "There's the goats and where they live, of course, and the barn."

"Don't forget the caves," Glen told her. He pulled out May's chair. "They're thousands of years old. Probably used by the original indigenous tribes as a form of shelter. There might be treasure."

Heidi sighed. "They're not that interesting. I use them to age my cheese. The temperature is perfect, and I don't have to worry about space. There's plenty."

Rafe stood. "Cheese and goats. Great."

"You don't have to come with us," she said. "Perhaps you'd like to stay here and phone your office."

One eyebrow rose, as if he were surprised she was willing to take him on. She lifted her chin slightly, not sure it would help, but even the tiniest psychological edge would be welcome. She had a feeling that Rafe not only brought a lot more resources to the battlefield, but that he was also used to winning at any price. Her idea of a good fight was facing down Athena when the goat escaped.

"I wouldn't want to miss the treasure," Rafe said, his mouth curving into a smile.

It was, she realized, the first time she'd seen him smile. For a second he looked approachable, appealing and unbelievably sexy. She wanted to smile back and then say something funny so he would smile again. Her toes curled in her athletic shoes, and she had an overwhelming urge to flip her hair, the fact that she was wearing her usual braids notwithstanding.

Get a grip! Rafe wasn't some handsome guy hanging out so she could flirt with him. He was the enemy. He was dangerous. He was trying to steal her home. The fact that she could be undone by a smile simply proved how pathetic her love life had been for what felt like decades. And when all this was resolved, she would find someone nice and have a relationship. But for now she had to remember what was at stake and act accordingly.

They all went outside and walked to where she kept the goats. Heidi had picked a nice, large area for her small herd. Most of the fencing was still in place, which meant she'd been able to focus her money on what she referred to as the goat house. A solid structure she used for milking. There was room for the goats when the weather got cold or when one of them was giving birth. Large sliding doors allowed the goats to come and go as they pleased.

May leaned against the fence and studied the goats. "They're not all the same."

"No. I have three Alpines and five Nubians." Heidi glanced at Rafe. "You met Athena the other day."

"Yes. She was charming."

Heidi was pretty sure he was being sarcastic, so she ignored his response. "Athena sort of runs things around here. Persephone and Hera are the ones who are pregnant."

She thought about mentioning she would put the money she received for their kids toward the debt, but then decided it wasn't going to be enough to impress anyone. What she needed was a steady market for her cheese. One that went beyond Fool's Gold.

She'd contacted a few stores in Sacramento and San Francisco about carrying her cheese. While they'd been interested, getting samples to the stores meant leaving the ranch and her goats. What she needed was a sales rep who could do the legwork for her. Someone with experience. Finding such a person seemed impossible. Give her a restless crowd and a game of ringtoss and she could take control in about fifteen seconds. But the business world was out of her realm of expertise. Something that hadn't concerned her until now.

"You named your goats after Greek goddesses?" Rafe asked.

"I thought it would be fun for them and for me."

"They read the classics, do they?"

"Oh, Rafe." May shook her head. "You'll have to forgive my son. He doesn't have much of a sense of humor."

"I have a fine sense of humor."

Heidi tilted her head. "Yes, and all those people who try out for *American Idol* think they can sing."

Rafe turned toward her, his dark gaze settling on

her face. His expression was unreadable, but she had a good idea of what he was thinking. Something along the lines of *Who do you think you are, trying to take me on? Be prepared to be squashed, little bug.*

She squared her shoulders. He might be richer and bigger and a whole lot scarier, but that didn't mean she would go down without a fight.

"What do they eat?" May asked.

"Good-quality hay and alfalfa. They need lots of water. They love to be out eating grass and pretty much any kind of brush. I move them around to different parts of the ranch. We also get calls all summer from people wanting to borrow our goats to clear land."

They left the goat area and went through the main barn, where most of the stalls were held together more by wishful thinking than actual wood. One section was still sound, and there Heidi boarded two horses, including her friend Charlie's large gelding.

The more they toured, the more Heidi became aware of the broken fence line, the weeds and the sad condition of nearly every building on her property. She'd been making steady progress. The goats had been her main concern. Now that they had the hooved equivalent of a five-star hotel, she planned to focus on the house and the barn. Or she had, before Glen had put them both so deeply into debt.

Back in the house, Heidi served samples of her goat cheese.

"Very nice," May said, nibbling on her pieces, then

taking seconds. "Really delicious. Tell me about the soap."

"I make it from goat milk. It's mild and very moisturizing. The lower pH level can help with some skin conditions. I sell it to several mothers in town who have kids with eczema. It seems to help."

"I'd love to try a bar."

"Of course." Heidi walked to the cupboard where she kept her inventory. She picked two scented with lavender and carried them back. She handed one each to May and Rafe.

"Thank you," he said. "I enjoy smelling like flowers."

"Maybe you should try it," his mother told him. "Women might like it." May turned to Heidi. "Rafe has a terrible time in relationships."

"Mother."

"You do. And now you're dealing with that Nina person. A matchmaker. Can you believe it? That's how bad he is at getting his own girl."

Heidi could practically hear Rafe's jaw grinding. Rafe might be a pain in the ass, but Heidi had a feeling she was going to like May just fine.

Keeping her expression as neutral as possible, she turned to Rafe. "There are a lot of single women in Fool's Gold. Would you like me to ask my friends if they know anyone who would go out with you?"

"No. Thank you, but no."

She had to press her lips together to keep from grinning. "You're sure?"

"Very."

May took another piece of cheese. "It's all so beautiful here. My children grew up on this ranch."

"I'd heard," Heidi said.

Glen went over to the coffeemaker and started a pot. "One of these days I'm hoping Heidi gives me a great-grandchild. I'm still waiting."

Now it was Heidi's turn to squirm.

"You have three children?" Glen asked.

"Four," May told him, wandering across the kitchen, toward him. "Three boys and a girl. Shane breeds horses, and Evangeline is a dancer. Clay—"

"Tell me about the goat manure," Rafe said, interrupting.

Heidi blinked at him. "Excuse me?"

"You sell it?"

"Yes. It makes a great fertilizer. Do you need some?"

"No."

It took her a second to realize he wasn't interested in talking about the goats as much as he'd wanted to change the subject. Talk about subtle avoidance. She replayed in her mind what May had been saying and realized he'd been keeping his mother from talking about Clay.

"If you change your mind..." she murmured, wondering if there was bad blood in the family.

Glen collected clean mugs from the cupboard.

May smiled at him. "You know your way around the kitchen."

"I've been on my own for a long time. A man does what he has to. This one—" he pointed to Heidi "—showed up in my life when she was three. Cutest little thing ever, but her daddy was long grown, and I'd forgotten everything I'd known about raising kids. Not that I'd been around much for mine. I was the kind of man who'd taken off first chance he could. Not proud of that. Still, I muddled along with Heidi, and we became a family."

May sighed. "What a wonderful story. So many men wouldn't have bothered."

Heidi held in a groan. While Glen had taken her in and raised her, she knew the story was more about impressing May than recounting the past. Her grandfather had always had a way with the ladies. Unfortunately, he didn't exactly have much of a track record when it came to long-term romantic relationships. She was going to have to remind him that he'd already stolen two hundred and fifty thousand dollars from May. Breaking her heart on top of that wouldn't be helpful.

He poured coffee. Heidi collected milk from the refrigerator and asked if anyone wanted sugar. Rafe, of course, drank his coffee black.

"Is it goat milk?" May asked, picking up the small pitcher and pouring.

"Yes."

"I can't wait to try it." She took a sip and smiled. "Perfect. In fact, everything is perfect. From what I can tell, there's no reason why we can't work out some kind of compromise."

"Mom," Rafe began.

His mother waved him into silence. "I want this, Rafe. I want to be a part of the ranch, and I don't think there's any reason Heidi and Glen can't be a part of it, too. There's room for all of us."

Heidi liked the sound of a compromise, but she would reserve judgment until she heard all the terms. Or had the money to pay May back. Although she had a feeling that the latter was going to take a little longer.

"What did you have in mind?" Heidi asked.

"I want to make a few improvements," May said. "The barn needs to be fixed and the fence lines. This house..." She glanced at the aging appliances. "Those were old when I lived here. I hated that oven."

"Me, too," Heidi admitted. "One side doesn't heat."

"So you have to keep turning everything. I remember. There's painting to be done and maybe new floors."

"Slow down," Rafe told her. "Let's take things one at a time."

May set her mouth. "I'm sorry, Rafe, but I've been waiting to get back to this ranch for twenty years. I'm here now. At my age, I can't afford to slow down."

"At your age." Glen shook his head. "You're barely out of your teens and too young for me. More's the pity."

May ducked her head. "I have four grown children."

"Even looking at Rafe here, I can barely believe it."

Rafe's jaw twitched. "Maybe if you made a list."

Everyone stared at him.

"Of what you'd like to do at the ranch," he clarified.

"Good idea," his mother said.

"Even a blind squirrel finds an acorn from time to time," he muttered.

Heidi hid her grin behind her mug and thought maybe she'd been a bit hasty in judging Rafe's sense of humor. As much as she liked May, she could see that the older woman wouldn't be all that easy to deal with. The combination of sweetness and determination could be daunting. Not that Glen was any less complicated.

May put down her mug. "Rafe and I should be going. I want to get right on making that list. You know where we're staying, right? At Ronan's Lodge? Oh, let me give you my cell number, and I'll take yours."

"You're staying in town, then?" Heidi asked.

Rafe answered. "Yes. Until this is settled, we're not going anywhere."

More threat than promise.

"Lucky us." Glen took May's hand in his. "I look forward to seeing you again, very soon."

"Me, too," May whispered back, her gaze locking with his.

Heidi didn't know if she should leave the older couple alone or insist on being a chaperone. Either way, she was going to have a very long talk with her grandfather.

Even as she wondered how she was going to convince him to see reason, she saw Rafe studying Glen.

Because they weren't in enough trouble already, she thought grimly, confident he would continue to protect what was his. She could only hope his matchmaker person found someone fast. With Rafe distracted, she might have a prayer of surviving the disaster that was her life.

HEIDI WAITED UNTIL RAFE and his mother had driven away, then walked into the family room and stood in front of her grandfather. Glen had already settled into his favorite chair to watch TV.

"Not so fast," she said, taking the remote from him. "We have to talk."

"About what?"

He sounded so innocent, she thought grimly. "May Stryker. You have to stop it. I can see what you're up to."

"She's a beautiful woman."

"Yes, she is, and not someone you can get involved with." She sank onto the ottoman in front of him. "Glen, I mean it. Don't do this. Don't mess with her. You know what will happen. You'll sleep with her a few times, get her to fall in love with you and then you'll lose interest."

"Heidi, that's harsh."

"Maybe, but it's true. This is important."

"I know." He leaned toward her. "I'm not playing around."

"You're flirting."

"I like her."

"You like all women."

His expression turned serious. "No. I like her. This is different."

She stared at his familiar face and wondered if she was strong enough to shake some sense into him. "There's no way you're going to get me to believe this would be more than a fling. All my life you've told me that love is only for the foolish and weak-minded. That if I felt myself falling in love, I should run in the other direction."

"I know, I know." He held up both hands. "You've got me dead to rights on that one. But I'm getting older, Heidi. Even I have to admit that. And growing old alone is starting to feel like an unnecessary mistake. What if there's something to this 'till death do you part' thing—with the right woman."

Heidi shook her head. "No. You don't get to suddenly announce everything you believed in was wrong."

"Why not? People once thought the world was flat. That's not true. Like I said, maybe I was wrong. And May's not like any other woman I've met. I can't ignore that."

Heidi covered her face in her hands. "Don't do this to me."

He leaned in and kissed her forehead. "You're a good girl, Heidi. I love you. You know that, right?"

"Yes, Glen. I love you, too."

"Then have a little faith."

"MARGARITA WITH AN EXTRA shot," Heidi said.

Jo, the owner and main bartender at Jo's Bar, raised both eyebrows. "You're not an extra shot kind of girl."

"I am tonight."

"You driving?"

Some people would find the question annoying or presumptuous. Heidi loved it. The concern, the meddling, were all vintage Fool's Gold and only one of many reasons she and her grandfather had wanted to settle here.

"Glen dropped me off," Heidi said. "He'll be picking me up when I call."

"Okay, then. An extra shot it is."

Jo left. A few minutes later, Annabelle and Charlie walked in together. They scanned the place, saw Heidi had already claimed a booth and hurried toward her.

"You won't believe the rumors," Annabelle said, sliding in first. "Did the judge really order you to sleep with Rafe Stryker?"

Heidi choked. "No. Of course not."

"Too bad," the petite, redheaded librarian said with a sigh. "I saw him yesterday. He's delicious."

"Is that really the rumor? The sleeping part," Heidi added. "Not him being delicious."

Charlie rolled her eyes. "No. Annabelle, I swear, you need a man. You're getting desperate."

"Tell me about it. I promised myself that I was done with relationships. The good guys never fall for me. I just didn't think the sex thing through. Do you think the judge would order Rafe to have sex with me?" She brushed her long, wavy hair out of her face and turned to Charlie. "You know everyone in town. Could you ask her?"

Charlie groaned. "You probably shouldn't have alcohol tonight. Lord knows what you'd do."

"I'm a librarian," Annabelle said with a sniff. "Haven't you heard? We're very prim."

"I think that's a story put out by the librarian council to distract people from the truth," Charlie muttered. "You're all a little wilder than you want people to know."

Heidi chuckled. This was exactly what she needed. Time with her friends. People who cared about her and made her laugh. The perfect combination.

Nevada Janack joined them. "Am I late? Tucker's in China, and we were talking and I lost track of time."

"Spare me the annoyance of those who are in love," Charlie said.

Heidi shifted to make room and Nevada slid in next to her.

"I won't apologize for having the perfect husband," she said, her eyes dancing with humor. "But I am sympathetic toward you for not having Tucker."

"Too bad there's only one of him," Annabelle said with a sigh. "Or Rafe."

Nevada turned to Heidi. "I've been hearing rumors."

Jo returned to the table. "Margaritas all around? I'll warn you, Heidi wants hers with an extra shot."

Heidi held up both hands. "In a few minutes you'll

all know what's been going on, and then you'll be sympathetic."

"Okay," Charlie said. "I can't wait for details. Margarita for me, no extra shot."

The others agreed. They ordered their usual food—chips, salsa and guacamole, and a couple of plates of nachos. Not exactly nutritious, Heidi thought, her stomach growling, but still extra-right for the occasion.

She and Glen had only been in town a few months when she'd become friends with the other women at the table. Nevada, one of the Hendrix triplets, had married the previous New Year's Eve, in a ceremony she'd shared with her two sisters. Although Nevada was as friendly as ever, there was a difference now. She had Tucker and they were madly in love. Heidi didn't begrudge her any happiness, but sometimes it was hard to be around happy newlyweds. Every touch, every stolen glance, was a reminder of her own desperately single state. Not that she was looking for someone in the judicial system to order her to sleep with Rafe Stryker as a remedy.

Thank goodness for Charlie and Annabelle. They were all in the same position, and that reality had only enhanced their friendship.

Conversation flowed around her. For a second, Heidi let herself remember another friendship—one that had been nearly as good as the camaraderie she shared with these women today. Melinda, her best friend for years, would have been turning twenty-eight now. But Melinda had died six years ago. A senseless and tragic loss.

"You okay?" Annabelle asked.

Heidi nodded and pushed the memories away. She would mourn later—when she was alone. For now, she would appreciate the time with her friends.

Jo returned with their drinks and promised the food would be delivered shortly. When she'd walked back to the bar, Annabelle leaned toward Heidi.

"Start at the beginning and tell us everything. What did the judge really say?"

Heidi sipped her margarita. "Basically that we have to share and play nice until she decides what to do about the problem." She went over the details of the temporary plan, including the fact that "improvements," as May called them, were allowed.

"I don't get it," Charlie said. "Why would May Stryker want to pay for stuff at a ranch she might not own?"

"I think she's pretty confident in the outcome," Heidi admitted, trying not to wince as she thought about losing her home. "I tell myself the good news is May is a sweetie, and at least Glen isn't in jail."

"Why is she so hot for the ranch?" Annabelle asked. "Why not buy something somewhere else?"

"They used to live here," Nevada told them. "It was a long time ago. I was a kid, and I don't think any of the Stryker boys were in my class. I think the youngest boy, Clay, was a year older." She wrinkled her forehead in thought. "There's a baby sister, too. I don't remember much about her. What I do remember is that the family was dirt poor. I mean going-without-food poor. My mom wanted to send over clothes my brothers had worn, but by the time they'd worked their way through all three of them, there wasn't much left in them. She did take over food, though. And toys. The town kind of adopted the family."

Heidi couldn't imagine the very proud Rafe accepting charity from anyone. "That must have been difficult for all of them. In court, they said that the old man who owned the ranch promised it to May when he died. But he left it to distant relatives instead. Now she's been cheated out of the place twice."

Nevada gave Heidi a quick hug. "You didn't do anything wrong. Glen did. I know he was trying to help a friend, but now you've put yourself on the line for him. You'll get through this and we'll be right here with you. Tell us how we can help."

Heidi appreciated the assumption that they would simply do what had to be done and the problem would be fixed. It was one of the many reasons she loved Fool's Gold and why she would fight for her home. The fact that Rafe and his mother had more resources wasn't going to matter. She had heart on her side.

"My attorney wants me to sleep with him," she admitted, then downed her extra shot. The tequila burned a pleasant path to her stomach. When she swallowed, she saw all three women staring at her.

"Did she say why?" Charlie asked.

"She thought it would soften him up toward me."

Charlie raised her eyebrows. "If you're softening him up, you're doing it wrong."

The four women looked at each other and then burst into laughter.

When she'd caught her breath, Annabelle sagged back in her seat. "You must be really good. I can't see anyone paying two hundred fifty thousand dollars to have sex with me."

"Do you have a price you're comfortable with?" Charlie asked Annabelle.

"I don't know. Maybe a couple of thousand. Of course, if you started an affair, and added up the number of times you did it..." She stopped talking. "What?"

Nevada cleared her throat. "I think Heidi's attorney was speaking in more metaphorical terms. That if Heidi slept with Rafe, he might forgive the debt. I doubt she was suggesting a sexual installment plan."

"Oh." Annabelle flushed. "Sorry."

"No, it's fine," Heidi said, grinning. "But Charlie's right. You have it bad. You need to find a man."

"Show me a good one who's interested and I'm so there. Or not. It probably wouldn't go well. But back to the issue at hand. Maybe we should find Rafe a woman. Distract him. He would be so busy falling in love that he would forget to be mean to Heidi."

"It's not a bad idea," Charlie murmured.

Jo returned with plates of food. Heidi was already feeling a pleasant buzz. But she knew the danger of drinking on an empty stomach, so she picked up a chip and dug it into the guacamole.

"Who are you thinking of sacrificing?" Nevada asked, reaching for the nachos.

"You make the most sense," Charlie said.

Heidi paused in the act of dipping a second chip into salsa, then realized Charlie was looking at her. In fact, they all were.

"What? No. Not me."

"You're there," Nevada pointed out. "The two of you will be spending time together on the ranch."

"He hates me. He looks at me with contempt. He's some big-city rich guy. I loathe that type. He thinks he's better than everyone else."

"Maybe on the surface," Annabelle said, "but if he grew up poor, it may just be a facade. Maybe you could find out about the real man lurking beneath."

"You make him sound like a sea monster."

Annabelle grinned. "I'm saying it's worth a shot. What have you got to lose? The guy is hot."

"Okay, sure. Ruggedly handsome with broad shoulders," Heidi said.

"Don't forget his ass," Charlie told her. "I've seen him walking around town. Very nice."

"It would be for a good cause," Nevada added.

"Sleeping with the enemy? Wasn't that a movie and didn't it end badly?" Heidi asked.

Annabelle grinned. "Only for the guy. He'll be overwhelmed by your charms."

"I don't have any charms. If I did, they got lost

in the move. Rafe isn't going to fall for me. I'm not his type. He's certainly not mine. I just need to get through this transition without making things worse. And coming on to him would definitely be worse."

She also needed to figure out how to earn two hundred and fifty thousand dollars to pay May back, but that wasn't anything she was going to discuss with her friends. Comfort was one thing, pity was another.

"You really could seduce him if you wanted," Annabelle said. Nevada and Charlie both nodded in agreement.

Heidi clutched her margarita in both hands and laughed. "I appreciate the vote of confidence, however misplaced." She raised her glass. "To the best friends ever."

THANKS TO SEVERAL GLASSES of water, aspirin and her grandfather's secret remedy, Heidi woke the next morning feeling perfectly fine. No headache, no upset stomach. Maybe she should forget about goat cheese and sell his formula instead.

After working her way through her usual chores, she headed for the barn. Last night, Charlie had mentioned she wouldn't be able to make it to the ranch for a couple of days. That meant Mason, Charlie's big gelding, would need to be exercised. Hardly a chore, Heidi thought, anticipating a ride in the cool but sunny April day. She could take Mason out for a couple of hours and still be home in time for lunch. Later, she would take Kermit, their other boarder, on his ride.

"Hard work but someone has to do it," she murmured happily to herself as she pulled on riding boots. She slathered on sunscreen, picked up a cowboy hat, then headed for the front door. As she stepped onto the porch, a familiar Mercedes pulled up by the house. Instantly, her good mood vanished.

May Stryker bounced out of the passenger seat, waving and smiling. "Hello! I hope I'm not being a bother. I just can't stay away."

"You're not a bother," Heidi assured her. In May's case, she was telling the truth. The older woman was lovely, and if she was the only Stryker involved, Heidi believed they could easily come to terms.

The bigger issue—all six-plus feet of him—climbed out of the car more slowly. Rafe stared at her over the roof of his vehicle.

"Morning."

The single word, spoken in a low voice, caused an odd sort of quivering in her stomach.

This was her friends' fault, Heidi realized. All that talk last night about sleeping with Rafe had somehow latched onto a synapse in her brain. Yesterday he'd just been an evil corporate guy bent on her destruction. Now he was someone with a great butt she should try to seduce in a pitiful effort to save her home.

"Go away."

She only thought the words, rather than spoke them, but that didn't lessen the intensity of her wish. Why him? Why couldn't May have had a nice son who understood that people made mistakes?

"I was, um, going for a ride," she said. "To exercise the horses we're boarding."

May walked toward her. "That sounds like fun. How many horses are there?"

"The two you saw on the tour."

"Oh, perfect. Rafe, why don't you help Heidi? If you ride one of the horses, she can be done in half the time."

Or they could go into town and each get a root canal. That would be fun, too.

Heidi did her best to keep her expression neutral. "It's not necessary. I'm fine. Besides, I doubt if Rafe would enjoy riding." Or know how. Although, she had to admit, the thought of him flopping around in a saddle was kind of nice. Maybe he would fall off, hit his head and get amnesia. Then she could pretend he wasn't furious with her, and her problems would be solved. If only…

Rafe raised one eyebrow. "Think I'm not up to the challenge?"

"I didn't say that."

"You didn't have to." He reached into the car and pulled out a pair of sunglasses, then motioned to the barn. "After you."

CHAPTER FIVE

"YOU REALLY DON'T HAVE to do this," Heidi protested as they walked into the barn.

"I know my way around a horse."

"You're a guy who probably wears a five-thousand-dollar suit."

"You're forgetting, I grew up here. Besides, I want to check out my mother's land."

He walked toward the corral where Mason and Kermit were lounging in the sun. Rafe gave a piercing whistle that had both horses turning toward him.

Heidi told herself not to be impressed. Except the horses moved toward him, as if drawn by a force she couldn't see. Rafe stepped into the corral.

"Where do you want them?"

"In the barn."

He guided the horses easily. She let him lead the way, her gaze lingering on the butt Charlie had mentioned. She had to admit it was nice. Athletic rather than flat. Okay, sure, Rafe was a good-looking guy, but a coral snake was beautiful and still deadly.

Once inside, they set to work. Rafe might have a job in San Francisco in a high-rise, yet he hadn't forgotten how to saddle a horse. After using a brush to clean off Mason's back, he set the pad in place with practiced ease. She worked on Kermit, the smaller of the two horses, huffing only a little as she gently set the saddle on Kermit's back.

Bridles were next. Both Mason and Kermit were calm horses, taking the bit without trying to spit it out. From the corner of her eye, she saw Rafe making one last check to make sure everything was fastened securely, but not too tight, and that there weren't any wrinkles or spots that would rub. They led the horses outside.

There was a mounting block on the far side of the barn. As both Mason and Kermit were good-size horses, she turned in that direction, but Rafe stopped her.

"I'll give you a hand up."

"You don't have to."

"I know I don't."

He draped Mason's reins over a post, then walked toward her. He waited until she'd taken the reins in her left hand and grabbed the saddle. Then he laced his fingers together.

She stepped onto his hand. Despite the fact that they weren't touching anywhere, the act felt oddly intimate. She told herself he was just being polite. That his mother had trained him well. Still, she felt flustered as he counted to three, then lifted her toward the saddle.

She swung her leg over Kermit and settled lightly into place.

"Thanks."

"You're welcome." He continued to look at her. "You're a little touchy."

"You've threatened me and my home more than once. I think being cautious shows wisdom."

"I'm protecting what's mine."

"So am I." Which meant what? That they had something in common? "This would be a lot easier if we could get along."

His mouth curved into a slow, sexy smile. "I don't do easy."

"I'm not surprised."

He chuckled, then walked over to Mason. Rafe settled in the saddle, and they moved away from the barn.

"You have a route you usually take?" he asked.

She adjusted her hat, trying not to notice that, for a guy who drove a Mercedes, Rafe looked pretty comfortable on his horse.

"Uh-huh. It's a big circle that takes us over most of the land."

"Good."

Right. Because he wanted to claim what he considered his. "You're not going to start peeing on trees to mark everything, are you?"

He laughed. "Maybe when we know each other better."

He was joking. Unfortunately, his words made her remember her friends' suggestion from the previous evening. That seducing Rafe was the answer to her problems.

She glanced at him, taking in the straight back and

broad shoulders. Was he the kind of lover who took his time and made sure everyone enjoyed the event, or was he selfish in bed? She'd known both kinds of guys, more of the latter than the former.

Not that it mattered, she reminded herself. Sleeping with Rafe would be stupid.

"Is the fence line like this everywhere?" he asked, pointing to the broken or missing posts, the downed line.

"Some of it is in better shape, but only for small sections. What was it like when you lived here before?" she asked before she could stop herself.

"Things were in better shape. Old man Castle might have paid his employees shit, but he cared about the ranch."

She heard a trace of bitterness in his voice, and knew he had cause to resent what his family had gone through. But she still had trouble reconciling the vision of a hungry little boy with the successful man riding next to her.

"He kept a lot of cattle," she said, watching the dark, moving shapes in the distance. "They're everywhere and very wild."

Rafe glanced at her. "Wild?"

"You know. Feral."

He laughed again. "Been attacked by a few feral cows, have you?"

"No, but I stay clear of them. They make trouble with the goats. I swear, they come in the night and show Athena how to break out."

"You're giving them way more credit than they deserve."

"I don't think so." While he was in such a good mood, even if it was at her expense, she risked a potentially dangerous question. "What does your mom want to do with the ranch?"

"I have no idea. I'd say restore it to its former glory, but it never had much of any. She has an emotional connection to this place. She wants to make it...better. She's talking about fence lines and fixing up the barn."

"Does she want to run cattle?"

"I don't think so."

"You could ask."

"Then I'd know, and with my mother, that's not always a good thing."

"Not knowing is the reason you're here now. How come you signed the contract?"

He shook his head. "A few years ago, one of my mom's friends died unexpectedly. Her affairs weren't in order and that made a mess for her kids. My mother decided that wasn't going to happen and made sure she was fully prepared for her eventual passing."

"That's both considerate and a little creepy. She's not that old."

"I know, but once she gets her mind set on something, she can't be budged."

"Oh, so you inherited that from her." Heidi winced, wishing she could remember to think before she spoke.

"Are you saying I'm stubborn?"

"Pretty much."

The sun was high in the sky. The temperature was in the mid-sixties and there were no clouds to be seen. Some of the trees were budding, others had pale pink and creamy-white flowers all along the branches. She could hear birds, and if she ignored the wild cattle off in the distance, the moment would be about perfect.

"Part of her plan to get things in order involved me," Rafe said after a few minutes. "I have to cosign every financial transaction she makes. She uses an online bill-pay, so I'm not involved in those, but every other check or document with a signature comes to me first. It adds up."

"So, that's how come you didn't read the contract to buy the ranch."

"Yeah. It's my own fault."

"Glen's not a bad man."

"No one said he is."

"You implied it."

"He did steal two hundred and fifty thousand dollars."

"But it was for a good reason. To help a friend."

Rafe stared at her. She met his dark gaze and sighed.

"Your point is, stealing is stealing and trying to justify it doesn't change the act itself. He was wrong."

"Something like that," Rafe admitted. "Glen may not be evil, but he's not big on consequences."

Heidi wouldn't admit it out loud, but Rafe was right about her grandfather. Glen skated through life using his charm to get him out of most of the world's unpleasantness.

"I don't suppose it would help to say I'm sure he's sorry."

"No."

They rode in silence for a few minutes. She tried to work up a good indignation or some old-fashioned annoyance, but couldn't. Sure, Rafe threatened her and her home, and she would do anything she could to stop him from tossing her out, but there was a part of her that understood.

Glen had defrauded an innocent woman, and there was no way to make that okay.

"He took me in," she said, keeping her gaze on the beautiful, untamed land around them. They were riding east, with the mountains in front of them. Snow was still visible. The snow line would move higher throughout the summer, but it would never completely disappear. The Sierras were too high for that.

"He told us that, but it's not going to change my mind about him."

She sighed. "I'm pointing out that he's not a bad man. And why I'm not furious with him. I'm frustrated, but I know he's basically a good person. My parents died when I was three. I don't remember much about them. I'd only met Glen a couple of times, so he was a stranger to me. But he didn't even hesitate to become my caretaker."

"What did he do?"

"He was a carny. Working for a carnival. It comes

through here every year, which is how I knew about Fool's Gold."

"I don't know much about carnival life," he admitted.

"It's a unique world. Transient and insular at the same time. We're always in a new place, so we find a sense of home with the people we work with."

"How did you go to school?"

"There were a few kids around, so different adults took on various subjects. Glen taught math."

"That had to have been interesting."

"He was actually pretty good. My friend Melinda aced the SATs and got into a great college." Heidi hadn't been interested in getting a degree, but she and Melinda had still stayed close. If only she'd gone to college with her, maybe everything would have been different.

She told herself not to think about that now. That she couldn't afford to be distracted around Rafe. Not if she wanted to hold her own.

She turned her attention to the man. He rode easily, looking as if he spent daily time in the saddle.

"You weren't kidding about having grown up on a ranch," she admitted.

He patted Mason's neck. "It's coming back to me. Maybe being here won't be so bad, this time around."

"Or you could, you know, leave."

His dark gaze settled on her face. "Not likely."

"You can't blame a girl for trying."

"I can but I won't." He straightened. "It's unfortunate we both want the same thing."

She nodded. "Home and a place to belong."

"I was thinking more of the land."

"One means the other. At least to me. That's all I wanted. Somewhere to settle, a place for Glen and me. And the goats."

"You're not going to get rich raising goats."

"I never needed to be rich. Until now."

AFTER LUNCH, RAFE WENT into town. While he'd been out riding with Heidi, his mother had thoughtfully put together a list of projects she would like to see him take care of over the next few weeks. When he'd pointed out he still had a business to run, she'd actually patted him on the head and said he would figure out a way to get both done.

He loved his mother. He really did. But there were days, and this was one of them, when he would cheerfully walk away from his entire family and never have anything to do with them again.

He parked by the lumber supply yard, but instead of going inside the small office, he headed for the center of town. Stiff muscles protested the walking. As his ride with Heidi had only been an hour at best, he was going to have to step up his workouts when he got back to San Francisco. Weight training and miles on a treadmill didn't prepare a man for life on a ranch, and according to his mother, he was going to be here for a while.

Despite how much he didn't want to be anywhere near Fool's Gold, he'd found himself enjoying being on a horse again. Riding in the sunlight, surveying relatively untamed land, had been kind of nice. Either the pleasure was primal, or he'd been watching too many Westerns.

He ducked into a Starbucks and bought a drip coffee and a scone. As he stepped outside, he had the thought that he should have brought Heidi along with him. She would have—

He paused in midgulp of the hot coffee, then nearly choked. Brought Heidi? Into town? What? So he could make friends with her? She wasn't a friend, she was trouble. All sweet and pretty, with those damn, big green eyes. Yesterday he'd nearly bought into her innocent act. Sure, maybe she hadn't known what Glen was doing, but he still couldn't trust her. Or her goats.

He ate the scone and tossed the paper bag into a nearby trash can. He wasn't going to think about Heidi. Not how good she'd looked on the horse, or how she'd smelled like vanilla and flowers when he'd given her a hand up to the saddle. Not the way her eyes crinkled when she smiled, or how he'd been aware of her body moving with each step of the horse. Nope, not him. Not the least bit aware. She was someone in his way—nothing more.

He turned to walk back to the lumber supply yard when an older woman came toward him. She was well dressed, wearing a dark blue suit and pearls. Her white hair was carefully styled in that poufy bubble old ladies seemed to like.

When she smiled at him, he came to a stop.

"Rafe Stryker."

"Yes, ma'am."

"I'm Mayor Marsha Tilson."

The combination of her name and the steady gaze of her blue eyes triggered a memory. Rafe frowned. "You're the lady who gave me the bike." She was also part of the group that had regularly delivered food and clothing to his mother, but as a kid, the bike had been more significant.

Her smile widened. "Yes. I'm delighted you remember."

"You were kind to us. Thank you."

The words were tough to get out. Even after all this time, he didn't like to recall the past—when he'd gone hungry and his mother had cried all the time.

"You were an impressive little boy," the mayor told him. "So determined to take care of your family. So proud. You made sure your brothers and sister didn't have to worry."

He cleared his throat, not sure how to respond to her statements. "I did what had to be done."

"You were nine or ten. Far too young to be shouldering life's responsibilities. Now, I understand, you're a successful businessman."

He nodded.

"Fool's Gold needs men like you."

"I'm not here to stay. I'm helping out my mother."

The mayor's eyes twinkled. "Maybe we can change your mind. We have a very progressive business climate here. In fact, there's a new casino and hotel going in right outside of town. The Lucky Lady."

That caught his attention. "I hadn't heard."

"You should take a look at what they're doing. The developer is Janack Construction."

"I've heard of them," Rafe admitted. Janack was multinational. They took on massive projects, like suspension bridges in developing countries and high-rises in China. If they were building something here, it was significant.

"I appreciate the information," he told her.

"You could fit right in here, Rafe."

Unlikely, but rather than say that, he wished her a good day and hurried to the lumber store.

He stepped around the side of the building and pulled out his phone. He dialed a familiar number.

"Jefferson," his friend Dante barked.

"Having a bad day?"

"Rafe." Dante chuckled. "No. I was expecting another lawyer to be calling me. You know, it's all about attitude. What's going on? Convince your mother to come back to life in the big city?"

"Like that's going to happen."

"She's a determined woman."

"Tell me about it. And while you're at it, tell me what you know about a hotel casino project called the Lucky Lady."

He waited while Dante typed on his computer.

There was a second of silence, followed by a low whistle. "Impressive." He read off the statistics, how many rooms, number of acres, the approximate cost of the project. "Janack Construction has this sewn up. We can't get in on it."

"We don't have to." He thought about his mother's ranch and the thousands of acres with nothing on them. "Maybe my time here isn't a complete waste. That hotel and casino is going to need employees. There can't be enough housing in Fool's Gold, which means a potential opportunity for us."

"I'll put somebody on the preliminaries," Dante told him. "Find out zoning restrictions, if anyone else has been getting permits, that sort of thing. You know...." Dante paused. "You could use this to help with the judge."

"How?"

"Your mom wants you to fix up the ranch. I say go for it. Putting money into the house and the land might give you a stronger case. Even if the judge rules against you, you can appeal. With that casino and hotel going in, you've got even more reason you want to win."

Potentially several million in profit, Rafe thought. Money always worked for him.

"If you get involved in the community, you'll look good to the judge," Rafe added.

"I'm not getting involved."

"It wouldn't kill you."

"It might," Rafe said. "We have to win this case,

Dante. I'm not going to be defeated by a woman who raises goats."

"She's pretty enough."

"I'm unmoved."

"Maybe I'm moved enough for both of us."

Rafe laughed. "She's not your type."

Dante preferred his women well dressed, sophisticated and easy. Heidi might have a string of excellent qualities, but none of them matched Dante's interests.

"Keeping her for yourself?" his friend asked. "Should I be worried?"

"That I'm going to fall for goat girl and go soft?"

"Okay. When you put it like that… I'll get you a report on the potential for your mom's land by the end of the day."

"Thanks."

Rafe hung up and went inside the lumber store. He was approached by an old guy wearing an apron and a name tag that said Frank.

"How can I help you?" the man asked.

"I need about ten miles of fence line and to repair an old barn." He pulled out of his shirt pocket a list of supplies he'd made and handed it over. Since learning about the Lucky Lady, he was more enthused about his mother's projects. "You know anybody looking for a few days' work?"

Frank scanned the list, then gave a low whistle. "You're serious. Okay, then, let's get your supplies ordered. As for guys to help, the best place to get them is through Ethan Hendrix. He owns the biggest home construction firm in town. Also the most reliable and experienced. Hendrix Construction. I have a card up front."

Rafe followed the man, ducking around a teenager with two-by-fours on his shoulder. Interesting that Ethan Hendrix had been recommended. Rafe remembered the name and the kid who'd gone with it. Rafe and Ethan had been friends, along with another kid. Josh Golden. He knew that the latter, the former professional cyclist and Tour de France winner had settled in Fool's Gold, but he hadn't realized that Ethan was still here.

Frank took him out into the lumber yard and pointed out the various options for the fencing. Rafe made his decision, then picked lumber for the barn. Frank showed him the small selection of roofing material they kept on hand, and made sure they had plenty of what Rafe needed. Just as they were wrapping up their conversation, two massive construction trucks backed into the yard, sending men scattering.

"Those guys mean business," Rafe said once he and Frank were inside. Big trucks meant big projects. "Are they here for the casino and hotel construction?"

"You've heard about that?"

"Yes."

Frank grinned. "Lucky for us, the contractor believes in buying local. They're employing lots of people, too. You looking for a job?"

Rafe shook his head. "No. Just curious."

He paid for the lumber and other supplies and arranged for them to be delivered in two days. When he returned to his car, he pulled out his cell and made a quick check of his email. There was a note from Nina Blanchard. He scanned it, then dialed her number.

He was put through immediately.

"Rafe," Nina purred.

Purred was not a word that would come to his mind under most circumstances, but there was no other way to think of the smooth tone of her voice.

"Nina."

"You're being elusive. Can you guess it's not my favorite characteristic in a client? All your rather formidable assistant would say was that you were out of town."

"She's right. I'm in Fool's Gold. Do you know it?"

"I've been a few times. They have charming festivals."

"So I've been told. I'm here on a family matter, and I'm not sure when I'll be back in San Francisco. We'll have to table our plans until then."

"Don't be silly. If you can't come to the ladies, then they'll come to you."

He glanced at the lumber yard. "I don't think that's a good idea."

"Why not? You'll be in neutral territory. If they won't make the drive, they're not worth the trouble, right? You've hired me to find you the perfect wife. I take that responsibility very seriously."

"Fine. If one of the candidates wants to come here, I'll meet her."

"Thank you. Now, let me get you some names and we'll take it from there."

"Sure."

He hung up, knowing he should probably be more enthused than he was about the whole idea of getting married. Honestly, if he didn't want kids, he wouldn't bother with a permanent relationship. But he couldn't seem to shake the traditional idea of a mother and a father when it came to children. He'd watched his mother struggle after his dad had died.

He had a feeling that his idea of perfect and Nina's might not be the same. He'd done his best to explain he wasn't looking for love. He'd tried that once and it had blown up in his face. This time, he was going to be realistic. Find someone he could be friends with, someone he would enjoy sleeping with, and with whom he could imagine raising children. Nothing else was required. Love was a myth, and he was too old to believe in fairy tales.

HEIDI RELEASED ATHENA back into the goat corral, then stripped off her gloves. Three very fat, very sassy cats gazed at her expectantly.

"Where did you come from?" she asked, even as she poured fresh, still-warm goat milk into an old pie pan and set it on the wooden floor of the goat house.

The first of the cats had shown up about a month after the goats had arrived. Heidi had been milking, minding her own business, only to be startled by a very demanding meow. Foolishly she'd given the black-and-white cat a taste of goat milk. From then on, the cat had shown up exactly at milking time, every day. Eventually it had been joined by a tabby and an all-gray cat with a pushed-in kind of face.

The cats waited until she put the pie dish on the floor, then began lapping the milk.

Their coats were in great shape and they were obviously well fed. They must live around here, but where? And how had they learned to tell time? She only milked once a day, and the cats always arrived a few minutes early, then waited patiently until she was finished.

She supposed she could simply stop giving them milk. After all, she wasn't much of a cat person. But there was something compelling about the way they stared at her, as if their feline minds should have the ability to direct her actions.

Still chuckling at the thought of cat mind-control, she carried the fresh milk toward the house. She was halfway across the yard when she realized that an SUV and a Mercedes were in the yard. Vehicles she recognized. Rafe and May had dropped by early.

It had been two days since their last visit—when she'd gone riding with Rafe and had found herself oddly attracted to the one person who was out to get her. Chemistry, she thought as she walked into the house. It could make a fool of you every time.

"Good morning," she said, setting the clean metal buckets on the counter.

May sat at the table with Glen, a box of pastries between them. Rafe leaned against the counter. While his mother was all smiles and hellos, Rafe regarded her with an unreadable expression.

"Oh, you were milking. I'd like to see that," May said. "Do you think I could learn how to do it?"

"Sure. It's not that hard. The main rule is to keep everything clean and sanitary. A challenge when it comes to goats."

"You sell raw milk?" Rafe asked, his tone very similar to the one a person would use to ask if the entrée contained poop.

"Every day."

"So many people see the benefits of organic goat's milk," May said with an enthusiastic smile. "Oh, Rafe, this is going to be so fun."

This? This, as in…

Rafe turned to Heidi. "My mother has decided she would prefer to stay here, rather than at the hotel. If it's all right with you, of course."

The latter was added simply to be polite. Heidi got that. May's decision to "work things out" was the only reason Glen wasn't currently in jail. Until the judge ruled, it made sense to play nice. But May living here and—

Heidi felt her mouth drop open. Rafe raised an eyebrow and nodded imperceptibly.

"Yes, I'll be joining her."

Because he wasn't leaving until the case was settled, and a guy like that wouldn't let his mother come live on the ranch by herself.

This couldn't be happening. Both of them at the house? May wasn't a problem, but Rafe?

She wanted to say the place wasn't big enough, but there were six bedrooms and a bathroom on each floor. Something May and Rafe would know, having lived here before.

"You know we haven't had the chance to remodel anything," Heidi said weakly. "The bathrooms are pretty ancient, and the beds are worn and not very comfortable."

"It will be perfect," May assured her.

Heidi glanced at her grandfather, but Glen was busy stirring his coffee. She had a bad feeling that the issue had been discussed while she was out with the goats and Glen had agreed without any protest.

"I hope you don't mind," May continued, "but Rafe and I have taken the liberty of picking out our rooms. I'm going to stay downstairs."

Heidi glared at her grandfather. Glen was downstairs. No doubt he was pleased by the arrangement, but if he thought sleeping with May was a good idea, he was beyond wrong. Heidi was going to have to figure out a way to talk some sense into him.

"Which makes us roommates," Rafe murmured. "All right. Housemates."

Heidi swung her gaze to his and wanted to stomp her foot at the amusement she saw lurking in his brown irises. Oh, sure. He thought this was funny.

"You know there's only one bathroom upstairs," she said.

"I can share."

"Fine. Of course, you're welcome to stay here." She would get through this, figure out a way to pay back the money owed and get on with her life. In a year or two, what was happening right now would be little more than a funny story to share with her friends.

"Let's get your things out of the car," Glen said, rising to his feet.

Heidi let him go without saying anything. She would corner her grandfather later and remind him why he had to act like a perfect gentleman around May. No seduction allowed.

She walked to the pantry and picked up several sterilized glass one-quart milk bottles. Rafe walked with her, grabbing four and following her back to the kitchen.

"I went upstairs," he told her.

"I'm not even surprised. Did you happen to go through my underwear drawer while you were there?"

"No. Did you want me to?"

She ignored that, and him. After setting a stainless steel funnel into the first bottle, she raised the bucket and began to pour.

"You're in my old room."

It was a testament to her upper-body strength that the flow from the bucket barely wavered.

"Do you want it back?"

"No, you keep it. I took the one next door." He walked toward the back door, then paused. "I hope you don't snore."

GLEN DID A GREAT JOB of avoiding his granddaughter, but Heidi tracked him down shortly before dinner. It took her standing outside the bathroom while he showered and shaved. She listened to the familiar old songs he hummed as he worked. They reminded her of when she was a little girl and had been frightened of the thunderstorms that rolled across the plains states. Glen had always held her tight during the storms, humming music popular a generation before she was born.

She enjoyed the memories, but refused to let them sway her. They were in a lot of trouble, and Glen had the power to make their situation much worse.

He opened the bathroom door, saw her and paused.

"Heidi!" His voice was falsely cheerful. "What can I do you for?"

She grabbed him by the arm and pulled him toward his bedroom. When they were safely inside, she closed the door behind him and planted her hands on her hips.

"Stay away from May."

His eyes widened in exaggerated innocence. "I have no idea what you're talking about."

"Yes, you do, Glen. I've seen how you look at her. I've watched the flirting. You like her, which is great, but this time the answer is no."

His back stiffened. "You're my granddaughter. That's not for you to say."

"It is for me to say," she told him. "If you hurt May, we'll lose everything for sure."

"I would never hurt her."

Heidi sighed. "Yes, you would. You know how you

are, Glen. Getting women has never been the problem. It's keeping them that you're not so crazy about. You walk away and the woman is crushed. If you do that to May, she'll take the ranch."

Her grandfather nodded slowly. "You're right. I'll be careful."

She studied him, not sure if he was saying what she wanted to hear, or if he meant what he was saying. "You promise?"

He kissed her cheek. "I'm sorry I got you into this mess, Heidi. I won't do anything to make it worse."

CHAPTER SIX

"DO YOU MIND?" MAY ASKED, her arms full of framed pictures. She paused in the middle of the living room, then turned to Heidi. "I'm intruding. My boys tell me all the time that I get too involved. I'm enthusiastic. Mostly that's a good thing, right?"

Despite the fact that Heidi was now living in the bedroom next to Rafe's, and that her grandfather was avoiding her, which meant he was either upset or still determined to seduce May, and that Heidi lacked money in her savings account, she found herself smiling.

"Not enough people are enthusiastic," she admitted. "I don't mind you personalizing the house. If you have a sofa or two in your suitcase, I'd love to see them."

May laughed. "You don't love the green-and-purple plaid?"

Heidi leaned against the hideous couch that had come with the place. "No. Weird, huh?"

"It was ugly back when we lived here. Now it's ugly and old. Poor thing."

She set three pictures on the sofa table. Heidi moved closer. She recognized Rafe at once, even though the photo was from at least a decade ago. He was wearing a black cap and gown, holding a diploma cover that clearly said Harvard. She wasn't even surprised.

May followed her gaze. "Rafe was on an academic scholarship. There's no way I could have paid for his books, let alone the tuition. But he worked hard and graduated at the top of his class." She pointed to the middle frame. The man was handsome, in a rugged way, with an easygoing smile. He was leaning against a horse, one arm on the animal's neck.

"My middle son, Shane. He raises horses. Breeds them. Mostly Arabians and stock for the rodeo. He's in Tennessee right now. And this is my baby. Clay."

Clay had the same dark hair as his brothers, and his features were similar enough to claim the familial relationship, but the similarities ended there. Clay was a whole new level of handsome. The plain navy T-shirt he wore outlined chiseled muscles and broad shoulders. He wasn't smiling, but Heidi found herself wishing he would. Just a little.

"Wow," she said, picking up the frame and staring at the picture. "He almost looks familiar."

May looked uncomfortable and quickly took the picture back. "Rafe doesn't like me to talk about Clay."

Why? Was he in prison? Or worse, although she wasn't sure what would qualify as worse.

"Then we won't talk about him." Heidi touched the other woman's arm. "It's all right."

May nodded, her mouth tight with worry.

"Don't you have a daughter, as well?"

May sorted through the other pictures she held and

passed one to Heidi, showing the boys and their sister at the holidays.

Rafe's baby sister was younger than Heidi had expected. The boys were obviously close in age, but Evangeline had to have been born six or eight years later. She didn't look anything like the rest of the family, either. Her hair was a honey-blond, her eyes deep green.

"She's lovely," Heidi told May. "I notice you don't have any other pictures of her. Is she…" Heidi paused, wishing she'd thought before speaking. "Did she, um, die?"

"Oh, no. She's a classically trained dancer. I've only seen her perform a few times, but she's wonderful. Elegant and graceful. I wish…" May drew in a breath. "We're not close. We don't speak much these days. Mothers and daughters. You know how that goes."

As Heidi barely remembered anything about her mother, she couldn't relate to any kind of mother-daughter relationship, but she nodded, mostly because she realized things in the Stryker household weren't as they had first seemed. Not quite so perfect.

May quickly put out the rest of the pictures. Heidi saw that, except for the one photo of Evangeline, they were all of the brothers. Complications and questions, but not so many answers.

"We should probably come up with some ground rules," May told her. "About the kitchen."

"What did you have in mind?" Heidi asked, not sure what she meant.

"I thought it would be easier if we shared our meals. The four of us. I love to cook, so I don't mind taking care of fixing dinner."

Cooking wasn't one of Heidi's favorite chores, so she was thrilled to let someone else handle that. But sitting down across from Rafe every night would be difficult. Or tempting, which made the situation problematic.

"I already asked Glen and he said it was fine with him."

Heidi held in a groan. "You're welcome to cook anytime you'd like. I hope you'll let me help. But, about Glen. You need to be careful. He's a bit of a flirt."

May blushed and turned away. She busied herself rearranging the pictures on the table. "I've heard a few things about him in town. Don't worry. I won't be taken in by his charm. It's just nice to have a man to talk to. My husband died so long ago. I'd nearly forgotten what it was like to have a man around."

Heidi didn't know how to press her point without sounding mean, so she hoped her warning would be enough.

"Is there any food you don't like?" May asked.

"No."

"Good. Rafe and I will go out tonight, but tomorrow I'll be cooking. Maybe lasagna."

"That sounds delicious." Heidi suspected May's lasagna didn't come in a red box from the frozen-food aisle.

The roar of a large truck engine shattered the quiet. May turned toward the sound and clapped her hands together. "They're here with the supplies. I can't wait to see everything."

Heidi followed her out onto the porch. Two trucks from the local lumber supply pulled into the yard, by the barn. From where she stood, she could see fence posts and two-by-fours, roofing material and what looked like a barn door. While the thought of getting the place fixed up was exciting, everything on the trucks represented more money she was probably going to have to pay back if she wanted May gone.

She wanted to complain, to say that until the judge ruled, this was still her house and her land. But she didn't dare annoy May. The other woman's generosity was the only reason Glen wasn't sitting in jail. Right now Heidi couldn't afford to speak her mind. Just one more thing on the list of what was very expensive these days.

Rafe pulled in behind the trucks. He climbed out of his car, wearing jeans, a plaid shirt and work boots—not exactly the high-powered executive she'd first met in the middle of the road. His jeans fit him well and, yes, his butt was very nice, but her interest was purely intellectual. She could admire a man and still not want to have anything to do with him. The long legs and narrow hips were Mother Nature's way of messing with her head. And maybe her hormones.

Oh, but it had been a very long time since a man had held her.

She'd had a few boyfriends during her teen years, and a serious relationship when she'd turned twenty. Mike had been a "townie" living in the small Arizona city where the carnival had settled for the winter. Heidi had always heard about the dangers of getting involved with locals, but Mike had swept her off her feet and she'd quickly succumbed to his charms. She'd given him her heart and her virginity. But when spring came, he didn't want to go with the carnival, and she couldn't leave the only family she had in the world. Although she and Mike had promised to stay in touch, he had eventually stopped calling. She'd heard through a mutual friend that he'd found someone else and was engaged. The following winter, the carnival went somewhere else.

She'd gotten over her broken heart, had enjoyed her life. The men who traveled with the carnival were either too old or too much like brothers for her to consider as romantic partners. Then, just when she'd started thinking it was time to find another way of life, Melinda, her best friend, had fallen in love.

Her relationship had burned hot and ended badly. Melinda, a softhearted young woman who always believed the best about everyone, had been devastated. Depression had followed. Two suicide attempts had shaken the small carnival community. Heidi had been determined to keep her friend alive, no matter what. But Melinda had been more determined to die.

Heidi walked around the back of the house and headed for the refuge that was her goats. Watching

Melinda suffer had made Heidi wary of love. Of the price it exacted. Very few of the carnival family were married, and she could only remember a handful of happy couplings. Which made her unclear on the benefits of falling in love. Could that kind of feeling really last, and was it worth the trouble?

As far as how long it had been since she'd found a man in her bed, that was a different sort of problem. One of the downsides of living in Fool's Gold was that, in a close-knit community like this one, there were no secrets. Going out of town for temporary romance might have been appealing, but she didn't know where or how to begin. She wasn't the bar type, and goats weren't exactly a guy magnet.

Glen always told her to be open to the possibilities. The next time one presented itself, she just might have to say yes.

HEIDI FINISHED PRINTING the new labels for her cheese and studied the result. The artwork was clean, the colors bright. The only way she knew to make more money was to sell more cheese. But would this new label appeal to consumers?

Glen was downstairs. She could show it to him and get at least one opinion. If only she knew a marketing person, she thought as she walked out of her bedroom and ran into something solid, warm and very male.

Heidi stepped back and looked up, then wished she hadn't.

Rafe had spent the afternoon unloading lumber and

other supplies for the barn and fence line. No doubt he'd worked up a sweat and had therefore wanted to shower before dinner. But none of that explained why he was standing in the middle of the upstairs hall, wearing nothing but a couple of towels and a sexy grin.

His hair was wet and standing in surprisingly appealing little spikes. He hadn't bothered shaving, so he was a combination of rough and naked. He smelled like her goat soap. The towel draped around his neck did little to conceal his bare chest, and the one at his waist teased with possibilities.

"What?" she snapped. "You can't get changed in the bathroom?"

That single damned eyebrow rose.

"Is there a problem?"

"No. And don't think I'm going to sleep with you, because I'm not. You're just stubborn enough that it wouldn't distract you from what you want, and then I would lose twice."

His mouth curved into a slow grin. "I don't recall asking you to sleep with me, but if you did, no one would lose."

Horrified to realize what she'd just said, Heidi turned and raced for the stairs. Laughter followed her down to the first floor, where she bolted outside.

Cool evening air filled her lungs, but it wasn't enough to ease the burning on her cheeks. Stupid man, she thought. Stupid man who looked really good in a towel. Whoever said life didn't have a sense of humor was fifteen kinds of wrong.

"DON'T TELL ME TO SLEEP with Rafe to fix the problem," Heidi said. Perhaps not the most professional way to begin the conversation with her lawyer, but she wanted to be clear. After last night's unfortunate verbal spill, she'd been avoiding Rafe and planned to continue to not see him. Perhaps forever.

Trisha shifted the folders in front of her. "You can't ask me to help you, then tie my hands and expect a miracle." She chuckled. "Okay. I won't mention it. I wonder if Rafe would be interested in sleeping with me? I wouldn't say no to that one, despite the age difference."

A visual Heidi didn't want, but at least the concept was a distraction.

"Rafe and May have moved in."

Trisha winced. "I don't like the sound of that. Getting them out could be a problem."

"With what the judge said about us sharing the ranch, I didn't think I could tell them no. The house is big enough." She wasn't going to mention her worries about Glen. As far as she was concerned, there'd already been too much sex talk.

"How's it working out?" Trisha asked.

"May is lovely. Very sweet and motherly. She cooks."

"Ask her to come live with me," Trisha said with a sigh. "I would kill for a home-cooked meal."

"Tell me about it. But Rafe is complicated."

"His type always is."

"I've heard more about what happened to May and her kids back when she worked for the previous owner. He was horrible to her."

"That may be true," Trisha said. "It shouldn't have an effect on the judge, but everybody's human."

"What do you know about Rafe's younger brother Clay?"

Trisha leaned back in her chair and sighed. "You don't know?" She laughed. "You really should."

"What are you talking about?"

"Have you seen his picture?"

"Sure. May put several out in the living room."

"Oh, not that kind." Trisha typed on her laptop, then turned the machine so it faced Heidi.

The photo of a man filled the screen. He was naked, the shot taken from the back—his butt front and center, so to speak. Trisha reached around and pushed a button. The picture changed to Clay Stryker in extremely tight bikini briefs. Unless he'd been Photoshopped, his, assets were impressive.

Heidi felt her eyes widen as she stared. "He's a—"

"An underwear model. Also a movie butt-double. Trust me, the studios pay big bucks to get his ass up on-screen. Very successful."

"Rafe talks about him like he's a criminal. Actually, he doesn't talk about him."

"Probably embarrassed. Rafe is a successful business guy. Do you think he likes having his little brother posing half-naked on a Times Square billboard?"

Heidi didn't know Rafe well enough to be sure. "But he's family."

"Not everyone thinks being family is enough. How's the financial plan coming?"

Heidi would rather talk about Clay's butt or nearly any other topic. "Not well. I'm going to try to sell more cheese, and I have a couple of pregnant goats. Their kids will bring in money."

"Am I right in thinking they don't go for a hundred thousand each?"

"Not exactly."

"How did you buy the ranch in the first place?"

Heidi shrugged. "I won a small lottery jackpot. It was enough for the down payment, closing costs and the goats. We had a few dollars in savings. I've started playing again, but I don't hold out hope I'll win a second time."

"Any rich relatives ready to die?"

"No."

"Too bad." She turned the computer around and closed the top. "You need to come up with a way to pay back a significant percentage of what Glen stole. The judge isn't going to want to hear about a plan that takes a decade. I'm serious, Heidi. You could lose the ranch, and Glen could go to prison. For real."

"I'll come up with something," Heidi promised, although she wasn't sure what or how.

RAFE SURVEYED THE FENCE. Most of the posts were leaning or missing, and the material between had either disappeared or was hanging by a single staple. The job would go faster if there were no fence at all. As it was, he would have to check each of the posts, pull the ones that weren't sturdy enough, get rid of all the old wire fencing and then start with new material.

"That's a lot of work."

Rafe turned and saw Glen walking toward him. The old man pulled a pair of gloves out of his jeans' back pocket.

"So we should probably get started."

"You planning on helping me?" Rafe asked. He would guess Glen had been eligible for social security for close to a decade. Sure, he looked wiry, but what about his heart? Rafe wasn't interested in putting the old man at risk.

"I put in my years as a roadie. Besides, it's not like you're digging holes the old-fashioned way." He pointed to the engine-powered auger Rafe had rented. "Hell, boy, I've been handling machines like that longer than you've been alive."

Boy? Rafe hid a grin. If Glen was trying to intimidate him, he was going to have to work a lot harder.

"You want to drill the postholes, you go ahead," Rafe told him, thinking it would be the easiest work of the day. The equipment would provide most of the muscle, and Rafe would handle the heavy lifting.

Rafe had barely pulled out the first of the leaning posts when two trucks drove onto the ranch. They headed right for the fence line and came to a stop only a few feet away. There was one guy in the first truck, and two in the second.

The first man climbed out and walked toward Rafe. He was tall, with dark hair, and there was something about him that seemed familiar. Almost as if Rafe had met him before.

The man laughed as he approached. “I wouldn’t have recognized you, either,” he said. “Not if I hadn’t heard you were back in town.”

Rafe studied the stranger. “Ethan? Ethan Hendrix?”

“That’s me.”

The two men shook hands.

“Welcome home,” Ethan said. “I remember you hating Fool’s Gold. I can’t believe you’re back.”

“I’m not back or home. This is temporary.”

Ethan glanced at the stacks of fence posts and rolls of fencing. “Looks pretty permanent to me.”

“My mother is planning to stay in town. I’m helping her out.”

“You always did take care of her.” Ethan motioned for the other two men to join them. “I’m going to let you have two of my best. Got a call from the lumber supply about what you were planning to do.” Ethan grinned, his dark eyes bright with amusement. “Last I heard, you were some finance guy. If you’ve gone soft, there’s no way you can do this yourself.”

“I haven’t gone soft,” Rafe told him, then introduced Glen, who waved away the words.

“I know Ethan,” the old man said. “And these two.

Come on, boys. We'll get started and show them how it's done."

Rafe and Ethan walked toward the larger truck.

"You never left?" Rafe asked. "I remember something about you wanting to get away, too."

Ethan shrugged. "That was the plan. Life intervened. Turned out staying here was the best thing that ever happened to me." He pulled out his wallet and removed a couple of pictures.

Rafe studied the pretty redhead and the three children. "You've been busy."

"I've been happy," Ethan said.

Rafe handed back the picture. "Good for you." While he didn't feel any regrets about his marriage having failed, he was sorry not to have children of his own.

"Where are you living?" Ethan asked.

"San Francisco. You still in construction?"

"Some. The company pretty much runs itself. Most of my time is spent building turbines." His smile flashed again. "Windmills, to you laypeople. Wind energy."

They talked about Ethan's business for a few minutes.

"We should get together," Ethan said. "I'll talk to Liz about having you over for dinner. Remember Josh Golden?"

"Sure."

"He's still in town. Married, with a kid. Fiona is a year now. Time flies. We'll have them over."

They discussed the other mutual friends they'd had in school—who was still around and who had moved on. After a few minutes, Ethan glanced at his watch.

"I need to get back. Keep my guys as long as you want. They know what they're doing."

"I appreciate the help. You'll send me a bill for their time?"

"Count on it," Ethan told him. "From what I've heard, you can afford it."

Rafe shrugged. "I get by."

"I'll be in touch to set up that dinner. It's good to have you back."

"I'm not back."

Ethan opened the driver's-side door of his truck. "People say that a lot around here, and yet they never seem to leave. You might be more 'back' than you think, Rafe."

AT SEVEN-THIRTY THAT NIGHT, the sun had yet to drift fully below the horizon. Rafe sat on the front-porch steps of the old house, a bottle of beer between his feet.

It had been a good day, he thought, shifting slightly. His muscles protested the movements, reminding him that building a fence was hard work, even with a motorized fence-post digger and plenty of help. His shoulders ached. Despite the gloves he'd worn, he had a few cuts on his hands, along with several blisters. He should probably be pissed, but he felt a sense of pride when he studied the straight, strong fence line. They'd made a good start. With the help of the guys Ethan had sent, it would only take a couple of weeks to get the fence line finished. Then they would move on to the barn.

He checked in with his office regularly. Ms. Jennings kept him informed on the most important projects. His days usually consisted of meetings and negotiations, contracts and travel. At the end of twelve or fourteen hours, he'd done plenty but couldn't point to any one thing that had been finished. When a deal finally closed, he was already so deep into the next one, he rarely stopped to notice, let alone celebrate.

He'd thought being stuck in Fool's Gold would be like serving time in hell. Maybe it would come to that, but today it hadn't been too bad.

His cell phone rang. He pulled it from his shirt pocket. "Stryker."

"Miss me?"

He grinned at his friend's words. "No."

Dante chuckled. "How wrong you are, and you'll know it, too, when I tell you what happened today."

Dante explained how he'd filed court documents, charmed a judge and done his best to once again make sure the company didn't just win, but also crushed the opposition.

"Impressive," Rafe said, then took a swallow of his beer.

Instead of paying attention to the details that would gain him millions, he found himself listening to the sounds from inside. The low rumble of conversation and the familiar intro music to his mother's favorite game show. Heidi had gone upstairs after dinner. Would she come down again later?

Except for raving about his mother's lasagna, Heidi had been silent at the table. She hadn't looked at him once and had resisted any attempts at conversation. May had fussed over her, wondering if she didn't feel well. Rafe suspected Heidi's actions were more about what she'd said yesterday than any health issues.

When had she started thinking about them sleeping together? And, while it was all fine and good that she'd decided she wouldn't sleep with him, her announcement had had the opposite effect on him. He'd been unable to think about much else.

"You're not listening to me," Dante said.

"Sorry. Distractions."

"Goats?"

"Not exactly."

"A woman?"

"Any other business?" Rafe asked.

"That's a yes. Goat girl? She's not your type."

"What does that mean?"

"Since your divorce, you've preferred a different kind of woman. Beautiful, sure, but the kind who wouldn't know a real emotion if it bit her on the ass. Heidi's different."

"When did you become an expert?"

"I'm just saying."

"I'm hanging up now."

Rafe pushed the button to end the call, then slipped the phone back into his shirt pocket. He took another swallow of his beer, knowing Dante was right. Heidi wasn't like the other women who drifted in and out of his life. She was more down-to-earth. Besides, his plans for the ranch included making sure his mother owned it and Heidi didn't. All the more reason to avoid her.

The screen door opened, and the woman on his mind stepped out, into the rapidly cooling evening air. She walked onto the porch, then came to a stop when she saw him.

"Oh, sorry." She started to turn around.

"Wait." He moved to the side on the step, making room for her. "Join me."

"I don't want to intrude."

"I'm not doing anything."

Her gaze darted around the porch, as if searching for an excuse to say no, then she sighed, and moved toward him.

She sat down, holding herself stiffly. The scent of vanilla drifted to him. For once, her blond hair was loose rather than in the braids she favored. She wore a long-sleeved T-shirt over jeans and boots. Nothing sexy or enticing. Nothing that should have appealed to him. Yet he was aware of her, of how it would be to close the distance and have her lean against him.

"The fence looks good," she said.

"Uh-huh."

"Glen said you worked hard."

"You sound surprised."

She glanced at him, then faced front again. "You seem like more of a manager."

"Better at giving orders than taking them?"

Her mouth turned up in a smile. "We both know that's true."

"Fair enough, but I can put in a fence if I have to. Until now, I've done my best to make sure I don't have to."

She wasn't wearing any makeup, he realized as he stared at her. Her skin looked soft, as did her mouth. He lowered his gaze to her hands. Short nails and a few calluses. She worked hard with her hands.

"May said you've found someone to take the cows," she said.

He picked up the bottle and took a drink. "The price is fair. He'll be by in a couple of days to get them."

"They're going to end up on someone's dinner table, aren't they?"

"Is that concern I hear in your voice?"

She sighed. "I don't want them hurt. I just don't want them here. Maybe a zoo would take them."

He swallowed just then and started to choke. She watched him anxiously until he'd recovered.

"You okay?"

He nodded and cleared his throat. "You want to offer your wild cows to a zoo?"

"I can't think of them being killed and eaten."

"Where do you think your steaks come from?"

"That's different. I don't know those cows."

"You don't know these, either. You're scared of

them. Heidi, it's a lot of money." He told himself not to remind her of that again. After all, every cent she made would go toward paying off his mother. If she got enough together, she might be able to sway the judge.

"Let me think about it. If he would promise not to kill them, then I would be okay with it."

"What's he supposed to do with your herd?"

"You're being logical. I just want to have my goats and not deal with other animals. At least not the kind you eat."

"People eat goats."

"Not mine."

"Your goats do have a good life here."

Heidi told herself that her awareness of the evening came from the natural beauty of the surroundings and the quiet of the night. The goats had already settled down, the birds had nested and the crickets were out. She was one with nature. She was calm.

Then Rafe shifted on the step and she jumped. Her heart thudded so loudly, she was surprised the crickets didn't all scream in terror, assuming crickets made any sound other than the chirpy one.

So much for being calm.

It wasn't her fault, she told herself. It was what she'd said before. About not sleeping with him. Now he knew she'd been thinking about it. The man had an ego the size of the Grand Canyon. He probably thought she was desperate to have him in her bed, when the truth was she'd only been thinking about sex as a way to convince him to not take her ranch. A really dumb idea, especially considering she was reasonably sure she wasn't good enough—bed-wise—to convince him of anything.

"Heidi?"

"Hmm?"

"You okay? You look like maybe you're in pain."

"I'm fine." Or she would be. Eventually. "Dinner was great."

"That's what you were thinking about?"

"No, but that's the conversational gambit I'm putting forth."

He angled toward her, his leg now millimeters from her thigh. "You can do better than talking about my mom's lasagna."

"Fine. Do you miss San Francisco?"

"Yes."

She rolled her eyes. "You're in my hometown. You could at least pretend to have to think about your answer."

"Why? I like living in the city."

"The shopping and access to the ballet?"

One corner of his sexy, well-shaped, come-kiss-me mouth turned up. She found her attention very much settled on his mouth, and wondered what it would feel like against her own. If he, you know, wanted to—

She mentally slammed the door on those thoughts and stared out at the barn. The silhouette was very meaningful, she told herself. Or at least safer than Rafe.

"I like fine dining and easy access to work."

"Missing the corporate lifestyle?"

"Yes. I don't have enough power here. I'm not a ranch hand, I'm a power broker."

Despite her awareness and the steady hum of need that had taken up residence inside her belly, she laughed. "Maybe you should go back. To make sure everything is okay."

"I have staff. They make sure everything is okay."

"Must be nice."

"It is."

"Are you rubbing in your richness? I'm very aware that you could buy and sell me a hundred times over. It doesn't matter. I'm not a city girl. And I don't like townies."

"Townies? You don't seriously call people that."

"Yes. They live in towns. They're different." Some of them had hurt her best friend, and Heidi knew she would never get over that.

"You should embrace townies," Rafe told her. "They buy your cheese." He leaned back against the railing. "What markets are you in?"

She blinked at the question. "You mean like, what are the names of the stores that sell my cheese?"

The smile returned. "No. What market segments do you find most profitable? Organic, local, wine stores?"

"Oh." She folded her hands together on top of her thighs. The faint tingling had faded, leaving her feeling uneasy and inadequate. "I sell in town. To places I can deliver to. During the festivals, I usually set up a booth."

His expression remained expectant, as if he thought she was saving the best for last.

"That's pretty much it."

"How are you going to make a living doing that? You need to expand your market. Whole Foods and Trader Joe's are obvious, but what about smaller organic and specialty chains? You're within a few hours of San Francisco, and not that much farther from L.A. Both could be huge markets for you. Plenty of upscale stores, with shoppers interested in buying local and organic. You could try the food shows. Trade shows. Hell, send samples to Rachael Ray. What about your sales reps? What do they say?"

"You're the only one out here with staff. I can't afford to pay someone to sell my cheese."

"It's the only way you're going to take things to the next level. Otherwise, you'll be scrambling to pay the bills forever. One decent rep could pay for him- or herself in three months. You could put the rest of your profits back into the business. There are dozens of markets. Of course, that assumes you have extra cheese to sell."

"I do."

"Then—"

He stopped talking suddenly, as if aware of what he was doing. Helping the enemy. Because if she became successful, she could pay back his mother and win the case.

"All good ideas," she admitted. "I'll think about them." Because they were smart business moves. Not that he had to worry, because even if she started right now, she couldn't have them up and running in time. It wasn't as if the judge was going to give her six or eight months.

"Heidi, I—" He stopped and shook his head.

She waited.

She thought he would tell her she couldn't use his ideas, or that even if her business grew to be the size of Kraft foods, he would still win, or that she was completely out of her league with him. Instead, he muttered something she couldn't quite hear, then leaned forward, grabbed her by her upper arms and kissed her.

She was so startled, she couldn't react, really couldn't even feel what was happening. Her brain couldn't wrap itself around the action. Kissing her? Rafe? Why?

But instead of trying to answer the question, she became aware of the warmth—no, the heat—of his lips on hers. Of how they seemed to fit together. His kiss was firm—he was obviously in charge. Yet there was an unexpected gentleness. He offered rather than took and, as crazy as it sounded, she sensed he wanted her to yield. As if her giving in, her surrender, was important.

Somewhere during the first flash of confusion, she closed her eyes. In the darkness, she felt his mouth moving against her. Instinctively, she leaned toward him, raising her arms to his shoulders. His shirt was smooth, his muscles hard. His hands dropped to her waist. She felt the pressure of each individual finger.

Against her mouth, the kiss lingered; heat grew. She told herself to pull back, that Rafe was dangerous to her on more levels than she could count. That, in any circumstance, he played to win, and she rarely played at all. Yet she couldn't seem to get the message to her body. Maybe because being close to him felt so good. She gave in to the inevitable and tilted her head, then parted her lips.

He swept inside, claiming her with a deep kiss that stirred long-dormant needs. Her blood moved more quickly. Her breasts began to ache and between her thighs a telltale throbbing pulsed in time with her heartbeat.

As his tongue danced with hers, he moved his hands up and down her back. His touch was part caress, part promise. She got lost in the sensations, wanted him to touch other places, to cup her breasts and maybe slip lower.

He broke the kiss, then pressed his lips against her jaw. From there, he trailed his way to her neck, then her collarbone. Lips teased, teeth scraped, each action making her shiver and ache and need. Wanting grew, until she was ready to grab his hands and place them where she wanted them most. Right at this second, being really stupid sounded like the best plan ever.

She'd barely moved her arms to grab his wrists when his phone rang. She heard the shrill sound, felt the vibration in his shirt pocket and jumped back. Her eyes flew open.

Rafe pulled out the phone. She saw his thumb hit the ignore button, but not before she saw the name on the screen.

Nina.

"Girlfriend?" she asked into the silence that followed.

As usual, Rafe's expression was unreadable, his dark gaze steady as he looked at her.

"No."

She waited. Whoever the woman was, she was important enough to be in Rafe's contact list. While it was too late for Heidi to take back the kiss, it wasn't too late to find out how dumb she'd been.

"My matchmaker."

She wasn't sure if that was better or worse than a girlfriend. Better, she decided. He wasn't involved. He was looking to get into a relationship, but not with anyone like her, of course. Which was fine. She wasn't interested in him, either. Despite the evidence to the contrary.

She managed to stand and step back onto the porch. She crossed to the screen door and opened it.

"You should call her back," she said, pleased her voice was so calm. "It might be important."

CHAPTER SEVEN

RAFE HEARD HEIDI HEADING DOWN the stairs. He didn't have to glance at the clock to know it was still early. The pale light at the edge of the curtains warned him that most people were still sound asleep. He waited until he heard the back door close, then got up and quickly dressed.

It had been three days since he'd kissed her. Three days of her carefully avoiding him, and his mother watching, as if aware there was a problem. He hadn't mentioned the kiss to May, and he would bet money Heidi hadn't said anything to her grandfather, either. But still, May had guessed something had happened. He made it a point to avoid talking about his personal life with his mother, so he had a problem. The only way he could see to fix it was to get things back to normal with Heidi.

He walked down the stairs, through the living room and kitchen, and out back. Heidi was already in the goat house. As he crossed the yard, he saw three cats scampering in front of him. They slipped through the partially open door, and he followed.

Heidi was already milking Athena when he arrived. The three cats were sitting, watching her.

"When did you get cats?" he asked.

Heidi didn't look up from the rhythmic movements of her hands. Milk flowed steadily into the gleaming metal bucket.

"They're not mine. They show up when I milk. I don't know how they know."

He studied her movements, wondering if he could master the art of goat milking. Not a lot of call for that skill in his world.

"Can I help?"

She snorted. "I don't think so."

He counted the goats obviously waiting for their turns. There were only six. "You're not milking all of them?"

"Two are pregnant. No milking then."

"How often do they get pregnant?"

"Generally once a year."

He knew this meant there was a fair amount of nonmilking time with each goat. "That cuts into your cheese making."

"I know. I need to expand the herd a little more, but not so much that it's unmanageable."

He wanted to ask if she'd thought about their conversation, the advice he'd given her. He might not know much about goats, but he did know business, and the principles of selling were universal.

"Will you keep any of the kids?" he asked.

"Probably not. I'd rather expand the bloodline. I know a few breeders. I might be able to work a trade."

She finished with Athena. The goat stepped away.

The next took her place. Heidi carefully washed the udders before starting to milk again.

"If you still have the name of that guy, I'm willing to sell the steers," she said, concentrating on her work.

"I'll call him. He was available to come by this week."

"Good."

Heidi worked efficiently, neither of them speaking. What had happened before—the kiss—hung between them.

He wasn't sure why he'd done it. He wanted to say it was because she'd been there and he hadn't had anything better to do. But he knew that was a lie. He'd wanted to kiss Heidi. He'd wanted to know what she felt like in his arms. He'd wanted to touch her and taste her. Now that he'd kissed her, he wanted more. Which was why he'd called Nina back and confirmed his date. Because Heidi wasn't part of his plan, and he doubted she was the type to have sex because it felt good. She would want more, and he'd given up on more a long time ago.

"About the other night..." he began.

Her hands slowed, then picked up speed.

"I didn't mean to make things awkward between us."

"Too bad," she said, still not looking at him. "Because if that had been your goal, you could be happy now."

"You're pissed."

"No. I'm confused. Tell me about Nina, the matchmaker. Did you really hire someone to find you a wife? Do you know what century we're living in?"

"I hire the best. She's the best."

She turned to him. "You can't get your own girl?"

"I tried that once. It didn't work."

She returned her attention to the milking, finishing with the second goat. The third took her place.

"I was married before," he admitted. "We were young and in love and we got married. I thought everything was fine. Then one day, she said she didn't love me anymore, and left. I kept waiting to feel devastated or humiliated. All I felt was relief that we hadn't had kids. So that was the end, and I was left thinking there should be more to it. But I guess there isn't."

Love was an illusion—an excuse for people to get into relationships. Something he didn't need.

"So why get married again?"

"I want kids. I'm traditional enough to believe that, in a perfect world, there are two parents."

"Let me guess," she said. "You want Nina to find you the right sort of woman. Educated, probably with a career, but not one that takes up too much of her time. You're willing to let her work, but you'd prefer it if she would stay home with the kids. Smart, but not too smart. Pretty, but you're not interested in beautiful. She should be entertaining and talk about current events. Someone who won't stray. You plan on being faithful, but you don't expect her to touch your heart. You're saving what's left of it for your children.

Oh, you'll settle for two, but you'd really like three. And a dog."

Rafe stayed where he was, which took a whole lot more effort than it should have. He felt as if she had cut him open and laid him bare for everyone to see. She'd managed to reduce the sum of him and his wants to a mockable list. How had she guessed? He'd always been told he was tough to read. Was he showing his cards, or did she have some kind of insight? Even his mother hadn't been able to guess all of that.

"You don't approve."

"I don't have an opinion," she told him. "I guess the part I don't understand is wanting to spend your life with someone you're not in love with."

"Love is an illusion."

"You're wrong about that. Love is very real and it's dangerous. People do crazy things in the name of love. Bad things. Love is powerful and shouldn't be played with. So, when do you get to meet the first of your candidates?"

"In a couple of days."

Heidi glanced at him. "She's coming to Fool's Gold? For a date?"

He shrugged. "I tried to put Nina off, but she said it wasn't a problem."

"That's because you're quite the catch, Rafe."

She wasn't exactly laughing, but he saw the humor in her eyes. When they'd first met, he'd been in control of everything going on around him. Somehow that had shifted. He felt as if he were walking on floating logs, and in danger of slipping and falling. It wasn't a sensation he enjoyed.

"Will we get to meet her?" she asked.

"No."

With that he stalked out of the goat house and headed back for the kitchen. He had a fence line to finish and a company to run. As for Heidi, he'd been wrong to think he'd offended her by kissing her. She was a lot less fragile than he'd thought. In fact, she was a formidable opponent. He was done playing nice. After all, he was in Fool's Gold for only one reason, and that was to win.

HEIDI CARRIED THE MILK into the kitchen. She'd already seen Rafe heading out to work, so she knew she was safe. Thank goodness. She wasn't sure she could stomach another encounter with him today. The last one had nearly done her in.

Everything about their relationship was unfair. How tall he was, how sexy, the way his smile made her feel weak in the knees. And that had been with her sitting down. Imagine if she'd been standing.

It was the kiss, she thought, as she poured the milk into containers and then put them in the second refrigerator in the mudroom. The way he'd touched her and made her feel. Now she knew the possibilities, and she couldn't make herself forget them. While he was busy looking for his perfect wife, she was left wanting more kisses followed by long, languid nights in his bed.

She had a feeling she'd guessed right about the kind

of woman he was looking for. Coming up with the list had been easy. She'd simply imagined everything she wasn't.

She told herself it didn't matter. That when she and Glen won their case, May and Rafe would return to San Francisco. She would forget all about this interruption of her regularly scheduled life, and all would be well.

She poured herself a cup of coffee and walked through to the living room. She'd barely swallowed her first sip when she was brought to a halt by the sound of soft laughter. Soft, intimate laughter. She heard Glen's voice coming from his room. Seconds later, May answered. Also in his room.

No, no, no, she thought, freezing in place, like a mouse caught out in the open. Not already. They couldn't be… She'd warned May, had talked to her grandfather. They were old enough to know better.

She backed into the kitchen and sank into a chair by the table. Now what? If Glen broke May's heart, then they were in serious trouble. An angry May could have a fair amount of sway with the judge. Heidi was going to have to have a serious talk with him again, and then go look for someone else who would be on her side. Even if that meant having to deal with the one person she most wanted to avoid.

IT TOOK HEIDI TWENTY-FOUR hours to find the courage to speak with Rafe. He hadn't come to dinner the previous night. May had mentioned something about him meeting friends in town. Heidi wasn't sure if she believed that.

Regardless, he'd been gone, so she'd been unable to force herself to talk to him when he finally got home. Now she knew she couldn't wait much longer. Glen was the kind of man who knew how to seduce a woman. While it wasn't something she wanted to think about, protecting May was paramount.

She'd heard a couple of big trucks arrive and had assumed they were delivering more supplies for the fence line or barn. But when she stepped outside, what she found instead was a handful of men she didn't know, her feral cows being herded into corrals and Rafe on a horse.

The sun was high in the bright, clear sky, the temperature still in the fifties. Despite the coolness, she found herself oddly warm as she looked at the man riding Mason.

He had a cowboy hat on his head and a rope in his hands. Worn jeans hugged powerful thighs. His jaw was chiseled, his eyes narrowed. She stumbled to a stop, caught up in the moment. One of the other men yelled something she couldn't hear. Rafe's mouth, the mouth she couldn't stop thinking about, curved into a smile. She knew right then she was in more trouble than she'd realized.

As she watched, he urged Mason forward, then swung the rope in a lazy circle and dropped it around the neck of a cow. Mason sat back on his heels, bringing the cow to a quick stop.

Heidi wasn't sure who had surprised her more—Rafe or the horse. For a man who looked as good as he did in a suit, he seemed to know his way around the ranch. She supposed the lessons learned as a child weren't easily forgotten.

She returned to the house, where she made calls and answered emails. For all the danger Rafe presented to her personally, he'd made some great suggestions about her business. She'd already contacted several small stores in San Francisco and Los Angeles about carrying her cheese, and was asking around to see if she could hire a sales rep, at least part-time. With the money the cattle would bring, she could afford to take the risk and still put the majority of the funds aside in her Pay Back May account.

Glen strolled into her small office, close to lunchtime. "They're nearly done loading cattle," he said.

"I'm glad to hear it." She glanced at him. "I thought we had a deal."

Her grandfather, the person she loved most in the world, didn't bother looking the least bit chagrined. "Now, Heidi, I'm a grown man. You don't get to dictate my love life."

"Isn't it enough you stole two hundred and fifty thousand dollars from May? Now you're going to break her heart?"

"Don't say that. She's a fine woman. Maybe she's the one."

"There's never been a 'one' with you, Glen. I thought

you might slow down as you got older, but you haven't at all. You slept with your attorney."

"That was when we first arrived. She wasn't my attorney then." He walked over and patted her on the shoulder. "Don't worry about me. It'll all work out."

"I'm not worried about you," Heidi said, exasperated. "I'm worried about May. And you don't know that it's going to work out. If you hurt her, she'll go to the judge, and we'll lose everything. Have you thought about that?"

Glen's humor faded. "Heidi, you can't dictate love. If there's anything I've taught you, it's that matters of the heart are unpredictable. May is unexpected. And maybe unexpected is what I've needed all along."

"I agree, but whatever pretty words you put on it, you don't fall in love. You don't believe in love. You've said it a thousand times. You have fun and then you move on. May's been a widow for years. She's not the type to understand. You're risking our home."

"I'm not. I promise you that. She gets to me, and I can't let her go. I don't want to lose her, Heidi. And I won't. Trust me. Just trust me, little girl."

With that, he left.

She watched him leave, knowing he was asking for too much. She loved him, but she didn't trust him.

She worked a couple more hours, then heard footsteps in the mudroom. She logged off her computer and went into the kitchen. Rafe stood by the sink, drinking water. He'd dropped his hat onto a chair by the table and rolled up his sleeves. Sweat darkened his shirt and dust stained his jeans. He looked like an ad for something manly and vaguely sexy.

He finished the glass, then refilled it from a pitcher he'd pulled out of the refrigerator. As he poured, he glanced at her.

"They're gone. You can roam your land in peace, without fear of being attacked by feral cattle."

"Thanks for arranging that."

"No problem." He quickly drank the second glass of water, then turned to her. "What?"

"I'm worried about your mother."

"Because?"

"She's getting involved with Glen. Trust me, no good will come of that."

Rafe chuckled. "He's in his seventies. What's the worst that could happen?"

"Don't dismiss him because he's over sixty-five. Glen has been charming women for decades. They find him irresistible. He's not into long-term relationships, which means your mom could be hurt."

The chuckle turned into laughter.

She folded her arms across her chest. "You're not taking me seriously."

"I can't. Glen and my mom?"

"She was in his room. I heard her laughing."

"She was probably delivering laundry."

"They were having sex."

The humor faded. "No way."

"I've talked to Glen, but he won't listen. You need to talk to your mom. Glen isn't the kind of guy who settles down. If that's what she's expecting, it's not going to happen."

"I'm not discussing my mother's personal life with her."

"You'd rather deal with her broken heart after the fact?"

"She and Glen aren't involved."

"You know this how?"

"I just do."

She groaned. "So this is what you do. If you don't like something, you pretend it's not real?"

"You don't know what you're talking about."

"What about Clay? He's your brother and you don't talk about him."

Rafe's gaze hardened. "He's not your business."

"You act like he's a criminal. He's an underwear model. He probably makes more money than you. What's the big deal?"

"He could have done something with his life."

"He is."

"Nothing to be proud of."

Heidi dropped her hands to her hips. "You're a prude. You're embarrassed by what Clay does, so you don't talk about it."

"I'm not."

"You're embarrassed to talk to your mom, too. Is it sex?"

"I don't have a problem with sex," he growled.

"You have a problem with something."

"Right now, mostly you." He set down the water

and faced her. "I worked my ass off when I was a kid, taking care of my family. I went hungry, did a man's job, and I was ten years old. So I have the right to say whether or not my brother is wasting his life. The same with my sister."

That confused her. "I thought she was a dancer."

"God only knows. She walked away from..." He shook his head. "I'm not talking about her."

"You're the one who brought her up."

She thought about all she'd learned about him and his past. About how hard that time must have been for him. He'd managed to go to college on a scholarship and create a business empire. But how much of that small, frightened, hungry boy remained?

"Just because Clay became a model doesn't mean he doesn't appreciate what you did."

"Don't try to get inside my head. It won't happen."

"I'm saying maybe you need to give him a break."

"This advice comes from all the experience you have with a big family?"

She raised her chin. "I grew up with plenty of family. Maybe not the traditional kind, but I know exactly what it's like to live with a lot of people in a small space." She held up both hands. "Fine. We'll let the Clay thing go. But please talk to your mother about Glen."

"No."

"For a man who was married before, you really don't know much about women. No wonder you need to use a matchmaker. Fine. Don't talk to May. But don't say I didn't warn you."

HEIDI PUSHED HER EMPTY GLASS to the edge of the table. She looked across the room to the bar and waited until Jo looked up. When the bartender raised her eyebrows, Heidi tapped her glass and nodded.

Yes, thank you very much, she would like another margarita and maybe even one after that.

"I'm budgeting a hundred and thirty-five thousand dollars," Annabelle was saying. "I'm hoping to get it for around eighty or ninety, and have the rest for refurbishing and stocking."

"A bookmobile?" Charlie asked.

Annabelle nodded. "We have a lot of people in our community who can't get to the library. The last big fundraiser completed the media center, which is great. Plus, if I could get a couple of laptops and a mobile hotspot, we could take the internet to people who've never experienced it before."

Charlie grimaced. "I find you annoying when you're this earnest. It confuses me."

"I know. I'm more natural being sarcastic, but I really care about the bookmobile. I've been thinking about a festival fundraiser. I need to talk to Pia."

Pia was responsible for the dozens of festivals in Fool's Gold. She worked miracles out of a tiny office. Due to her extraordinary planning, decorative flags went up on time, vendors arrived and Porta Potties were delivered.

"We'll help," Heidi said. "Just tell us what you want to do."

Charlie shook her head. "I'm not volunteering."

"Yes, you are," Heidi told her. "You know you are."

Charlie sighed. "Fine. I'll be there."

"I'm still in the planning stage, but I'll let you know when that changes to action."

Jo delivered Heidi's margarita. She promised their burgers would be out shortly, then went to check on other customers. Heidi reached for her glass only to realize her friends were staring at her.

"What?"

"That's your second," Charlie said.

"I know."

"You usually don't get a second drink until the food arrives. Sometimes not at all."

"I'm having a bad day." Heidi slumped back in the booth. "I don't even know where to begin."

Annabelle patted her arm. "Jump in wherever you want. We'll catch up."

"Glen is sleeping with May. At least I think he is. She was in his room and they were laughing, and it sounded very intimate. I'm worried about her, about Glen breaking her heart. That's what he does. He's not a one-woman kind of guy. But when I tried to talk to Rafe, he wouldn't listen. He thinks Glen is too old to have sex. Stupid man. And all my life, Glen told me love wasn't real, and if it was, it was for suckers. Now suddenly he's saying May is the one, and his feelings are real. That he was wrong about love, and I should forget everything he told me before."

She paused to draw in a breath. "And Rafe has a matchmaker, if you can believe it, and he's on a date tonight. Because if you had a chance to land someone like him, what's a three-hour drive to Fool's Gold, right? And the cows are gone, which is good, because I need the money, and I'm hiring a sales rep for my cheese, which is scary. It was Rafe's idea, so he's helping me and trying to take my home from me at the same time." She drew in another breath. "There's a lot going on."

She reached for her margarita and took a long drink.

Annabelle and Charlie exchanged a look.

"That's quite a list," Annabelle said.

"Most of it was about Rafe, and she's drinking more than usual," Charlie added. "You know what that means."

"Trouble." Annabelle shook her head. "Big trouble."

"Man trouble."

"There's no man trouble," Heidi announced. "None. Zero. Zip. I'm not attracted to Rafe."

"But you've kissed him," Annabelle said smoothly.

"Yes, but it was—" Heidi slapped her hand over her mouth. She hadn't meant to mention the kiss. She dropped her arm to her side. "It's not what you think."

"Was there tongue?" Charlie asked.

Prepared now, Heidi pressed her lips together and didn't speak.

"That's a yes," Annabelle said with a sigh. "I miss tongue. Or any kind of kissing. I miss sex and men and orgasms." She sighed again. "I'm sorry. What was the question?"

"Tongue is exactly what I think," Charlie said.

Jo brought their burgers. When she left, Heidi grabbed a fry from her plate.

"No, it was an accident. Or meaningless, or both. He has a matchmaker. Who does that? I don't know why he can't get his own girl. The man is rich and good-looking. And when he rides Mason… Oh!" She turned to Charlie. "Did you know your horse knows how to rope a steer? Well, the horse part of it. He's not the one throwing the rope."

Charlie picked up her burger. "Seeing as I bought Mason, yes, I knew. So Rafe is sexy on a horse?"

"More than should be legal. With those shoulders and in that hat?"

"Oh, no. You have it bad." Annabelle stared at her. "I thought you were going to sleep with him to keep him from getting the ranch. Not fall for him."

Heidi took a bite of her burger and chewed. She swallowed, then flicked her fingers at both of them. "I'm not falling for him. He's not my type. He's a townie. I know better."

"Townie?" Charlie mouthed. "I can figure that out in context, but it's not like you're still in the carnival. You live in a town. You're a townie now."

"Not in my heart." Heidi drank more of her margarita.

The tequila went down smoothly. If her brain was a little fuzzy, that was a good thing. Soon she wouldn't have to think about Rafe on a date. With some San Francisco-based bimbo.

"Stupid man," she muttered. "Who does he think he is, looking that good on a horse? It's not like I started the kissing, either. He kissed me."

"Was it amazing?" Annabelle asked wistfully.

"Yes. But it's not like he wanted to have sex with me."

"Not that you're bitter," Charlie murmured.

"I'm not. Stupid man."

"You said that already," Annabelle told her.

Heidi gulped the rest of her margarita and signaled for another.

"You really don't want that," Charlie told her. "You're plenty drunk as it is."

"You're not the boss of me," Heidi announced.

"It's too late," Annabelle said. "There's nothing we can do."

"You're going to be hating life, come morning."

Maybe Charlie was right, but at this moment, Heidi didn't care.

CHAPTER EIGHT

"BUT I NEED MY CAR," HEIDI said, leaning against the door in Charlie's truck. "Not that I would have driven, but we could have towed it. Or herded it. Like the cows." She giggled at the image of herds of cars following faithfully behind. "They should make a commercial."

"What are you talking about?" Charlie asked.

"Nothin'. My cheeks are numb."

"You'll be throwing up soon enough."

"Na-ah." Heidi liked the way the sounds felt in her mouth and made them again, then laughed. Her amusement ended in a snort that had her covering her mouth. "That wasn't me."

"That is so the least of what you're going to be doing tonight," Charlie told her, as she pulled around the ranch house and stopped by the front porch. "When next we see each other, I'm going to say, 'I told you so,' and I don't care how pitiful you look. You're going to be living in a world of regret."

"Already there," Heidi said, fumbling with her suddenly complicated seat belt. There were many regrets, most of them fuzzy. A few of the more clear ones were about Rafe and his date.

"I hate her."

"Who?" Charlie asked.

"I don't know yet. But her."

"Okay, then."

Charlie climbed out and came around the truck. As she reached for the door, Heidi saw someone on the porch. The shape moved toward them and she recognized Rafe.

"You shouldn't be back," Heidi said as Charlie opened the door. "You should be out with her."

"Oh, Lord," Charlie muttered. "Come on. Let's get you inside."

"What happened?" Rafe asked.

He was tall. With big man-shoulders. Heidi remembered how he'd looked in that towel—all wet and sexy. She would like to see him naked again. She hadn't seen a penis in a long time, and she had a feeling his would be especially nice.

"Too many margaritas," Charlie said, unfastening the seat belt. "Heidi's not much of a drinker. She's going to have a difficult night. Come on, kid. There's going to be a big step."

"I'll get her," Rafe said, stepping closer.

Charlie moved back, giving him room. Heidi found herself at eye level with Rafe.

"This is your fault," she told him.

"I'm sure that's true. Come on, goat girl. Let's get you inside."

She wanted to protest the "goat girl" title, except the way he'd said it sounded kind of nice. Friendly.

Maybe teasing. Like they were friends. Not that Rafe was the friend type. He was more the kind of man who took what he wanted, leaving women broken and desperate and…

"What's so funny?" he asked.

"What?"

"You're laughing."

Heidi felt her face. "No, I'm not."

He glanced over his shoulder. "How much did she drink?"

"Let's just say, around two in the morning, I wouldn't get between her and the bathroom."

"Thanks for the warning." He turned back to Heidi. "You ready to get out of the truck?"

"All right."

She took a step forward, only to realize she hadn't gotten out of the truck yet. Her feet got tangled, and she would have fallen out of the cab face-first if Rafe hadn't grabbed her.

He muttered something she didn't catch and wrapped his arms around her. "I guess we're doing this the hard way."

He eased her out of the truck and stood her next to him on the driveway. Balancing was harder than she remembered, she thought, as she swayed and tried to stay upright. She had a vague idea that she should see Glen, and go get some of his post-bender elixir, but the notion faded as quickly as it had arrived.

"You're not getting up the stairs on your own, are you?" he asked.

She was too busy staring at his mouth to answer. She liked his mouth, especially how it felt when it was busy touching hers.

"Charlie asked if there was tongue and I wouldn't answer, but I think she guessed the truth."

Rafe was sure Heidi thought she was whispering. Unfortunately, she was wrong. He glanced at the tall, broad-shouldered woman who'd driven Heidi home.

"You Charlie?"

"Uh-huh."

"Mason's your horse?"

Charlie nodded. "I heard you were riding him. I appreciate you giving him the workout. I'm less sure you should be messing around with Heidi."

"Me, too. And I'm not."

Her steady gaze didn't waver.

"It was one kiss," he added.

"That's generally how it starts. She's my friend. Don't make me hurt you."

Rafe sighed and put his arm around Heidi. As he helped her to the porch, he wondered why he couldn't be back in San Francisco, at a baseball game with Dante, or even working late. Right now a financial crisis or lawsuit threat sounded pretty damned good.

"I promise not to hurt her," he said. "Good enough?"

"We'll see."

He half led, half carried Heidi to the porch. Charlie closed the passenger door and went around to the driver's side. She got into her truck and drove away.

"Bye, Charlie," Heidi called after the retreating vehicle. She tried to wave and nearly slid to the ground.

He caught her and pulled her back to her feet. She rubbed his arm. "You're so strong."

"Thanks."

"It's very nice. I've seen you in a towel and that's nice, too. If you weren't trying to steal my home, I'd like you more. Want to change your mind about that?"

"This isn't the time to have that conversation."

"Sure it is. Or we could kiss." She stared up at him hopefully.

"Are those my only two options?"

She nodded her head, then stopped. "You had a date." Her tone was accusing. "With a woman."

"Would you be happier if it had been with a man?"

She considered the question, then blinked. "I don't know."

He had a feeling that for her, it was a brand-new day.

"Did I mention the kissing?" she asked.

"You did."

"Any thoughts?"

"None you want to hear."

He knew he could break the mood by mentioning his date, but he didn't want to talk about it. Bad enough he'd lived through it once already. While Julia had been perfectly lovely, he'd spent their two hours together trying not to get caught staring at his watch. He'd found himself thinking about Heidi and the ranch, wondering why he would rather be there than out to dinner with a charming companion. He'd ducked out early, and had turned off his cell phone so Nina couldn't call to ask how the date had gone.

"Let's get inside."

He managed to guide Heidi up to the porch and into the house. Rather than risk her navigating the stairs, he picked her up in his arms and carried her to the second floor. From there, it was a short trip to her bedroom.

Once inside, he set her on her feet and turned on the light. She gazed up at him with wonder.

"You carried me."

He nodded.

"That was so romantic." She smiled. "You can kiss me now."

She obligingly closed her eyes and pursed her lips.

The smartest thing would be to walk away. She was drunk, and he was just trying to get through the days without stepping in too much crap.

But there was something about Heidi. Something that tempted him beyond what was reasonable. She wasn't his usual type, but that didn't make her any less...appealing. He was drawn to everything about her. She was unguarded and funny. She worked hard, was loyal to those she cared about and, right now, even drunk, she was sexy as hell.

He leaned in and lightly brushed his mouth against hers. The heat was instant, as was the need. She swayed again, and he put his hands on her shoulders to steady her.

The second he touched her, he knew he was lost.

That wanting couldn't be reasoned with, and he wanted her bad. Taking advantage of a woman who was drunk wasn't his style, though. Besides, he had enough ego to want Heidi to know what she was doing when she came to his bed. He drew back.

Her eyes were wide and unfocused. She yawned. "That was nice, but I'm sleepy."

Despite the painful throbbing in his groin, he smiled. "You're not tired—you're about to pass out."

She waved one hand. "Tomato, tomahto." She edged toward the bed.

He helped her. When she sat on the mattress, he pulled off her shoes. No way he was taking off her clothes, he thought. The hows and whys of undressing her weren't a conversation he wanted to have.

She stretched out on the bed, and he covered her with the comforter. He kissed her forehead.

"You're going to be in a world of hurt tomorrow," he murmured.

"No. If I drink Glen's secret mixture, I'll be fine."

"Want me to fix it?"

She closed her eyes and drew in a deep breath. "'Night, Rafe," she murmured, sounding half-asleep already.

He took that as a no. "'Night, goat girl."

He walked out, leaving her door open. After using the bathroom, he left the light on so it would be easier to find in a few hours, then made his way to his own room. He was about to close the door when he heard a strange sound. Was Heidi sick already?

He stepped out into the hall and listened. The sound came again. He realized the source was downstairs. A cry. Not of distress, exactly, it sounded like…

His mother?

He flinched and hurried back to his room. After closing the door, he grabbed his iPod and shoved the buds into his ears, then cranked up the volume. Fool's Gold was, as he'd always known, his own version of hell. A place where his mother made time with the guy who had ripped her off, and where Rafe couldn't have the one who seemed to be the only woman he wanted.

RAFE HAD FALLEN ASLEEP close to midnight, only to be awakened about an hour later by the sound of rapid footsteps in the hallway. The bathroom door had slammed. He'd rolled over and gone back to sleep. His phone had beeped at him just before dawn.

He dressed quickly, then grabbed his boots and stepped into the hall. He knocked once on Heidi's door.

"Go away."

The voice was weak and full of pain.

He opened the door and saw a huddled shape in the bed. "I'll take care of the goats this morning."

"You don't know how."

"I'll figure it out."

"You have to sanitize everything."

"I've seen you do it."

Heidi shifted and one swollen, bloodshot eye peeked out from under the covers. The bit of skin around it was an uncomfortable combination of green and gray.

"What time did you stop throwing up?" he asked.

"I'm not sure I have."

"I'll deal with the goats," he repeated.

"Thank you." She collapsed back on the bed, then groaned. "Lars is coming."

"Lars?"

"He trims their hooves."

"I'll handle it. Actually, Lars will handle it and I'll supervise. I like watching other people work."

"Thank you. I'm probably going to die later."

"Sorry, no such luck. You'll wish you were dead, but you'll make it."

"You don't know that for sure."

He wondered how much she remembered from the night before, and figured, even if she recalled begging him to kiss her, she would pretend she didn't.

"Try to get some sleep," he told her. "I'll milk the goats and deal with Lars."

He stepped out of her room and went downstairs. As he passed through the kitchen, he heard soft laughter from the direction of Glen's bedroom. Being a regular kind of guy, he kept his head down and walked faster. No way he was having that conversation with his mother. At least, not before coffee.

He headed for the goat house and found the goats waiting for their morning milking. Athena's ears flicked back and forth when she spotted him, as if she'd already guessed there was a change. Her eyes narrowed and she took a step back.

"It's okay," Rafe reassured her. She didn't look convinced.

He washed his hands, then collected the supplies he would need. After everything was set up, he walked toward Athena. She glared at him and stepped to the side, obviously torn between the need to be milked and the fact that he wasn't Heidi.

The other goats watched. If Athena went easily, they would follow. If she didn't… He decided not to think about that.

The door pushed open a little and the three cats strolled in. They trotted toward him, mewing in anticipation. The gray cat wound around his ankles, leaving a coat of light-colored hair on his jeans.

"Nice," he told it.

The cat blinked at him, then purred.

The rumbling sound was loud, yet relaxing. Athena flicked her ears again, then stepped into place, by the short stool.

"All hail the cat," Rafe murmured, and put on fresh gloves. He sat on the stool, wiped Athena's teats with disinfectant and went to work.

Five minutes later, he was willing to admit that milking was harder than it looked when Heidi did it. Athena kept glancing at him, as if wondering why she had gotten stuck with the inept human, but finally he finished. The next goat took her place, and so on.

When they were all done, he gave the cats their

share, then propped open the doors, so the goats would have the run of the large yard. Usually, Heidi took them to different parts of the ranch to feed on the wild plants, but with the hoof guy coming, Rafe decided to keep them close.

He made sure they had water, then took the milk inside and stored it in the extra refrigerator in the mudroom. He grabbed a quick breakfast, mercifully avoiding his mother, before heading back out to get Ethan's guys working on the fence line.

Shortly before nine, a battered red truck pulled in next to the goat house. The guy who climbed out was a big bear of a man, with blond hair, a light-colored beard and the kind of muscles that could double for roof supports.

"You must be Lars," Rafe said as he approached.

Lars frowned. "Where's Heidi?" he asked in a thick accent.

"She's not feeling well this morning and asked me to make sure you had what you needed."

"But I see Heidi."

Rafe couldn't tell if Lars wasn't all there or simply determined.

"Usually, yes, but she's sick. The goats are here." He pointed to the gate, where Athena had come to investigate.

"Who are you?" Lars asked, as he collected a wooden toolbox filled with files and what looked like odd scissors, along with jars and brushes.

"Rafe Stryker."

"You're with Heidi?"

There was a complicated question. "I'm staying here for now."

"With Heidi?" Outrage added volume to the question.

Rafe leaned against the fence and allowed himself to smile. "Yes, with Heidi."

Lars's face reddened and his tire-size hands curled into fists. The man was a good five or six inches taller and probably seventy pounds heavier than Rafe. He knew he could handle himself in a fair fight, but against a mountain? Then he shrugged. What the hell. He'd beaten worse odds in his life.

But Lars didn't attack. Instead, his shoulders deflated and he reached for his toolbox.

"I see the goats now."

HEIDI INHALED CAUTIOUSLY. May had something baking in the oven, and while normally the smell of cake would make her day, this afternoon she wasn't sure even the most delicious of aromas was safe.

She'd stopped throwing up sometime before dawn, but it had taken until close to noon for her to decide that maybe she wasn't going to die. Sometime around ten, Rafe had appeared with weak tea and toast. The man had simply left the plate and mug, then backed out without speaking. Something for which she was grateful. Last night was very much a blur, but she did have one distinct memory. That of her telling Rafe he could kiss her.

Because feeling like roadkill wasn't punishment enough. She also got to be humiliated. Talk about not fair.

She crossed the kitchen and poured herself a cup of coffee. The first sip of the dark liquid went a long way toward restoring her belief in a brighter tomorrow, although the pounding behind her eyes didn't lessen. Maybe if she moved very, very slowly. She vowed she would never be this stupid again and, if she was, next time she would wake up her grandfather, regardless of the hour, so he could fix her his magic remedy.

"You're up!"

The bright, cheerful, loud words made her jump. Her headache turned into a vise grip, and she had to hold in a whimper.

Heidi turned and tried to smile at May. "Yes. I've decided I'm going to make it."

"You must have had quite the night."

"I guess." She glanced toward the window. "I didn't drive home, did I?"

"No. One of your friends brought you. Glen and Rafe went into town to get your truck. They should be back in a little while." May took her by the elbow and led her to the kitchen table. "You should sit down. You're still a little gray."

"I feel gray," Heidi admitted, grateful she wasn't at risk of having to face Rafe anytime soon. "Too much tequila."

"At least you had fun."

"I hope so. I don't remember very much." She'd

been with her friends, and Rafe had been on his date. That had upset her—well, that and the fact that he'd kissed her. It was more the one-two punch of events than either on its own.

She glanced at May. "Did I wake you when I came in?"

May blushed, then hurried toward the pantry and pulled out a loaf of bread. "I didn't hear a thing. Rafe mentioned you had a difficult night, though."

Heidi winced as she remembered puking up her guts. "Let's just say, whoever told me alcohol really is a poison wasn't lying."

May popped a slice into the toaster. "You'll get better today. Hydrate. That will help."

Heidi nodded, even though the thought of facing a glass of water made her want to gag.

"It's nice that you have friends here," May said as she poured Heidi more coffee. "I've met a few of the women I used to know, from when we lived here before. So many of them stayed. I envy them that."

She returned the carafe to the stand and looked out the window. "I never forgot the view from this sink. How I could watch the changing of the seasons." She glanced at Heidi and smiled. "I was raised in the Midwest. When we first moved here, I couldn't get over how tall the mountains are. How beautiful. After my husband died, I knew I didn't want to be anywhere else. Money was tough, but we had this house and the town."

Heidi's head had cleared enough for her to be able

to follow the conversation. "Rafe mentioned the man who owned this land, Mr. Castle, promised you would inherit it."

May nodded. The toast popped. She set the slice on a plate and lightly buttered it, then carried it over to Heidi.

"He did. I hate to speak ill of the dead, but he was a mean old man. I believed him and trusted him, and in the end, lost it all. When he died and it turned out he'd left the ranch to a relative, I was devastated. I had to move. I probably should have stayed in Fool's Gold, where I had friends, but I was humiliated."

"You didn't do anything wrong."

May settled across from her. "I know that now, but at the time, I couldn't get past the fact that Mr. Castle had taken advantage of me. I'd lost my husband a few years before, and then the ranch. So we moved and started over."

Heidi nibbled the toast. Her headache was a little better. Unfortunately, without the distraction of the throbbing, she was able to imagine May's plight more easily. Four little kids, no home, no money. Talk about desperate.

"You must have done something right. Look at your children."

May laughed. "They are wonderful, and while I want to take all the credit, they did a lot of it themselves. Rafe went to Harvard."

"I saw the picture."

"Shane works magic with horses. He breeds them and he's working on his own herd. Clay…"

Heidi reached across the table. "I know about Clay. He's very successful."

May's eyes danced with humor. "Rafe doesn't approve, so I try not to talk about Clay around him, but I think it's funny. My son, the butt model. He does well for himself, though."

"Which is part of what pisses off Rafe."

"True."

The timer went off. May walked to the stove and pulled open the oven. She drew out the cake, then shook her head as she surveyed the uncooked side. "Oops. I forgot to turn it." May spun the pan and reset the timer. "This old place. It needs a lot of fixing."

"A new oven."

"A bigger hot-water heater."

Heidi really didn't want to think about why May might need more hot water than the average person, but she knew the answer. Showers for two tended to last a long time. She worked very hard to keep the visual out of her brain, then drank a few swallows of coffee for courage.

"May, you're a lovely woman."

May leaned against the counter. "That's an ominous beginning. If you were my doctor, I would know I was a goner for sure."

"It's Glen. I'm worried about you. He won't listen, but I'm hoping you will."

"You're afraid he's going to break my heart."

"Yes."

May nodded. "You're sweet to worry. Glen told me the same thing himself. That he's not the kind to settle down, that I'm the kind of woman looking to find something permanent."

She brushed her hand through her short, dark hair. "My husband died over twenty years ago. I've accepted I'll never care about anyone the way I cared about him. He gave me my boys, and he will always be my first true love. But it's time for me to have a little fun." Her mouth curved into a smile. "I don't want to marry Glen, Heidi. I want to play, and he's the right man to help me remember how."

Pure TMI, Heidi thought. Or whatever qualified for *more* than too much information.

The timer went off. May pulled out the cake. It was still lopsided, although slightly less so.

"Maybe it will be better with frosting?" Heidi offered. "And sprinkles?"

May laughed. "You're my kind of girl. What crisis can't be fixed with frosting and sprinkles?"

Heidi knew she was supposed to laugh, too. But in that moment she was too overwhelmed by a sense of loss. She'd always told herself that she couldn't miss what she'd never had. That when her parents had died, she was so young that she didn't remember anything about them. But at this moment, with May, she found herself longing for a chance to have grown up with a mother. Someone who baked and offered advice on boys and knew how to pick out a prom dress.

The past couldn't be changed, which left only the future. Somehow, she would have to get out of the mess of the ranch and the money, without losing everything and without hurting May.

CHAPTER NINE

RAFE WALKED ACROSS THE barn's roof. From that height, he could see across much of the ranch. The goats had been taken to the north end of the property. He could see them munching their way through fresh spring grass, no doubt as happy as goats could be.

The fence line was finished. He didn't want to think about how many posts had been dug out and replaced, how many miles of wire fencing were carefully stapled into place. To his mind, it was a whole lot of work for eight goats, but his mother had insisted.

"Rafe!"

He turned, and one of the guys tossed him a plastic water bottle. His mother filled them each night and put them in the freezer. By midmorning, they were still cold but had melted enough to drink. He unscrewed the cap and took a long swallow.

His days were supposed to be spent in meetings. He excelled at getting what he wanted and assigning action items to others. Dante frequently joked that if Rafe left a meeting with actual work to do himself, he considered it a failure.

These days he spent his hours sweating. Roping, riding, building fences and now repairing the barn.

He no longer bothered showering and shaving in the morning. Instead, he rolled out of bed, pulled on jeans and boots, and headed out to work until his muscles ached.

He'd gone back in time, living in the same house as his mother, in a place he swore he would never return to. Except everything was different. He didn't mind the hard physical work. He enjoyed being able to point to the proof of his labor, to run his hands across a post or part of the barn and know that it was better, it was there, because of him.

Instead of going out to restaurants with beautiful women, he found himself in the ranch house's old dining room, across from Heidi, with Glen and his mother at the table. But the conversation flowed easily. Glen had a hundred stories about life in the carnival. Heidi had a few of her own, and Rafe enjoyed listening to them. He also enjoyed the sound of her laughter and the anticipation he felt when she smiled at him.

Some days, after he'd finished his work and headed for his shower, he thought about dragging her along with him. About her being naked with him, under the spray, his mouth on hers, his hands everywhere. The thought of slick soap and wet skin and the things they could do to each other. Then he reminded himself that she wasn't who he was looking for, and getting involved would be a level of stupid he wouldn't allow.

But a man could still dream.

He finished his bottle of water and dropped the empty container to the ground below. The repair work on the barn was going steadily. He figured they would be done by tomorrow. Of course, by then his mother would have a whole new list of projects. When he'd gone in for lunch a couple of days ago, she'd been ordering a new stove.

He wanted to remind her that getting the ranch wasn't a sure thing, but he knew he would be wasting his breath. Better to just work his way through the chores.

He'd barely picked up his hammer when a large animal transport truck pulled into the ranch. Rafe watched the vehicle slow and then stop. He hadn't spent much time with Heidi in the past couple of days. Not since the night she'd gotten drunk. He figured she was embarrassed and avoiding him. Even so, he was pretty sure he would have heard about any new goats showing up.

He made his way to the edge of the roof and carefully climbed down a ladder. His mother burst out of the house.

"They're here!"

In her jeans and T-shirt, she looked closer to thirty-five than fifty. She clapped her hands together and practically danced with excitement. Rafe felt something sinking in his stomach.

"Mom, what did you do?"

"You're going to have to see for yourself."

She met the driver. His helper came around back and started unlatching the trailer's big door and lowering a ramp. Rafe heard sounds from inside the transport, but couldn't place them.

He didn't think she would have ordered more goats without talking to Heidi, and he doubted she would get a horse without Shane's advice.

His mother signed the last of the paperwork and joined him. Just then, Heidi came out of the house.

"What's going on?" she asked.

"We have to wait and see," Rafe told her.

"It's a surprise." May hugged him. "I'm so excited."

"Really? I couldn't tell."

The two men went into the trailer. The helper came down the ramp first, leading…

"A llama?" Rafe asked, staring at the tall, off-white, fuzzy animal.

"Isn't he beautiful? At least, I think that's the boy. I can't tell for sure. It always seems so rude to look. But yes. A llama. Three, altogether."

Rafe glanced at Heidi, who looked as surprised as he felt.

"Are you going to raise them for their hair or fur or whatever it is?" Heidi asked. "Aren't they related to camels?"

"They're social herd animals," May told her. "And so beautiful. I saw them on eBay and couldn't resist. Plus, they'll protect the goats. I read an article, and several ranchers are using llamas to protect their livestock. Especially with the pregnant goats. We're so close to the mountains. There could be a coyote or wolf. We wouldn't want anything happening to one of the girls."

"Of course not," Rafe murmured. Llamas? What was his mother going to do with them if the judge ruled against her? Her condo in San Francisco wasn't llama-friendly.

Heidi drew in a breath. "Okay, where are you putting them?"

"I was thinking of that section of the ranch." May pointed west. "It gets plenty of light. There are trees and that hillside for them to climb."

And running water, Rafe thought grimly, remembering his mother had insisted he run a pipe out to the area.

May moved toward the llama. "Hello, sweet one. You'll be happy here." She glanced back at Heidi. "They're a little older, so I thought they could use a good home."

May moved off with the helper and showed him where to put the animal. The driver appeared with a light brown, slightly smaller llama, and followed the first.

"Old llamas?" Heidi murmured, moving closer to Rafe. "I kind of admire her philosophy."

"Sure. She bought them to protect your pregnant goats. What's not to like?"

"Feeling a little stressed, are we?"

"Someone needs to rein her in."

"She's your mother."

"Someone other than me." He glanced longingly

toward the west. Somewhere in San Francisco was a meeting he should probably be attending.

Once the three llamas were in place, two elderly sheep were led down the ramp. They went in the fenced area next to the llamas.

"Anything else?" Rafe asked, almost afraid to look in the trailer.

"That's it," the driver said, and handed over the receipts.

May took them happily and gazed out at her animals. "I've been doing research on how to care for them. Glen's been a big help."

"Lots of animals in the carnival?" Rafe asked, wondering how much worse things were going to get before they shifted to better.

"Not really," Heidi admitted. "A couple of goats and a few dogs. It wasn't a circus. You're going to need a large-animal vet. I use Cameron McKenzie. I'll get you his number."

A vet. Right, because old animals would need plenty of care.

"You couldn't start taking in cats, like other women your age?" he asked his mother.

She swatted his arm. "Don't act like I'm losing it. I've thought this over, and having these animals on the ranch is what I want to do. They make me happy."

He didn't know what to say to that. It wasn't as if he could tell her not to be happy, nor did he want to.

May wandered toward the fencing, where she could gaze at her new critters. Rafe rubbed his forehead.

"I really admire your mother," Heidi admitted. "She's full of life."

"That's not all she's full of."

Heidi grinned. "You love her and would do anything for her."

"It's my downfall. Why couldn't I be one of those guys who hates his mother? Life would be a lot easier."

"You don't walk away from your responsibilities. Except when it comes to Clay. I find that very interesting."

A statement that had come out of nowhere. "I have llamas and sheep in my life now. Can we not talk about my brother for a few days? Unless you'd rather discuss your recent drunkenness."

Heidi pressed her lips together. "No. We don't have to talk about that."

"See? Compromise can be your friend." He put his arm around her and guided her toward the barn. "Come on, goat girl. God knows what else my mother has bought on eBay. So, you can pass me nails while I finish the roof on this barn."

"Oh, wow. That's practically a date. Later, can I wear your letterman's jacket while we go get a milk shake?"

"Sure." He glanced down at her. "I'll bet you were cute in high school."

"I'm cute now."

He laughed. "You've been hanging around my mother a little too much. You're adopting her attitude."

"I'm learning from the master, which is going to be a whole lot of trouble for you."

He had a feeling she was right about that.

HEIDI CAREFULLY REMOVED octagon-shaped bars of soap from molds. The tiny dried flowers she'd placed at the bottom of the molds had set perfectly, in the center, just visible through a thin layer of creamy soap.

While her basic soap recipe had remained the same, she was experimenting, trying to make the bars more attractive. She'd been doing a lot of research online and checking out different bulletin boards devoted to small-scale retail endeavors like hers. Rafe had been right—there was a whole world out there looking for handmade, organic, natural products.

She set the soaps on a rack. She would let them cure for a couple of weeks before wrapping them in the specialty paper she'd bought. One of her new online friends had introduced her to a graphic-arts student, who had designed an appealing logo in exchange for being able to use the design as part of a school project. Heidi had received her first shipment of logo stickers that afternoon.

She picked up a bar of soap she'd made two weeks ago and neatly wrapped it, sealing the edges with a sticker.

"How's it going?"

She jumped, then turned, feeling both guilty and defiant.

Rafe stood in the doorway of the small bedroom

she'd taken over for her office. It was tucked in back of the house, by the mudroom, giving her easy access to her supplies, and it was far from Glen's room, so she didn't have to hear the wild noises at night.

"I'm fine. Are you checking up on me?"

As soon as the words popped out, she wanted to slap her hand over her mouth.

Both his dark eyebrows rose. He reached up, grabbing the top of the door frame and stretching just enough to make his T-shirt ride up to the waistband of his jeans, although not high enough to expose anything interesting. It was about seven in the evening. Rafe had showered after his long day, and they'd had dinner. May and Glen were watching TV and, last Heidi had seen, Rafe had been on the porch, checking his email.

Now Rafe dropped his arms to his sides and strolled into the room. "You're making soap."

"So?"

"You look like a kid caught smoking behind the school. Unless you're smuggling military secrets, why are you so jumpy?"

"I'm not." She sighed. She'd never been a very good liar. "I took your advice and researched other markets. I found a couple of online communities that had a lot of information. I've been sending soap samples to different stores and to a couple of reps, and I have my first orders."

He walked over to the straight-back chair by her desk and sat down. "That's good."

"From my point of view."

She saw the second he put it all together. If her business became successful, she could pay back the money and make a case for keeping the ranch.

"I'm glad it's going well," he told her.

"Because you don't think I can do well enough in time?"

He surprised her by gently touching her cheek. "This was a whole lot easier before I got to know you."

"Agreed, but I still need to win."

"Me, too." He dropped his hand. "Tell me about your soap empire."

"It's not an empire yet, but I have orders and the promise of more. I'm getting word out on the internet. I'm going to need a website. Annabelle says she knows somebody in town who can do it." Probably time to change the subject. "Are the animals settled for the night?"

"Last I checked. Llamas and sheep. What was she thinking?"

Heidi wasn't sure, but still admired May for doing exactly what she wanted.

Rafe leaned back in the chair. "We'll have to have Lars check their hooves next time he's around."

"I hadn't thought of that. Do sheep and llamas need their hooves trimmed?"

"Lars will know."

"Why do you say it like that?"

He gave her a slow, knowing smile. "Lars wasn't happy dealing with me instead of you. He seemed… smitten."

"Oh, please." She returned her attention to her soap wrappers. "I barely know him."

"You've made an impression."

"Speaking of that sort of thing, how was your night out with your matchmaker girl?"

He shrugged. "Fine."

"Oooh, when you say it like that, I want to know when you two are setting the date."

"It was one date."

"You were home early."

"I'm surprised you remember that."

She didn't remember much else about the evening, but she did recall that Rafe had beaten her home, and she hadn't been out all that late. There were some other blurry images, something about kissing, but she wasn't going there.

"She wasn't the one?"

"No."

"But she drove all the way out here to see you. That has to be worth something."

"Not to get too cynical, but do you have any idea how much I'm worth?"

"Not really." She thought about the little she knew and what Trisha, her lawyer, had told her. "A lot?"

The slow, sexy smile returned, making her fingers

fumble on the soap wrapping. “That’s as good a number as any.”

“You’re saying she was in it for the money and not your sparkling personality?”

“It’s a concern.”

Probably a realistic one, she thought. “Maybe you should have your matchmaker play down your fortune. So you can find someone who loves you for who you are.”

“I’m not in it for love. I want a partnership.”

“That’s romantic.”

“I tried the romantic route. It didn’t go well.”

Heidi had a feeling that if Rafe and his ex-wife had walked away from their marriage with no regrets, then they’d never been in love. Her experience with the emotion was entirely different. Love could hold you in its grip and never let go. She thought of Melinda and knew people died in the name of love.

“Where did you take her?” she asked.

“Who?”

“Your date.”

“To the hotel restaurant.”

She sighed. “That’s your problem. You need to do something more special.”

“A moonlit horseback ride?”

“Not if you don’t warn her to dress right. Fool’s Gold is a great town. There are lots of little restaurants that have more ambience than the one at the hotel. Or take her up to the Gold Rush Ski Lodge and Resort.

At least you could ride the gondola to the top of the mountain. That's romantic."

"It's cold."

She rolled her eyes. "You could put your arm around her and keep her warm. Jeez. No wonder you're forced to use a matchmaker. You're not very good at the whole dating thing."

"I'm very good at it. The problem isn't me, it's the town. Being here. Being back."

"Too many memories?"

"Yeah."

She thought about what May had told her about Rafe and how difficult things had been back then. "You're not that kid anymore. You can take care of your family."

He drew in a breath and picked up one of the wrapped packages of soap. "They brought us baskets every holiday. There was plenty of food. Not leftovers that someone dug out of the back of his pantry, but real food. Turkeys and hams, big roasts. All the fixings. Pies and cakes. There would be movies for us kids and books for my mom."

"That sounds nice."

"It wasn't. I always knew when they were coming. I answered the door and I could see the pity in their eyes."

As he spoke, Heidi knew he wasn't the Rafe Stryker she'd met, but instead, a ten-year-old boy who couldn't provide for those he loved. The one who had been left with an impossible task—providing for his family.

"It wasn't your job to take care of everyone," she murmured.

"Someone had to."

"Your mom was doing it."

"She was overwhelmed. There was too much work and no help."

"So you did what you could."

"It wasn't enough."

She understood why he was so concerned about May. Back then, he'd been unable to protect her. Now he could protect them all. Yet that attention came at a price. When one of his siblings didn't measure up, Rafe was unforgiving.

"Tell me about your sister."

He stared at her. "What do you want to know?"

"What is she like?"

"Younger. I was nine when she was born."

"I thought your dad died when you were eight."

"He did."

"Oh." Heidi couldn't make the math work.

"It was a few months after. Mom was having a tough time coping." He put the soap back on her desk. "Shane brought some guy home. A cowboy here for the rodeo. I guess my mom spent the night with him. He left before we were up, and we never saw him again. A few months later, she told us she was having a baby. Then Evangeline was born."

"That can't have been easy," Heidi said.

"Mom is strong."

"I meant for your sister. To know she doesn't completely fit in with the family. That she's a constant reminder of what your mom did."

"It's not like that. Not for either of them." He hesitated. "I don't know. Maybe it is. Evie's never around. Shane and Clay come by to see Mom every few months, but not Evie."

Heidi guessed that Rafe was much more clear on the problem than he wanted to let on. But admitting it would mean dealing with it. As long as he didn't see there was an issue, he could ignore the situation. "Where's your sister now?"

"She's a dancer. She went to Juilliard. She's very gifted."

Heidi waited, but Rafe didn't say any more.

"You never said what she's like?"

"I don't spend much time with her. When she was a kid, she was always dancing."

"Was she always the outsider?"

He stood. "Is this another of your townie things? For someone who embraces the idea of community, you like to put people into groups. Us versus them."

"That's not fair."

"Maybe not, but it's accurate. Evangeline is my sister. I love her. Sure, I don't know every detail of her life, but if she was ever in trouble, if she ever needed anything, I would be there for her. We all would. We're a family."

He stalked out of the room. Heidi watched him go,

wondering if Evangeline would agree. May had decorated the living room with pictures of her sons, but there was only one of her daughter. She had a feeling Rafe hadn't spoken to his sister in months. Maybe longer. She supposed every family had secrets, even from each other. The trick was loving your family, despite the secrets…or maybe because of them.

MAY SMOOTHED THE PAPER on the kitchen table. "What do you think?" she asked anxiously.

Heidi studied the drawing. She saw the outline of the barn as it existed today, and then how it would nearly double in size if May had her way. There were plenty of stalls for horses, storage areas for feed and other supplies, wide doors and an open second story for hay.

"It's wonderful." And expensive, and would only add to her bill should she win the case.

"Good. I was hoping you'd say that," May told her. "I've spoken to Shane and mentioned the ranch to him. I'm hoping he'll want to come here."

"Shane?" Heidi pulled out a chair and sat down. "Here?"

She didn't think she could survive a second Stryker brother. She was having enough trouble with Rafe.

"You'll like Shane. He's much more easygoing than Rafe. I'm sure that comes with not being the oldest."

Heidi traced the drawing and knew there was no way to say no. The last thing she needed was May upset with her. But if she wasn't careful, the Strykers would weave their way into every part of her world. If that happened, there would be no win—for any of them.

CHAPTER TEN

RAFE WATCHED YET MORE lumber being unloaded. Thanks to his mother's grand plans for the barn, what had started out as a simple repair job had turned into major renovation. When she'd shown him her drawing the previous day, he'd made a few minor changes and promised to look into getting it done. This morning she'd informed him she'd spoken with Ethan, had hired his men for the remainder of the summer and had already ordered the necessary supplies. Now Rafe figured he would be lucky to ever get back to his office in San Francisco.

He should be annoyed and itching to return to the city, but somehow, he found himself not minding too much. He spent his mornings working with Ethan's guys. After lunch, he dealt with his company, giving instructions to Ms. Jennings and talking to Dante about what was going on in the office. Around three, he went back out to join the guys and finished before dinner. Evenings were spent on his computer. Sometimes he and Heidi watched a baseball game or went for a walk.

Not exactly the life of a sought-after bachelor, he thought, pulling on gloves. No dinners out, no evenings at the theater. Pretty much the only thing he missed about his old life was hanging out with Dante and his season tickets at the Giants' stadium.

He had thought he would be bored here. Restless. So far, he was enjoying himself more than he had expected. There were calluses on his hands and a pleasant ache after a day of physical labor. He and Mason took long rides together, to the point where Charlie had noticed that her horse had never been in better shape.

There was an honesty to the land, he thought, then chuckled. He'd better be careful, or he'd turn into the cowboy his mother had always wanted him to be.

The truck driver walked over with a clipboard and paperwork. "You keep goats here?" he asked as he handed Rafe a pen.

"Sure. Why?"

"I would swear I saw some goats walking down the road when I was driving here. You might want to make sure yours didn't get out."

Rafe scrawled his signature on the paperwork, then turned toward the house. He didn't know where Heidi had taken the goats that morning. Before he'd taken more than a couple of steps, the back door opened and Heidi hurried out.

"The goats?" he asked.

She nodded. "My friend Nevada just called. Athena led three of them to the casino construction site. She did this last year and apparently remembered the way."

"How do you get them back?" he asked, following her to the goat house.

Heidi ducked inside, then stepped back out with several ropes. "I catch them and walk them home. I don't have a truck big enough to transport them. What I want to know is how she gets the gates open."

He fell into step with her. "Think of it as forced exercise."

"I'm worried about Persephone. She's pregnant. I'm not sure that much walking is good for her."

"Don't goats travel in the wild?"

"Yes, but they eat as they go. When Athena gets a burr up her butt, it's more a forced march. I'll call the vet when I get back."

He took the ropes from her. "I'm sure she'll be fine."

"I hope so. This is only her second pregnancy."

"Why isn't Athena pregnant?"

"Alpine goats breed in the fall. That's one of the reasons I have both Nubians and Alpines—to stagger their pregnancies, so I never go without fresh goat milk. It's less of an issue with the cheese. With the aging process, I always have cheese at various stages. But the fresh milk is important to several of the families in the area."

"Today's milk will be aerated by the walk."

She smiled. "I'm not sure it works that way. I swear, Athena needs a hobby."

"Too bad you can't teach her to read."

"I'd worry if she learned, she would take over the world."

"You should put the goats with the llamas. If they

really will protect the herd, then the llamas can keep the goats from getting out. Or at least alert you if Athena makes a run for it."

"I could try. I haven't wanted to put them together in case they get attached."

Because one way or another, this arrangement was only temporary, and Heidi wouldn't want her goats hurt by missing a friend.

Dante would say she was taking her goat responsibilities too seriously. A few weeks ago, Rafe would have agreed. Now he knew that Heidi was sensitive to those she considered to be on the outside. Those who didn't belong.

They walked down the main road. About three miles from the ranch, a path cut through the trees. The branches overhead were thick enough to block direct sunlight. The temperature was a good ten or fifteen degrees cooler, and leaves and pine needles crunched underfoot.

Just when Rafe was sure she was lost, they stepped into a clearing and a whole other world.

The sound of large construction equipment echoed off the trees and the side of the mountain. From where he stood, at the west end of the site, he would guess about eighty or ninety acres had been cleared. The main building was massive—right now just poured foundation and steel beams—but he could see what it would be. Several stories, with a view of the mountains.

When he'd heard about the casino, he'd had Dante

pull information and had studied it on his computer. Still, the renderings hadn't prepared him for the sheer size of the project.

"Impressive, don't you think?" She pointed to the far end. "That's one of the parking lots. There will be a multilevel structure on the other side. The big building is the casino and resort. I'm not sure how many hotel rooms they're talking about. At least a couple hundred, maybe more."

She kept talking, explaining the layout and how the design had kept old-growth trees to line a walking path. That there would be a spa and several restaurants.

A pretty blonde woman with short hair and a ready smile joined them.

"You and your bad goats," she said with a laugh. "What's up with Athena?"

"I know." Heidi gave her a quick hug. "She'd ride a motorcycle if she could get a license. Nevada, this is Rafe Stryker. Rafe, Nevada Janack."

He shook hands with the woman, then glanced at the signs on the sides of the construction trailers. "Any relation?"

"I married into the family. Tucker's around here somewhere. Come on. I'll introduce you."

Rafe went willingly. He wanted to know a lot more about the project. He and Dante hadn't talked about what was going on here since Rafe had first discovered the casino. Now that he saw the scope of the project, he was reminded of the possibilities.

RAFE HELD THE PHONE to his ear with his left hand and made notes with his right. “I need to see everything you’ve pulled on the casino project. Not just the plans, which you sent me.”

He waited while Dante typed in his computer. “Got it,” his friend said.

“The guy in charge, Tucker Janack, says there will be over three hundred hotel rooms. There’s a casino, spa, golf course. There’s also going to be an outlet mall, but another company is developing that.”

“Too small for Janack?” Dante asked.

“Probably. Depending on time of year, staffing and events. They could have upward of five hundred employees there. No way Fool’s Gold has that kind of labor force just sitting around. Which means bringing people in. Lots of people.”

“They’re going to have to live somewhere.”

“Exactly.” Rafe pressed a few keys on his computer. “You have it?”

“Right in front of me.”

Rafe stared at the outline of the Castle Ranch. Done to scale, it showed the main house, the barn and the fence line. The main road was to the south, and several smaller roads provided natural boundaries.

Assuming a standard lot size of five thousand square feet, a modest three-bedroom house with attached garage, keeping a few acres around the ranch buildings for his mother and her animals, there was more than enough room for a hundred homes. With plenty left over for future development.

"You doing the math?" Rafe asked.

"It's a sweet, sweet number. Considering how cheap the land is, I'm a happy guy. You're talking serious profit levels."

"Tell me about it. We wouldn't have to do anything fancy. We'll add the most popular upgrades. Some landscaping."

"With employees coming to work for the casino, they'll be desperate to buy. That means motivated buyers."

Rafe wrote frantically. "We can arrange our own financing. Give people a break for going with our lender and make more money on the mortgage. We'll have to get the town to agree."

"I've done some preliminary research. The town is business-friendly. The mayor has a reputation for being easy to work with. No crazy zoning requirements. As long as we're building up to their standards and not playing fast and loose with the rules, they'll make it go smoothly for us."

"Good." Rafe wasn't interested in building crap, he just didn't want to waste profit when he didn't have to. "To think this all started because my mother wanted to buy back this damned old ranch. Now this could be one of our biggest projects of the year."

"As long as the judge rules in our favor."

"She will. Heidi won't be able to come up with the money."

"Plus, we can show that our plan helps the community," Dante added. "Your goat girl is going to find herself out on the street."

Dante chuckled, but Rafe didn't join in. While he still wanted to win, he found it difficult to imagine the Castle Ranch without Heidi and her goats. Where would she go?

He told himself it wasn't his problem, but wasn't sure he believed the words. Not anymore.

"We could give her a couple of acres. For the goats."

Dante laughed. "Good one, Rafe. Like you've ever given anyone anything."

His partner was still laughing when he hung up. Rafe set down his phone and stared out the window. Profit over anything—he'd long believed that. Money was the only way out, the only way up. He'd been poor, and it sucked.

In high school, his English teacher had made them all read *Gone with the Wind* and then watch the movie. In class, his friends had laughed when Scarlett O'Hara had held up the wizened turnips, declaring that, as God was her witness, she would never be hungry again. He hadn't found the words funny. He'd lived them.

He'd taken the charity baskets the town had given, vowing that when he grew up, he would be the richest man he knew. That no one would ever take advantage of him. That he would always win.

Dante was right. Giving away a few acres for Heidi and her goats made no sense. When the judge ruled and he got the ranch, she would be out, and he would have it all.

HEIDI WAITED ANXIOUSLY while Cameron McKenzie listened to Persephone's heartbeat. He'd already examined the goat, checking her legs and hooves, feeling her pregnant tummy. He removed the stethoscope from his ears.

"She's fine."

Heidi released the breath she'd been holding. "You're sure? I can't believe how far she walked today. All the way to the construction site and back."

"Goats walk. They like it. She's a healthy girl." Cameron stood and petted the goat. Persephone nuzzled his hand.

"Now, if only we could figure out how to keep Athena contained," May said from her place by the door of the goat house.

"She's a smart girl," Cameron said, packing up his bag. "You're going to need a more secure lock on the gate."

"This is my third attempt to find a lock she can't open," Heidi said. "It's tough having a goat who's smarter than me."

"We should put Rafe onto the problem," May told Heidi. "He's good at that sort of thing."

Heidi wasn't sure there was anything Rafe wasn't good at, which made him dangerous. She couldn't seem to stop thinking about him, wondering what he was doing and when she would see him next. When he smiled, she felt all gooey inside. The man was trouble, and she already had enough problems.

The three of them walked out of the goat house. Cameron looked past the barn, to the corral where the three llamas grazed.

"You're doing wonders for my large-animal practice," he told May. "I've handled a few alpacas, not so many llamas. I'll read up on them."

"There are sheep, too," May told him.

"Sheep are easy," he said. "Any others on the way?"

May smiled. "I don't want to spoil the surprise."

Uh-oh. "Does Rafe know?" Heidi asked.

"Of course not. He would tell me I'm being silly. You'll have to wait and see, like everyone else."

Heidi held up both her hands. "I'm okay with that." She glanced toward the house, where Rafe was on his cell phone, pacing back and forth on the porch, obviously in an intense conversation with someone.

"I look forward to whatever else you bring to the ranch," Cameron said. "Nice to meet you, May."

"You, as well."

They shook hands. Cameron turned to Heidi. "You okay now?"

"Yes. Thanks for coming. I guess I'm an overly concerned goat parent."

"I like that in my clients. You know how to get in touch with me."

He walked to his truck and climbed in.

"What a nice young man," May said, as Cameron started the engine, then waved before turning his truck around and driving away. "Very handsome."

Heidi thought about Cameron's dark hair and green eyes. "I guess. I don't think of him that way."

"Is he married?"

"Yes. Cameron got married a couple of months ago. But it wouldn't matter if he was single. He's not my type."

"No chemistry?"

"None."

"I see." May glanced toward the porch. "It's hard to predict which way the heart will fall."

Heidi opened her mouth, then closed it. Talk about a minefield. She was going to stay safely out of that conversation, she thought. If she was smart, she would also stay away from Rafe, but she didn't seem to be very bright when it came to him.

Fine—she would risk her feelings, but she would stay out of his bed. Because to cross that line would be to gamble with everything she had.

THE FOOL'S GOLD SPRING Festival always fell on Mother's Day weekend. Many a father had taken advantage of that fact, bringing his wife to the event and letting her choose her own gift. Sunday morning, the food vendors served brunch fare, and the jewelry designers did an especially brisk business.

The weekend celebration started on Friday evening with a chili cook-off. The winners (and losers) sold their entries all weekend long. Saturday morning, there was a parade featuring kids on bikes and pulled in wagons, all decorated with flowers and ribbons. Family dogs accompanied the children, the furry family members also festively dressed.

Rafe winced as a Great Dane in a dress strolled by. "That's just wrong," he muttered. "What happened to dog dignity?"

Heidi laughed. "She looks adorable."

"She's humiliated."

Heidi looked at the dog's happy face and wagging tail. "I think she's channeling her inner diva. Maybe next year I'll dress up Athena and bring her to be in the parade."

"She'll eat the dress."

"Maybe. But she'll be pretty until then."

The streets were crowded with locals and tourists. Even though it was still a couple of hours before noon, the smell of barbecue filled the air. Heidi sniffed the scent.

"You did say something about lunch, right?" she asked.

"Don't worry. I'll feed you."

After she'd come in from milking, she'd found Rafe sitting at the kitchen table. Weekends had a different rhythm at the ranch. The hired construction guys had the two days off. While Rafe often went out and continued the construction projects on his own, the pace always seemed slower.

After she'd stored the fresh milk in the mudroom

refrigerator, he'd surprised her by asking her if she wanted to go to the festival with him. She'd known that saying yes was risky, but she had been unable to resist. So here they were, blending in with the other people watching the parade.

When the last of the kids on bikes had gone by, Rafe suggested they tour the booths.

"You sure you feel all right?" Heidi asked.

"I can play tourist."

"I'll believe that when you buy a Fool's Gold refrigerator magnet."

"Mom would love that."

"May enjoys most things."

He chuckled. "I'm ignoring the implication that I don't."

"I didn't say that. I'm sure you have your moments."

They walked toward the booths. The crowd grew around them, with kids running between them. When they reached the corner, Rafe grabbed her hand and drew her close.

"I need to make sure you don't get lost."

He was being nice, she told herself. Friendly. Nothing more. But the feel of his hand linked with hers was more than friendly. It felt…right. The strength of his fingers, the calluses. His hand was bigger than hers, and if she allowed herself a moment of girly foolishness, she would admit that being with him made her want to flutter her lashes and sigh.

She reminded herself that he wasn't for her. He would never be for her. He wanted someone sophisticated. A woman who fit in anywhere and looked good doing it. Someone who always knew what to say. Heidi's idea of high fashion was to wear her hair loose. While she technically knew how to wear makeup, she would rather just slap on some sunscreen and call it a day. Her clothing choices were driven by the fact that she started her day milking goats.

"Tell me where you met your wife," she said, blurting out the instruction abruptly.

Rafe glanced at her. "At work. My first job after college. She was an intern with a guy my boss wanted to do business with."

"Not exactly romantic."

He grinned. "It wasn't. The two principals couldn't agree on contract terms. Ansley and I escaped to the coffee room. I'd just made my first deal. It was small—I didn't have much extra money, but it had gone through, and I saw the potential."

They were by the park. Heidi pulled them toward one of the benches and sat down. Rafe settled next to her.

"Let me guess. Ansley was a tall, cool blonde with family money and a pedigree."

He angled toward Heidi on the bench. "You're partly right. She did have a pedigree, but she was a brunette. Smart. Her family had started out rich, but the money had been lost a couple of generations ago. She was ambitious. We had that in common. I asked her out and she said yes."

"Then you fell madly in love?"

"Then I got to know her. There wasn't any 'madly.' More of a certainty. That we could make a life together. We shared the same values, we both wanted children and to make our mark on the world." He stared past her. "We got married. Everything seemed fine until she told me she didn't love me and that it was over."

He shrugged. "I realized I didn't mind losing her."

The only romantic love Heidi had seen got bigger with time. Passion exploded and rational thought wasn't possible. Love consumed, and she knew she didn't want that. Didn't want to be ruled by emotions people couldn't control.

He returned his attention to her. "What about you? Any townies steal your heart?"

"No. I avoid townies."

"You're with me and you claim I'm one of them."

"You're not interested in me."

One eyebrow rose, but he didn't respond to her statement. "So, who's the guy who got away? He must be with the carnival. Unless it's Lars. And if it is him, I think you have a shot."

She swatted his arm. "Leave Lars alone. He's very nice. And there wasn't anyone. I've had boyfriends, but no one serious. A couple of times, I thought the relationship was going somewhere, but it didn't."

To be honest, she'd never felt that sick-to-her-stomach, intense longing Melinda had talked about. Or the desperate-to-be-with-him-even-though-he's-bad-for-me feeling Nevada had admitted to last summer.

Before Tucker had come to his senses and realized he was completely in love with her. The scary truth was the closest she'd felt to any sort of out-of-control emotion was when she thought about Rafe. And that was still an easily managed out-of-control.

"Maybe there's something wrong with me," she admitted.

"Maybe love is a myth," Rafe told her.

"You don't believe that. Look at your mom and how long she's loved your dad. It's been over twenty years, and she's never loved anyone else."

"Okay, I'll accept her feelings were genuine. Name three other people who have that."

"I can name a lot more than that. The Hendrix triplets all fell in love and got married last year. You mentioned you know their brother Ethan. He's wild about his wife. Their mother was happily married for years. After being a widow for a long time, she's back together with her first love, and they'd spent over thirty years apart. Love is real."

Maybe it wasn't just for suckers, she thought wistfully. Although she was still a little afraid of "falling" for anyone.

"Don't be sad, goat girl," he told her, then leaned in and kissed her.

She was aware of people walking just a few yards away. Of the sound of a band tuning up over by the main square, and happy squeals of children. The sun was warm on her arms, the scent of flowers and grass mingled with the smell of freshly brewed coffee and barbecue. But all that faded into the background as Rafe moved his mouth against hers.

Wanting to prolong the moment as much as possible, she put her fingers on his shoulder. He was all hard muscle under his cotton shirt. Masculine to her feminine. His palm cupped her arm, drawing her closer, then he stroked his tongue against her lower lip.

She parted her lips immediately. Even before he moved inside, her body began to melt. Liquid longing poured through her, causing her breasts to swell and her thighs to press tightly together.

She wanted to wrap both her arms around him and lose herself in the moment. She wanted more than his tongue brushing against hers. She wanted him naked, taking, pleasing, doing all the things a man like him would do to a woman. When it came to Rafe, she might not be willing to risk her heart, but apparently she was ready to put her body on the line.

But they were sitting in a park in Fool's Gold, and a little French kissing was all that they could get away with. So she kissed him back, getting lost in the desire that filled her, telling herself it was enough and almost believing it.

He drew back, his dark eyes bright with something she really hoped was lust.

"Nice," he murmured, then cleared his throat. He drew back. "We can sit here for a minute, right?"

The question confused her. "Why would we… Oh." Right. Because walking around would make a few things obvious. She risked a quick glance and saw an impressive erection making its presence known. A shiver raced through her.

He took her hand in his and lightly kissed her palm. "If you want to leave this bench anytime soon, you need to stop looking at me like that."

She wanted to ask, "Like what?" but had a feeling she knew what he was talking about. She was probably looking at him as if he were the one man on earth she had to have.

He shifted so that he was facing front, his ankle resting on his opposite knee. He draped an arm around her, drawing her close.

"Let's pick a more neutral topic," he suggested. "And if you could speak in a squeaky voice, that would help, too."

She laughed. "What's wrong with my regular voice?"

"It's sexy."

She cleared her throat, suddenly unable to think of anything to say. "You never did tell me about your date."

"And I'm not going to."

"Any dates planned in the future?"

He glanced at her, his dark eyes bright with amusement. "Could we not talk about me dating?"

"Sure. Um, the carnival is coming to town in a few weeks."

"Your carnival? The people who taught you to hate townies?"

"Yes, and they didn't teach me that. I learned on my own."

"Will someone show me how to tame a lion?"

"That's the circus. This is the rides and games."

"I always did like a good Tilt-A-Whirl."

"Then you'll have to go on it."

"You coming with me?"

She shook her head. "They make me throw up."

"Lightweight."

"Townie."

He laughed. He might have a thing for her voice, but she liked the sound of his laughter. It made her feel safe and happy, as did pressing against him, with his arm around her.

All dangerous, she thought. Good thing she wasn't the type to fall in love.

CHAPTER ELEVEN

HEIDI FINISHED THE LAST of the milking, then poured the still warm, creamy liquid into pans for the waiting cats.

"I should put a camera on the three of you," she said, as her feline guests lapped up the milk. "One of those pet cams, so I can find out where you live."

Or she could simply ask around. Someone would know who owned the cats. But she liked the idea of a mystery, of being able to pretend the cats had exciting secret lives after they left here.

She put away her stool, checked to make sure the goats had plenty of water, then picked up the buckets and walked back to the house. She entered to the smell of coffee. As she poured the raw milk from the stainless-steel bucket to the glass containers she would put in the refrigerator, she told herself it was nice that May had gotten up early and made coffee. That Rafe wouldn't be the one waiting for her when she walked into the kitchen. Because anticipating anything about him would be very, very bad. But anticipation nearly overwhelmed her now, as spending mornings with him was often the best part of her day.

She was finding it more and more difficult to remember that he was the enemy. Being around him was…nice. He made her laugh, and she looked forward to spending time with him. In other circumstances, she would have taken the chance and offered him her heart. But these weren't other circumstances, and if she forgot what he wanted, she could lose everything.

Heidi put away the milk, closed the refrigerator door and walked into the kitchen. Rafe stood leaning against the counter, his dark eyes brightening when he saw her.

With all the hard work he put in on the ranch during the day, he usually showered before dinner rather than first thing in the morning. There was something to be said for a man who wasn't so crisp around the edges. She liked the faint shadow of stubble on his jaw, the slight muss to his hair. He wore a plaid cotton shirt, the sleeves rolled up to the elbows, and faded jeans with a tear by the front pocket.

Somewhere along the way, he'd ceased to be the guy in the suit. Now he was just Rafe. And just Rafe was turning out to be a lot more dangerous.

"Morning," he said, handing her a mug of coffee.

"Hi."

She saw that he'd already added cream and, she would guess, sugar, preparing it just the way she liked.

"How are the girls?" he asked, moving toward the table.

"Good. Happy to see me."

They sat across from each other, as they did most

mornings. This was their quiet time together, before May and Glen were up and the work crew arrived.

He had a few sheets of paper on the table and now nudged them toward her. "I was thinking about your cheese and soap, and made some calls."

She glanced down and saw three names, along with phone numbers. Next to the names were countries. Two were China and one was Korea.

"These are sales reps who already have distributors for American products in select, upscale Asian markets. Right now, goat cheese is hot."

She looked from the paper to him, trying to understand. "They'll take my calls?"

"They're interested in what you have to sell, and they know how to get started in those countries. There's little risk to you, because you're using infrastructure in place. Why reinvent the wheel?" He tapped the list, next to the second name for China. "She'll want samples of your soap. If she likes it, she'll take it on consignment, carrying the shipping costs herself. The only risk on your end is paying to have it returned if it doesn't sell. However, she knows her customers and what they want to buy. From what I've heard, the biggest problem is how fast the orders tend to come in."

A problem she could totally handle, she thought, considering the bars of soap curing and how many more she could make in the next few weeks.

Selling locally was one thing, but getting into the overseas market, especially in Asia, could mean real money. Possibly enough money to pay back May. Rafe had to know that.

"This kind of business takes time," he said gently. "But it will pay off eventually."

So he was good at business and a mind reader, she thought. "Thanks for the contacts," she said. "I'll call them all today."

"They're waiting to hear from you."

Conversation shifted to work on the barn, but Heidi kept thinking about what Rafe had given her. Assuming he was right, and she had no reason to doubt him, she wouldn't see any profits before they were to meet with the judge again. But if she could show an aggressive payback plan, that would help her cause. So why was he taking the chance?

Did he have that much faith in his lawyer? Or was he starting to have feelings for her? She knew he liked her, that they had a good time together. Did he wonder what would have happened if they'd met under other circumstances? He'd turned out to be very different from what she'd expected. Maybe it was the same for him. Maybe they were both discovering an unexpected connection.

RAFE LIT THE COALS in the barbecue and watched in satisfaction as the blue flames jumped toward the sky. Sure, a gas grill would be faster, but there was something gratifying about cooking meat the old-fashioned way.

Heidi walked out onto the back porch. "No explosion?"

He chuckled. "The grill will be ready in about thirty minutes."

"Perfect. Your mom left us potato salad in the refrigerator. I finished a green salad. We're good to go."

"You forgot the wine."

Her green eyes crinkled as she made a face. "We're having hamburgers."

"A good wine goes with everything."

She followed him into the kitchen. He'd already picked out a bottle. Heidi stared at the label.

"Col Solare. Is it Italian?"

He reached for the bottle and removed the foil. "Washington State. It's a blend made in partnership." He smiled. "How many details do you want?"

"I think we've reached my limit. Is it expensive?"

"Define expensive."

"More than twenty dollars a bottle?"

"Yes."

"More than thirty?"

"Do you really want to know?"

She tilted her head. "It's just wine."

"You can't use the words 'just' and 'wine' in the same sentence. You live five miles from a vineyard. You should support the local industry."

"I'm more of a margarita kind of girl. What's the difference between a ten-dollar bottle and a hundred-dollar bottle?"

"This wine is mostly aged in new French oak barrels. The best grapes are used, and the barrels are washed out during the aging processes. That's a lot of expense and labor."

"Why do they wash out the barrels? And how? There's wine in them."

"The wine is moved to stainless-steel containers, and then the barrels are cleaned out. It gets rid of sediment. The wine is then returned to the barrel to continue aging."

He removed the cork and then got two wineglasses from the cupboard.

"Stainless steel because the wine won't react with it?"

"Right."

She took the glass he offered and sniffed. "It's nice. You're not going to talk about chocolate and black cherry are you? I've never understood that. It's grapes, not chocolate. And if you say it's pretentious, I'll throw this at you."

On his Nina-arranged date, he and the other woman had discussed wine because they'd had little else in common. That conversation had been slightly tedious and filled with "I know more than you" stories. He found he preferred Heidi's honest assessment of wine.

"Tell me if you like it," he said. "That's what matters."

"Do I swirl? Red wine drinkers like to swirl."

"It aerates the wine."

"I thought oxygen hurt wine."

"In the bottle, yes. Once it's opened and ready for drinking, oxygen opens up the flavors."

She dutifully swirled her glass, then took a sip. She let it sit on her tongue for a second, then swallowed.

"Oh." Her green eyes widened. "That's nice. Smooth, but with a lot of flavor. I thought it might have that weird bite, but it doesn't."

"I'm glad you like it."

They walked out onto the porch and sat on the steps.

They were a couple of hours from sunset. The days were getting longer and warmer as they inched toward summer. Buds had given way to leaves and flowers.

He and Heidi had brought the goats back for the evening. He could see the sheep and llamas grazing contentedly. He'd resisted coming to Fool's Gold, but looking around now, he had a hard time remembering why.

"It's Saturday night," Heidi told him. "What would you be doing if you were back in San Francisco?"

"Working."

"Not out on a date?"

"If I was dating, I wouldn't need Nina."

"There must be tons of women where you work or hang out."

He shifted on the step, uncomfortable with the topic, but unclear on how to change it. "I'm not interested in going out with someone I do business with. I also won't date an employee. There aren't a lot of other women in my life."

"You have a lot of rules."

"I'm not looking to get sued for sexual harassment."

"Good point. No likely candidates at your monthly tycoon meetings?"

He grinned. "No. All the good ones are married."

"What about your season tickets to the opera or ballet?"

"I'm more a baseball guy. But I do like theater."

"Musicals, where people randomly break into song?"

"Sometimes."

"You're full of surprises." She put down her wine and grabbed his free hand. With her fingertips, she traced the calluses on his palms. "What will your tycoon friends say about these?"

"To tell you the truth, they'll be envious."

Heidi released him, which made him want to put his arm around her and pull her close. He liked when they touched. Lately he wanted to do a lot more than just touch, which made for some timing issues. He did his best to be gone before she stepped into the shower in the morning. The last thing he wanted was to spend fifteen minutes listening to the water running and imagining her naked. Not that leaving the house erased the image, but it made dealing with it easier.

"You're a better cowboy than I would have thought," she admitted.

"I like the work. I can look out and see what I've accomplished in a day. I don't get a lot of that in my regular life."

"Be careful. This kind of life can be seductive."

He glanced at her and found her looking at him. She had beautiful eyes, he thought, staring into her green irises. A great smile. Her blond hair hung past her shoulders, all wavy from the braids.

He found himself wanting to touch the soft-looking strands, to pull her close and kiss her. But kissing would lead to other things, and that would be a mistake. Heidi might not be the enemy anymore, but she stood in the way of what he wanted. Sleeping with her would make an already complicated situation more difficult. But, damn, she was a temptation.

"Coals," he murmured, not quite ready to turn away.

"What?"

"I should check the coals."

"Oh, right. I'll get the burgers."

For a second, neither of them moved. Rafe knew he was seconds away from not caring about the consequences. But just as he was about to set down his glass and reach for her, she scrambled to her feet and walked into the kitchen.

Probably for the best, he told himself, ignoring the need building in his body, and the voice in his heart that whispered he was a fool to let Heidi be the one who got away.

HEIDI HAD A HARD TIME with dinner. The meal was great—there was no bad with hamburgers and potato salad—and she enjoyed the wine. Rafe was his usual, charming self. A funny, intelligent companion who could speak on any number of topics and still surprise her with his unexpected views on everything from the British royal family to his belief in renewable energy.

Her confusion came more from wondering why on earth any woman would have left Rafe. He was the kind of guy she would hold on to with both hands. Which led to the second problem… Unruly girl parts.

She'd moved past the tingling-in-anticipation stage and was firmly in "take me now." Every time he smiled, she felt a tug in her belly. When his hand casually brushed hers, she wanted to whimper. If the man took her in his arms and kissed her for longer than thirty seconds, she would probably have an orgasm.

With dinner finished and the dishes washed, the rest of the evening stretched before them. May and Glen planned to go to a movie after their meal, which meant they wouldn't be coming home for another three hours. Maybe more. The night was young, the sun just setting, and Heidi was terrified she was going to say or do something humiliating. Her only option seemed to be escape.

She swallowed the last of her wine, possibly a mistake considering she was already a little buzzed from her first glass, and stood.

"I, ah, should get some paperwork finished."

Rafe rose. "You sure? I thought we could go for a walk."

"In the dark?"

"I'll protect you."

She wanted to say yes. Wanted to spend time with him, talking to him and maybe more. But her fear was greater. With her blood pumping and her hormones doing their best to convince her to be wild, she was very likely to say or do something humiliating. Escape was the safest route.

"Maybe another time," she murmured, moving back, anxious to get to the door. Once there, she could run for the stairs and make it to her room before disaster struck.

"Are you all right?"

"Fine. Great. Better than great."

She gave him what she hoped was a brilliant smile and turned. Unfortunately she'd gone back farther than she'd realized and, in her haste, plowed directly into the cabinets. Her momentum was such that she staggered back and started to trip. Rafe caught her before she could tumble. He took hold of her arms and turned her so she was facing him.

His eyes were dark as night. His face all hard planes and sharp angles. Her gaze settled on his mouth as she remembered how good the kissing had been.

Then, she didn't have to rely on memories, because he drew her close and pressed his lips against hers.

He tasted of the wine. Strong arms surrounded her, making her feel both secure and delicate. Female to his male. Her body nestled into his, her breasts flattening against his chest, her thighs pillowing his. She lifted her arms to wrap around his neck, her fingers burying themselves in his hair.

The kiss was everything she remembered. Tender and demanding at the same time. Taking and yielding. She parted her lips and waited a heartbeat for his tongue to brush against hers. Wanting turned liquid. Hunger swept through her, like the tide coming in.

She tilted her head so they could deepen the kiss. He moved his hands up and down her back before sliding them to her waist. He paused there, as if waiting for her to decide what happened next.

There were options, she thought hazily. She could step back, say good-night and run away. The safe course, the sensible course. Or…

There it was. That delicious word. The road to possibilities. *Or.* Or she could give in to the need, find out if Rafe was as good as he looked, if she could satisfy him, if they were as well matched as she imagined. And she'd imagined a lot.

In truth, there wasn't a choice. She'd made it the second she'd kissed him back. So why pretend otherwise?

She dropped her hands to his shoulders and squeezed. A silent invitation for more.

He responded immediately, moving his hands higher. Even as his large hands closed over her breasts, he shifted so that he was kissing her jaw, then her neck. He trailed his mouth to her ear, where he nipped at the lobe before licking the sensitive skin beneath.

At the same time, his hands closed over her breasts. He took the weight of her in his palms, using his fingers and thumbs to tease her tight nipples.

The combination of sensations overwhelmed her. Pleasure poured through her, making her want to cry out. Her legs trembled. The sensitive flesh between her legs swelled. She ached for him to touch her everywhere.

He continued to kiss his way down her neck to her collarbone. When he reached the edge of her T-shirt, he dropped his hands to the hem, drew back and pulled it off in one easy tug. Her bra followed as quickly.

Heidi was startled by the progression, but before she could figure out if she was comfortable or not, he bent down and closed his mouth over her right nipple. He drew in the tight bud and sucked. His tongue circled and flicked, sending jolts of need directly to the center of her being. At the same time, he cupped the other breast, his fingers matching the movements of his tongue.

She found herself growing weaker by the second. Her head fell back, her hair brushing against her bare skin. She hung on to him for balance, and because he was the only stable part of her rapidly spinning world.

He switched places on her breasts, replacing his fingers with his mouth, and vice versa. Her breathing increased as she hung on to him. With each tug of his mouth, she found herself more and more aroused. Blood became sluggish; wanting grew. Every inch of her was sensitized, so that even the brush of his arm against her belly was erotic.

He moved his hands to her shoulders and pulled her hard against him. His mouth covered hers. She kissed him deeply, meeting him stroke for stroke. Their bodies strained together. She felt his erection, hard and thick, and rubbed herself against him.

He reached between them, fumbling with the waistband of her jeans. She felt his fingers tremble as he undid the button, then pulled down the zipper.

He turned her so her back was to his front. As her rear nestled his arousal, he cupped one of her breasts in his left hand and slipped his right inside her jeans and beneath her panties.

He found his way between her legs, to the wet, swollen heart of her. She felt as if she'd been ready for days, so the first stroke of his fingers caused her to gasp in both pleasure and approval. He circled and rubbed, moved his fingers back and forth.

Each stroke was perfection, every brush of skin on skin taking her higher and closer. Through the haze of need, she was pretty sure he considered this the play portion of the evening, that things would get serious later. But it had been too long, or maybe it was because of the man himself. Either way, about forty seconds in, she felt herself reaching for her release.

She pulsed her hips a couple of times and tried to hold back. But he touched her so right, and then there was his other hand on her breast, and the way he played with her nipples. When he bent his head and kissed the side of her neck, she lost what little self-control she had. Her muscles tensed and then released as her orgasm poured through her.

She came with a quiet cry and shudder, hanging

on to him. He continued to rub her, drawing out her pleasure until she went limp in his arms.

Heidi stood there, her back to Rafe, humiliation blending with satisfaction. How could she have done that so fast? With hardly any effort on his part. She wasn't completely sure he'd even expected things to go that far. What if he'd just wanted to make out?

If this was how seventeen-year-old boys felt when they were with a girl, she now had a whole lot more sympathy for them.

Before she could decide on a course of action, or what to say, Rafe turned her in his arms and kissed her hard.

"That was the sexiest thing I've ever seen," he muttered, his voice thick and hoarse.

He grabbed her shirt and bra, pushed both at her, then took her hand in his and half pulled, half guided her to the stairs.

She clutched the clothing to her bare breasts and followed him up to his bedroom. In less time than she would have thought possible, he'd taken off his boots and socks and ripped off his shirt. He spent a couple of seconds fumbling in his shaving kit, then dumped the contents onto the dresser and dug through until he pulled out a package of condoms. He threw the latter on the nightstand, then returned to her.

After tossing her shirt and bra on a chair, he cupped her face and kissed her.

Later she would explore why her first instinct had been to go to the bad place. She would remind herself that her body was beautiful, and physical pleasure was to be appreciated. But for now, it was enough to touch Rafe's bare skin, to feel how much he wanted her.

She traced his back and chest, her fingers brushing against his hard muscles. She undid his jeans and pushed them down, along with his briefs. After he stepped out of his clothes, she stroked his erection, learning the length and breadth of him. She pressed her mouth to his chest, and rubbed her thumb against the very tip of his arousal, enjoying the sharp intake of air.

He helped her out of her jeans and panties, then led her to the bed. When she stretched out on the sheets, he joined her. He knelt between her thighs and bent down to give her an open-mouthed kiss.

She would have thought she was done, but he quickly brought her back to trembling. As his tongue stroked and circled, he pushed one finger, then two, inside her. He imitated the act of love, moving rhythmically against her swollen flesh.

She dug her heels into the bed and pushed against him. He closed his lips around her clitoris and gently sucked. At the same time, he pushed his fingers in and up, stroking her from the inside. Again and again, until he had control of her body, until he decided the exact moment she would climax.

He moved more quickly, still rubbing, still sucking, then faster still, until every muscle tensed in that last second, before her release rushed through her and she surrendered to the moment.

The last of the rapturous ripples faded. He straightened enough to grab the condom and rip open the package. When the protection was in place, he braced himself and thrust into her.

She met his thrust with one of her own, causing him to fill her completely. He went in deep and hard, the friction sending shivers through her. She wrapped her legs around his hips as he began the steady pumping.

She opened her eyes and found him watching her. His dark eyes flashed with passion, and she could see him getting closer. Sex was intimate, but this was more so. She could experience his pleasure with him, and found herself getting breathless as he got closer.

She drew him in deeper, and at the moment when he stilled and shuddered, she tightened her muscles around him. He came in a rush, grasping her hips with his hands, his gaze never leaving hers.

IT WAS DARK WHEN HEIDI WOKE. In the few seconds it took for her to find the clock, she realized she wasn't in her bedroom and that there was a man sleeping beside her. As the time changed to three-seventeen, the memories of the previous evening surfaced. She smiled, enjoying the warmth of Rafe next to her.

Once they'd found their way to his bed, they hadn't left. Sometime close to eleven, Glen and May had returned, but hadn't ventured upstairs. Fortunately, the downstairs bedrooms were on the other side of the house, so no one heard when she and Rafe made love for the second time.

Heidi carefully got out of bed. There was enough moonlight spilling through the window for her to see her clothes in a pile on the floor. Although she would very much like to stay where she was, she didn't want to risk getting caught there.

She picked up her panties and slid them on. Sore muscles protested, and she smiled again. It had been a while, but Rafe had been worth the wait. The man was a god in bed. Actually, he'd turned out to be a pretty nice guy everywhere else, too.

She dressed quickly, then picked up her boots and tiptoed to the door. Being as quiet as possible, she turned the knob. As she stepped back to let the door swing open, her hip bumped the dresser, and the contents of his shaving kit rattled. She put up her hand to stop anything from falling and waking him. In the process, she jostled a stack of papers, and several of them floated to the floor.

She bent down to pick them up, only to pause. The first sheet was a crude rendering of a development. Small houses lined narrow streets. As Rafe's business included development, she wouldn't have thought anything of the sketch, if not for what was written on top.

Castle Ranch.

CHAPTER TWELVE

"YOU'RE SURE?" CHARLIE ASKED, then held up a hand. "I'm not taking his side. I'm just saying, you need to be certain before we move forward with any plan."

Heidi sat at a table in Jo's Bar. She'd asked her friends to join her for lunch. She needed help coming up with some way to defeat Rafe.

"I'm sure." Heidi held on to her anger. It was the only thing that kept her from giving in to tears. "I looked through all the papers he had. He has a survey of the ranch, and pretty much every acre is accounted for. I don't know how he managed that without us seeing—except there are always workmen coming and going. He generously left his mother the main house and the land around it for her animals. But that's it. Everywhere else are his ticky-tacky houses."

She clutched her glass of iced tea. "I was so stupid. He used me. All this time, I thought he was being nice. He actually gave me the names of three people to help me sell my cheese and soap in Asia. I thought it was because we were becoming friends. It wasn't. He feels guilty. Or worse, what if he was just trying to distract me? We're not friends. I'm in the way of his cheap-house empire. He's planning on taking all of it. He's going to turn that beautiful land into a development, and there's nothing I can do to stop him."

Despite being furious, she felt the first whisper of tears.

"I can't let him win. Where will Glen and I go? I have the goats—they need land. And the caves are perfect for aging my cheese. Plus, this is h-home." Her voice cracked and she grabbed a napkin. "I don't want to have to leave Fool's Gold."

She felt Charlie and Annabelle squeezing her arm.

"You're not going to leave," Annabelle promised. "We'll figure something out. I just can't believe he's doing this in secret."

"He expects to win," Charlie said flatly. "Why not? With his money and influence, he doesn't live like the rest of us. I'm sure he figures the judge will be dazzled by his plans."

"She doesn't have to be," Heidi said, wiping away tears. "Even if I get sales reps interested in my cheese, it's going to be a while until money's coming in. I don't have weeks, let alone months. Assuming we have until midsummer before we're called back before the judge, I'll be lucky to have saved ten thousand dollars. That's only ten percent of what Glen took from May. Plus, May is completely settling into the ranch. She's had Rafe fix the fence line, and now they're expanding the barn. She's bought animals."

More tears fell. "I can't pay her back for that."

"You're not going to be responsible for the repairs,"

Annabelle told her. "The judge never made that a condition."

"I know, but I'm worried the judge will think May is losing even more."

"Do you think May knows about Rafe's plan?" Charlie asked. "Is she in on it?"

Heidi had asked herself the same question. Slowly, she shook her head. "I can't believe that. She's genuinely sweet. She could have been angry at what Glen did. She could have insisted he go to jail, but she didn't. Plus, she loves the ranch and isn't that into business. This has to be Rafe."

There was so much more she couldn't bring herself to say. That she'd begun to fall for him. That she'd trusted him. That last night she'd made love with him, giving herself to him in every way possible. Talk about being a fool.

"He's trying to distract me from his real plan," she murmured, hoping the pain in her chest was more about wounded pride than a broken heart. "That's why he's being so helpful. It all started…" She swallowed as the truth fell into place. "It's the casino. That's who the houses are for. The people who will work there. I'm the one who took him there. Athena got out, and he came with me to collect the goats. He saw it then."

"We can fix this," Annabelle told her.

"Any idea how?" Charlie asked. "I don't mean to be difficult, but wanting something doesn't make it so."

"There has to be a roadblock." Annabelle leaned

both elbows on the table and rested her head in her hands. "What gets in the way of construction?"

"Rules, regulations. Zoning." Charlie brightened. "We could talk to the mayor. She has to like you more than she likes Rafe. She'd be on our side."

"I don't know the mayor that well," Heidi told them. "Besides, why would she be against him building all those houses? Doesn't she want Fool's Gold to grow?"

"Sure, but not this way," Annabelle said.

"Why not? Won't those workers need somewhere to live? The ranch is perfect." Heidi blinked back more tears. "That's the problem. Who cares about a few goats and my dreams when compared with all those people?"

"Don't give up," Charlie said. "We'll find something. If we can't use the law to help us, what about the media? Aren't there groups that hate what Rafe does? Maybe if we contacted one of them."

"Unfortunately, he has a good reputation in the industry," Annabelle said glumly. "He builds to code, pays a fair wage, takes care of the land while doing it. Blah. Blah. Blah."

"Just our luck. He's only a bastard personally." Charlie sank back in her chair. "This sucks."

Hopelessness joined Heidi's sense of betrayal. She should have known Rafe was too good to be true. He was—

"I've got it!" Annabelle slapped both hands on the table. "I know what to do."

Heidi stared at her. "What?"

Annabelle grinned, her green eyes dancing with excitement. "Remember last fall at the casino construction site? They blew away part of the mountain and exposed all that Máa-zib gold? The press came, and they had to stop construction on that part of the site. The museum people investigated."

"I doubt there's any Máa-zib gold on the ranch," Heidi told her. "There's no mountain."

"But there are caves."

Heidi was doubtful. "People have been going in them for decades. They would have found whatever is there."

"Maybe, maybe not. And maybe there's more than gold to be found."

"I have no idea what you're talking about," Heidi told her.

Annabelle leaned forward and lowered her voice. "Cave paintings. What if there were cave paintings? Priceless, ancient cave paintings?"

Jo brought their burgers. "Anything else?" she asked.

"We're good," Charlie told her, then waited until she'd left to speak. "Rafe is still in the planning stages. Finding cave paintings or gold can't shut down what hasn't been started."

"Agreed." Annabelle picked up a French fry. "But it can buy Heidi time." The librarian turned to her. "You said you had contacts, so you're going to start selling your cheese and soap in Asia. If you had an extra three or four months to get that business under way, wouldn't that help? Could you get more money to pay back May?"

"Maybe," Heidi said slowly, not confident doing the math in her head. "It might be enough to show the judge I'm serious. I'm not sure how much I'm going to sell, but if I do half as well as I hope, then, yes."

"The discovery buys time." Charlie nodded. "I get it. With experts swarming around the ranch, the judge won't want to rule." She grinned. "This could work."

Heidi drew in a breath. "This all sounds really great, but I don't know if I can do this. It's lying. Worse. It's fraud. What happens if the judge finds out? First Glen took two hundred and fifty thousand dollars from May, and now I'm doing this? She's going to think I come from a family of thieves."

"All you need is enough time to get the money to pay back May," Annabelle reminded her. "You're not taking anything from anyone. You're keeping what's yours. Besides, if this brings a few more tourists to the town, all the better."

Heidi wasn't sure. The idea didn't sit right with her, but she wasn't sure she had an alternative plan. For all she knew, the judge would be so pleased at the thought of Rafe's construction, she would simply hand the land over. After all, from the town's point of view, there would be more revenue from his houses than her goats.

"I don't want to lose my home," she whispered, her whole body aching. "I can't. This ranch is what I've wanted my whole life."

"So don't lose it," Charlie said. "We'll help."

"I can do some research," Annabelle offered. "Come up with examples of Máa-zib cave paintings. That way, if you want to go through with this, we'll be ready."

Heidi sighed. "Thank you. Both of you. I have to think about this. I'm just not sure. I do want to save my home. I have to. But I don't know that this is the right way."

"Not to be a bitch or anything, but you're kind of out of options," Charlie pointed out.

"I know. Give me a couple of days to think about this."

She would look for an alternative. If she couldn't find one, then she would use their plan.

"You think," Annabelle told her. "I'll get my thoughts together, and maybe sketch out a few ideas for the cave paintings. The women of the tribe were sophisticated for their time, so we're talking about a little bit more than stick figures. How are your artistic skills?"

"Not much more than basic. I used to draw, but I haven't for years."

"Let's hope it comes back to you."

Heidi felt that she'd been living on hope for too long. Waiting and wishing and dreaming. When she'd found out what Glen had done, she'd been so scared they would lose everything. Slowly, after meeting May and Rafe, she'd let down her guard. That had been a mistake. Rafe was ruthless. She saw that now. He would take what he wanted, and he didn't care who or what got in his way. She would have to be just as strong, just as determined. She'd come too far to lose it all now.

HEIDI HEADED BACK TO the ranch right after lunch. She was hoping to escape to her room for a couple of hours of private time. She needed to really think her friends' plan through. She'd always been an honest person, and deceiving the town didn't sit well with her. But she had a bad feeling that if she trusted in the system to take care of her, she would find herself and her goats out on the street. After all, May was the injured party in all this.

When she drove onto the property, she saw a large delivery truck parked outside the house. The big lettering and appliance pictures made it clear May hadn't ordered another set of llamas. Had the old stove finally died? Was May getting it repaired?

Heidi walked in through the mudroom and found May hovering as two guys hooked up a brand-new, stainless-steel stove. There were six gleaming burners and an oven big enough to roast a thirty-pound turkey.

May saw her and clapped her hands together. "You're back. I was hoping they'd be gone before your lunch was over. I guess it's still a surprise, though, right?"

May looked both guilty and pleased. "I couldn't bear the thought of cooking in that old oven again, and Glen told me that pie is his favorite. I hope you don't mind me going ahead with this. I should have asked first. I'm sorry."

Heidi studied the other woman—the hope and worry in her dark eyes, the slight quiver at the corner of her mouth. There was no way May knew what Rafe was up to. Heidi refused to believe that. May was open and giving and generous. Traits her son could learn, but hadn't.

"The stove is beautiful," Heidi told her. "I'm thrilled."

"Are you?" May hurried forward and hugged her. "That's a relief. I was worried you'd be annoyed. But when I went to look at appliances, I couldn't help myself."

She led Heidi to the range and pointed out the features. The guys finished the installation. May signed the paperwork, and they left.

May reverently touched the handles. "Think about what we can cook with this. I'm going to make fresh strawberry pie first. Did you see the strawberries they have at that farm stand on the way to town? They're huge and so delicious. I need to bake the crust, so it can cool." She glanced at the clock on the wall. "There's just enough time."

The back door opened and Rafe walked in.

"Mom, you've got to stop surprising us like this." He walked into the kitchen. "New stove, huh?"

"Isn't it wonderful?"

Heidi did her best to control her breathing. If she focused on inhaling and exhaling, she might not be so aware of Rafe standing next to her. Of the size of him and how, despite everything, she found herself longing to touch him.

Images from the previous night filled her brain. Sense memories tricked her fingers into recalling the feel of his skin. She could inhale the scent of him, feel the sensual kisses that had weakened her.

Without meaning to, she glanced at him. He winked and gave her a knowing smile. One that implied intimacy and connection. She couldn't decide if she wanted to scream or weep. Pain battled with anger, but before either won, another large truck drove by the house.

"What else did you order?" Rafe asked, stepping through the mudroom on his way out back.

"Nothing." May followed him. "Just the stove. I don't have any other animals coming this week."

Meaning there were more coming next week? Heidi didn't bother asking. She honestly didn't want to know.

She went out after them and saw a man walking around his truck to the horse trailer he had pulled behind. The trailer looked fancy, with a heating and air-conditioning unit on top and plenty of ventilation.

The man himself seemed familiar. Tall, with dark hair and a build very similar to Rafe's. In the time it took May to shriek and run toward him, Heidi recognized his features from the pictures all around the living room. Shane Stryker had decided to join his family in Fool's Gold. Lucky her.

"MOM TOLD ME TO COME," Shane said from his place in the living room.

"When did you start listening to her?" Rafe wanted to know. Not that he wasn't pleased to see his brother. He and Shane had always gotten along.

"It's time for me to make my move," Shane told him. "I've been working for other people long enough. I'm going to start my own bloodline. I'm already working on it. I bought a new stallion and he's perfect." Shane took another swallow from his bottle of beer, then shrugged. "Except for his damned temper. But I'll get him to come around."

Rafe glanced toward the kitchen, where May was happily cooking dinner for her middle son. "Did Mom mention we don't technically own the ranch yet? In theory, the judge could rule in Heidi's favor."

"In theory." Shane grinned. "Come on. You're not going to let that happen."

"True, but until we're sure, you shouldn't be making any plans."

"I have faith in you, big brother. You'll end up winning everything, like you always do."

Rafe glanced toward the ceiling, a little uncomfortable with the conversation. While he did plan to end up victorious, he wasn't ready for Heidi to know that. Especially after last night.

Just thinking about what had happened between them made him want to grin like a fool. Being with Heidi had been better than he'd imagined, and he'd imagined a whole hell of a lot. Just thinking about her in his bed had his blood heating. Not anything he wanted to experience with his brother in the room, so he shifted his attention to the horses Shane had unloaded.

"You drove here from Tennessee?" he asked. "With six racehorses?"

"The airlines don't let me buy them seats, so there wasn't much choice. They did fine. Now they can settle in while I finish up my business back east."

"You're leaving?"

"Driving back in a few days."

"What's going to happen with the horses?"

Shane took another swallow of his beer, then grinned. "Funny you should ask that."

"No way. I'm not taking care of them."

"Someone has to." Shane looked more annoyed than concerned. "What are you doing with your day that you don't have time to take care of my horses?"

"Running a business, for one thing." Not that he had spent much time on his business. Odd how he was only a few hours from San Francisco, yet he was a world away from all he remembered. The town was getting to him, and he couldn't seem to find it in himself to mind. Or maybe it wasn't the town. Maybe it was Heidi. Not that he could see the bad in that, either.

"I'll do it."

They both looked up. Rafe saw that Heidi had walked into the living room. At least they weren't still talking about him taking over the ranch. That sure would've changed the tenor of their relationship.

Shane stood. "Evening, ma'am."

Heidi laughed. "While May would be thrilled with your good manners, if you call me ma'am again, I'm going to give your favorite boots to my goats. I'm Heidi. You must be Shane. Nice to meet you."

Shane took a step forward and they shook hands. Rafe felt himself stiffen for that brief second of contact. The need to claim Heidi, to tell his brother to back off, nearly overwhelmed him. He held the words inside, because he and Heidi had agreed that no one would know about last night. But he sure didn't like the way his brother smiled at her.

"Good to meet you, too," Shane said.

"Now that we have that out of the way, tell me about your horses."

"I brought six. Thoroughbreds. A little temperamental, but good animals. You know anything about horses?"

Heidi slid her hands into her back pockets, which caused her chest to arch forward. Rafe told himself the act was unconscious. She wasn't flirting with his brother, trying to distract him with her feminine curves. Still, he wanted to step between them, to change the conversation.

"We board two horses here already. I take care of them. You're welcome to take a look, and I can give you the phone numbers of the owners. For reference purposes."

"If the price is fair, I'm interested," Shane told her.

"We could go take a look at the barn after dinner."

Heidi smiled. "You can tell me what you expect, and then we can negotiate."

"I like the sound of that."

"All right, all right." Unable to stand it, Rafe moved toward them. "Heidi's off-limits. Mom and I have been living here."

Shane frowned. "What does that have to do with anything?"

Rafe expected Heidi to understand, to appreciate his desire to protect her. Instead, she seemed annoyed.

"Rafe has some peculiar ideas about how things should be done," she said. "And what belongs to whom."

Rafe felt as if he'd missed a significant part of the conversation, which wasn't possible. He'd been standing right there. So why didn't he know what Heidi was talking about?

Shane put his arm around Heidi. "Rafe has a lot of peculiar ideas about a lot of different things."

Rafe didn't like where this was going, but before he could protest, his phone rang.

He took it out of his pocket and glanced at the screen, then groaned. "Nina," he muttered under his breath.

"Who's Nina?" his brother asked.

"His matchmaker. She's in San Francisco, and he's using her to find the perfect wife."

The only good to come out of this potentially disastrous topic of conversation was that Shane dropped his arm to his side as he turned to face his brother.

"You've hired a matchmaker?" Shane chuckled as he asked the question. The chuckle turned into laughter. He slapped Rafe on the back. "Are you telling me that, with all the millions you have, you still can't get a girl?"

Rafe pushed the ignore button on his phone. "I can get a girl just fine."

"I suppose that's true," Heidi said. "I guess the real question is, can you keep one?"

With that, Heidi left.

Shane gave a low whistle. "I don't know what's going on, but you sure stepped in something."

"Tell me about it."

Rafe couldn't blame Heidi for being pissed. They hadn't had a chance to talk that morning, and now he was getting calls from his matchmaker. He didn't blame her for wanting his head on a stick.

"Does Mom know?"

Rafe scowled at his brother. "Know what?"

"That you and Heidi are together."

"We're not together. Not exactly."

"You're sleeping with her." Shane wasn't asking a question.

"Yes."

"And you've hired a matchmaker to find you a wife."

"That was before."

"Nina's still calling, bro. Let me get this straight. You're having sex with the woman whose ranch you're trying to take, while living with your mother and trying to find a wife." Shane slapped him on the back again. "Must be good to be you."

"Go to hell."

"Why don't you tell me what it's like there, bro? Sounds like you already know."

CHAPTER THIRTEEN

HEIDI GLANCED DOWN AT THE PAD of paper in her hand. The notes on the care of Shane's horses covered three pages. "When I die, I want to come back as one of your horses."

"I've heard that before," Shane said, rubbing the side of the mare's face. "I believe in treating my animals well."

Heidi looked at the six horses Shane had brought with him. They were all beautiful. Their coats gleamed, defining the rippling muscles underneath. Their eyes contained curiosity and intelligence, and they'd all been friendly enough when Shane had introduced her.

"I'm going to be here a few more days," he said, stepping out of the stall and closing the door behind him. "We'll have a chance to go over everything again. I'll make sure you've ridden each of the horses before I go. These guys are easy. You shouldn't have any problems."

"I'm not sure I like the way you say that," she admitted, following him out of the barn. "It implies some of your horses are difficult."

"A few are temperamental," he admitted. "I have a

new stallion who's nothing but trouble. But he's physically perfect and too smart for his own good."

"You're a gambler."

"Only when it comes to horses. I put nearly everything I have into him, so this gamble better pay off."

"My cheese empire shows great potential. If this horse does you in, you can come work for me."

Shane chuckled. "I appreciate that."

They were standing by the main corral. Sometime in the past few days, summer had arrived in Fool's Gold. The sky was blue, the temperature warm. It was the kind of day that made her want to go play. But the only companion who interested her in that way had turned out to be a lying weasel dog. Too bad she hadn't fallen for Shane, she thought glumly. Rafe's brother was just as good-looking. He was nice and easygoing and safe. Safe, because she didn't feel the slightest tingle when he was around. Not that he'd shown any interest in her, but that wasn't the point. Even now, thinking about how angry Rafe made her, she still wanted him.

She told herself these feelings weren't love. She was smarter than that. All she felt was that stupid bonding thing women did after they had sex with a man. It would pass.

"Do I want to ask what you're thinking about?" Shane studied her. "You're looking fierce."

"I wish I didn't like your mother so much. It would make it a lot easier for me to maim one of her children."

"Seeing as I'm about the nicest guy you're ever going to meet, you must be talking about Rafe. He's screwed up, hasn't he? I'm not even surprised."

"He does that a lot?"

"More than he should, for a guy as smart as he claims to be. Sometimes he holds on too tight. Sometimes he doesn't hold on tight enough. Mostly, he expects people to do what he tells them."

Heidi agreed. Rafe probably expected her not to mind that he was going to steal her home from her. She could probably get over that. It was the fact that he'd slept with her while planning to build homes on every inch of her ranch that really fried her.

"Want to tell me what happened?" Shane asked.

"Not really."

He exhaled sharply. "Good. Because I was just being polite."

"Sure, blame your mother."

He chuckled. His dark gaze met hers. "I don't know what you and Rafe have going on between you, but I'll tell you this. If he lets you get away, he's even more stupid than I thought."

"Thank you."

"You're welcome." Shane stared at something over her shoulder. "Speaking of the boss man, here he comes. Want to really piss him off? Laugh as if I'm the funniest guy you've ever met. It'll drive him crazy."

The thought of Rafe uncomfortable cheered her enough to make it easy to toss her head back and laugh. She straightened and rested her hand on Shane's forearm.

"Thank you," she murmured.

"You're welcome. So, we're riding tomorrow?" He asked the question in a louder voice, as if wanting the sound to carry.

"Absolutely," Heidi told him, doing her best to sound enthused. "I'm looking forward to it."

"Good. Then it's a date. Hey, bro." Shane shifted his hat back on his head. "I've been showing Heidi my horses. And a few other things."

"I can see that."

Rafe glared at Shane, who glared right back. Heidi could have used the moment to feed her fragile ego, but knew there wasn't any point. Shane was pretending, and she had no clue what Rafe was doing. It's not as if he were genuinely interested in her.

"Then I guess I'll be going," Shane said, blinking first.

"I guess you will," Rafe told him.

Heidi ignored them both and started for the goat house.

Rafe fell into step beside her. "You're getting along with Shane real well."

"He's nice. I like him. I'm going to be looking after his horses while he's gone."

"That's a lot of work."

"I have the time and I need the money. I want to show the judge all the progress I've made on paying back your mother."

She stopped walking and turned to face him. "You get that, right? That this is my home and I don't want to leave? You understand what Fool's Gold means to me. To have a place to belong, friends. That makes sense to you, right?"

She waited, watching him watch her, hoping for a sign, some hint he wasn't doing what she thought. That she'd been wrong about him.

"I get it," he said.

His gaze met hers, his eyes steady, his expression kind. She didn't know how he could do that, how he could pretend to care and still be planning to take everything from her. Technically, he hadn't lied. Omission was different. She would guess that, in his world, winning was all about nuance. The wording of the contract, the strength of a clause. But this wasn't a court of law, and what was on the line mattered to her more than anything in the world.

"One thing I learned from moving around as much as I did as a kid was that the rules were always different. They were rarely universal. What would be considered a lie in one place was an acceptable tweak of the truth in another."

"Is this about townies again?"

She nodded. "I had a best friend growing up. Melinda. She was the pretty one and sometimes the smart one, but I was okay with that. We were the same age and we liked the same things. Except maybe for college. She was determined to go to a good one, and I was more than ready to be done with school when I got my GED."

She drew in a breath. As fragile as she was feeling right now, she wasn't sure she could get to the story. But it was too late to stop.

"You told me about her," Rafe said. "Isn't she the one who got into a good college?"

Heidi nodded. "She was studying to be a vet. And there was this guy."

"There's always a guy, Heidi. Or a girl. That's not about being a townie."

"It was this time. He was popular, and the girls at the college couldn't believe he'd fallen for Melinda. He swore he loved her. He swore he wanted to marry her. She gave him her heart, and that's when everything went wrong."

She paused, not sure how to tell the rest. "She came home for the summer. She was different. Broken. I thought being in love would make her stronger and happier, but it didn't. I found out that some of the girls at college were bullying her. They were leaving messages on her voice mail, and saying horrible things about her online. They pressured him to break up with her, and he did."

"Then he wasn't worth it."

"Something easy for us to figure out, but not so easy for Melinda. Because the bullying didn't stop there. Those girls wanted her punished. Even after she left college, they continued to harass her."

Heidi raised her chin. "She killed herself. After two

attempts, she finally succeeded. The police investigated, but the girls had done a good job of covering their tracks and were never charged."

Rafe swore. "I'm sorry."

"Me, too. Because I learned a lot of things from that time in my life. Mostly, I learned that there are consequences to making yourself vulnerable to others."

"What are you saying, Heidi?"

She wanted to tell him she knew, that he wasn't fooling her anymore. But telling him that would mean giving away the tiny amount of power that information gave her.

"Nothing," she said instead. "I have to go call a friend. Excuse me."

She hurried into the house and went upstairs. Once alone in her room, she called Charlie and Annabelle to tell them that she'd decided to follow their plan and accept their help. She could only pray it was going to be enough.

TWO DAYS LATER, RAFE WAS NO closer to figuring out the mystery that was Heidi. She was pleasant, but distant. He'd been unable to get her alone, and while he wanted to say she was avoiding him on purpose, he couldn't be sure.

Not that he had anything specific he wanted to say. But he felt as if she'd dismissed him, and he had no idea why.

She'd gone out to meet friends after dinner, leaving him alone and restless. He'd tried watching TV with his mother and Glen, but couldn't get interested in the show. He wandered outside, where he found Shane returning from a last trip to the barn.

"You check on your horses a lot," he commented, slouching into a wicker chair, part of a set that had been delivered the day before.

"New place after a long trip," Shane said, sitting on the love seat opposite. "They're nearly every penny I have, on the hoof. I'd be damned stupid not to make sure my investment was doing well."

"Point taken." Rafe squinted up at the sky. The sun still hadn't set and the air was warm. He could hear crickets and something rustling in the bushes. The night would be beautiful—just right for seducing a woman. Too bad the one he wanted had lost interest in him. He stared at his brother. Lost interest right after Shane showed up.

"Want to talk about it?" his brother asked. "Whatever it is that has your panties in a bunch?"

Rafe raised an eyebrow. "I can still take you, little brother."

"I have my doubts, but I think we're both too old to test the theory. We'd look foolish rolling around in the dirt."

"Agreed." He put his hands behind his head and leaned into them. "It's Heidi."

"I figured."

"She's...complicated."

"So's the situation. Neither of you knowing who's going to end up with the ranch."

"I know."

"That it's going to be you? Then what happens to her?"

A question he didn't have an answer for. While he expected to win the case, he didn't like the idea of her being tossed out. She belonged here, with her damned goats. Which, to him, meant what? That he should change his plans and make room for her? If he left her an acre or two and the caves, that would help. But it wouldn't be enough. The goats needed more land. From what he understood, she kept them close in the winter. During the rest of the year, she let them wander around the ranch. Once he built his houses, that wouldn't work.

A problem without a solution, he thought grimly. Not his favorite kind.

"Why are you here?" he asked, mostly to distract himself. "I thought you liked Tennessee."

"I do, but it's time for me to get out on my own. I'm looking at buying some land."

"Here? What if we don't win the case?"

Shane chuckled. "Then I guess the earth would fall off its axis and spin helplessly into space." He shrugged. "I like Fool's Gold. I'd like to settle here, regardless."

"Have a family?"

"Eventually."

Rafe looked at his brother. "Including a wife?"

"Sure. You?"

"Same."

"Why the matchmaker?"

"Because I didn't get it right on my own, and I don't know how to keep from screwing up again."

"Tell me about it."

Rafe grimaced. "Sorry. Didn't mean to put my foot in it."

"Don't sweat it. That was a long time ago."

True enough, but Rafe had a feeling that Shane still regretted his first marriage. His brother had fallen hard and fast, giving his heart to a wild beauty who didn't know the meaning of being faithful. Unable to deal with the other men in his wife's bed, Shane had left her.

Rafe's own marriage had ended a whole lot less spectacularly, but the breakup still bugged him. Not that he missed her—he didn't—but the fact that he couldn't figure out where things had gone wrong.

"I figure a professional will know what to do," he said. "Nina swears she can help me find someone who's exactly what I'm looking for."

"Do you believe her?"

"I don't trust myself to get it right."

Shane nodded slowly. "I want to tell you you're an idiot, but I can't. I'm not about to trust love again, either. We both need a sensible woman. Someone who's a friend. No highs, no lows."

Which should have sounded perfect, but left Rafe with an empty feeling in his chest.

"Let me know how that works out for you," he said.

His brother laughed. “I don’t have you convinced?”

“Sorry, no.”

SHANE LEANED AGAINST THE SIDE of the stall. “Seriously, he’s smart.”

Heidi had spent the past couple of hours confirming that she knew all she had to in order to take care of Shane’s expensive horses. She was willing to admit that they were beautiful animals, but were they as miraculous as their proud owner claimed?

“I don’t think so,” she murmured.

Shane pulled a small plastic bag of apple slices out of his shirt pocket. “Wesley, do you want some apple?”

The horse raised and lowered his head.

Heidi smiled. “Coincidence.”

“I knew you’d say that.” He turned his attention back to the horse. “How many slices?”

The horse hesitated for a second, as if considering the question, then hit the stall door twice.

“Two? Are you sure?”

The horse nodded.

Heidi laughed. “Okay, you win. I’m impressed. And you have too much time on your hands.”

“Sometimes the winters get long,” he admitted, feeding the horse the two slices.

Shane led the way outside.

“As long as Wesley doesn’t expect me to read to him or do math, we’ll get along fine.”

“I’m sure of it.”

“You do have insurance, right?”

Shane glanced at her. "Very funny."

A delivery truck pulled up and honked.

"I got a package for you," the woman behind the wheel yelled.

"Been shopping?" Shane asked.

"Sort of," Heidi said, suspecting the box contained the special paint Annabelle had suggested she order online.

The delivery woman circled around to the back of the truck and pulled out a small box. "You're going to need to sign," she said.

Heidi hurried forward and scrawled her signature on the electronic clipboard. Before she could reach for the box, Shane had collected it.

"Where do you want it?" he asked.

Heidi waved as the delivery truck drove away, then pointed to the goat house. "In there, please."

In a couple of days, Annabelle and Charlie would be by to help her with the cave paintings. Heidi knew she didn't have a choice, but she still felt badly about her decision to fake an archaeological find. Apparently, she wasn't suited for a life of crime or even deception.

Fortunately, Shane didn't ask about the content of the box and put it where she pointed without saying a word. They walked back outside.

"I should probably feel guilty about financing your life of crime."

She felt her eyes widen and instinctively took a step

back. "Excuse me?" How had he figured out what she was up to?

He drew his eyebrows together. "I was kidding, Heidi. I know about the problem with who owns the ranch, and that you want to earn enough to buy out my mom. What I'm paying you will go toward the debt."

She breathed an inward sigh of relief. "You're okay with that?"

"Honestly? No. I'd rather she stayed here. She loves the ranch. Always did. So did I. I'd prefer the two of you worked out a solution."

She thought about the plans Rafe had for the land. "I'm willing, but I don't think 'compromise' is your brother's favorite word."

"You've met him, then?"

She smiled. "More than once."

"Then you know Rafe is big on winning. It comes from when we were kids."

"Because he had to take care of the family? As much as a kid can?"

"You've heard the story."

"Not all of it, but bits and pieces. I know he's not a bad person."

"Just difficult?" Shane asked.

"That works."

She felt his gaze on her, but wasn't going to say any more. Her feelings for Rafe were complicated. If he wasn't going behind everyone's back with those houses, she could like him a lot more. If she hadn't made love with him, disliking him would be a whole lot easier.

"It's gonna be okay," Shane told her.

"Can I get that in writing."

He touched her arm. "Smell that?"

She took a breath. The blending of meat and barbecue sauce drifted to her. "What is it?"

"Dinner. Mom's making her famous ribs. Once you get a taste of them, everything will seem a whole lot better."

"You're a simple guy."

"I know what I like."

"An excellent quality," she agreed, thinking it was a shame she couldn't feel that sexual hum when she was around this Stryker brother. Falling for Shane would have made life so much easier.

HEIDI HAD A BATCH OF FETA to prep before dinner. She'd just collected all the equipment she would need when Rafe appeared at the door.

"Need some help?" he asked.

She wanted to tell him no, that she could handle this herself, but she made the mistake of looking at him before she spoke, and found she couldn't look away.

There was something about the man's eyes, she thought. Or maybe just the man himself. Something that made her want to get lost in him, to be held by him, even loved by him. And to think her grandfather had raised her to be smarter than that….

"I'm making feta," she said.

Rafe groaned. "Why do there have to be so many kinds of cheese? Can't you specialize in one kind? I could learn how to do one."

Despite her confusion, the ache in her chest and the way being around him made her breathing uneven, she laughed. "Learning about cheese isn't part of your job description."

"Can I help, anyway?"

"Sure."

He'd assisted her before, so he walked over to the sink to scrub his hands without being asked. When he'd dried them carefully, he pulled on plastic gloves and joined her at the table. Several molds lay on the table.

"Here's the plan," she began.

"There's a plan? This isn't just random?"

She removed the weights on the molds and then uncovered them. Rafe peered into the first mold.

"Not impressive."

"It's cheese. Did you expect it to break into song?"

"If it did, you'd make a lot more money. I'm just saying. So, what's the next step?"

"It needs salting before we age it."

He sighed. "Why do I know I'm not going to shake salt on the top and call it a day?"

"Because you're more than a pretty face." She pointed to the pans she'd already laid out and the large glass containers of water. "We need a twenty-three percent salt brine solution. They'll soak in that for twenty-four hours."

"Twenty-three percent? You're that precise?"

"If I want the flavor right. After that, the cheese will age in a fourteen percent salt brine solution for about sixty days. We do that at sixty degrees, which is why I use the front part of the cave, where it's warmer."

He shook his head. "How do you remember this?"

She pointed to the shelf above their heads. Several notebooks were lined up. "I've done a lot of research, I've taken classes and I've screwed up a lot. I find that's the best way to learn. I was smart enough to start with small batches, so I didn't lose too much in the process."

They carefully transferred the cheese from the molds to the trays, then Heidi and Rafe slowly added the twenty-three percent salt brine. She covered the trays with cloth and stripped off her gloves.

"That's it?" he asked.

"Until tomorrow. Then I'll put them into individual, airtight containers with the fourteen percent solution. From there, they go to the caves and do their thing."

"And it's cheese in sixty days?"

"That's the plan."

"Put me down for five containers," he told her. "I'll pay retail. I'm that kind of guy."

She thought about teasing him, saying that each container would cost him twenty thousand dollars, but found herself unable to speak. Probably because she'd just figured out that either she or Rafe wouldn't be here in sixty days. No doubt, by then the judge would have ruled and, regardless of the outcome, one of them would be gone.

CHAPTER FOURTEEN

"So, Rafe had this new bike that Mayor Marsha had given him," Shane was saying. "He rode it everywhere."

The five of them sat at an old wooden table Rafe and Shane had brought out from the barn. The trees around the house provided shade, and a light breeze cooled the air. On the table were the remnants of their meal. The ribs May had spent all afternoon slow cooking, homemade mac-and-cheese, salad and ice-cold beer.

Worried about the paint and her plan to deceive the world, Heidi would have sworn she couldn't eat anything. But a single bite of May's dinner had been enough to make her ravenous, and she'd eaten her share of everything. Now full and more relaxed than she'd been in days, she leaned back and listened to the brothers trade stories about their past.

"I loved that bike," Rafe said, narrowing his gaze. "You stole it."

"I traded it for horseback-riding lessons."

"It wasn't yours to trade."

"I wanted to learn to ride a horse."

"Things went downhill from there," May admitted.

"I found them fighting in the barn. Rafe had a black eye and Shane's nose was bloody." She glanced at her middle son. "You shouldn't have taken his bike."

"So you said at the time."

"Did you get it back?" Heidi asked.

Rafe nodded.

"Obviously, you learned to ride a horse," she said to Shane.

"Yup. Never did do that well on a bike, but that's okay."

Everyone laughed. Heidi saw Glen reach for May's hand. The older couple was still together, and if she didn't know her grandfather as well as she did, she would have sworn they were in love. Glen had always done his best to avoid any long-term entanglements, but with May, he was different. She didn't see any signs of him wanting to get away.

"Remember when Clay brought home that old dog?" May asked. She laughed. "I'd never seen a dog so ugly. He insisted it was a fine-looking animal and that we should keep it." Her smile faded. "We couldn't, of course. I could barely feed my children. There wasn't any extra for a pet. But it would have been nice."

"You have your animals now," Glen reminded her.

"I do, and there's plenty to eat." She raised her glass. "To my boys, who have made me proud."

Heidi joined in the toast.

After dinner, everyone helped clear the table. Heidi shooed May out of the kitchen, saying the other woman had done enough with dinner. She was going to clean up. Glen and Shane drifted away, but Rafe stayed.

"I can do this," she told him.

"I'll help."

They worked quickly together. She was aware of him standing next to her, taking the rinsed dishes and putting them in the ancient dishwasher. She wiped down the counters, then wondered how she was going to escape without having to talk. Something that turned out not to be a problem, she thought helplessly, as he waited until she'd rinsed and dried her hands before putting his hands on her shoulders and turning her to face him.

She'd thought he'd try to ask her what was wrong, or, being the kind of man he was, demand that she tell him. Instead, he leaned in and lightly kissed her.

She could have withstood a verbal assault, she thought, feeling the soft brush of his mouth on hers. If he'd insisted, she would have had righteous indignation on her side. But the gentle pressure was irresistible, as was the warmth of his fingers. He straightened and reached up to tug on one of her braids.

"You're the only woman I know who wears her hair like this."

"I know it's not sophisticated," she began, then wanted to slap herself for admitting that.

"I like it, goat girl." His dark eyes stared into hers. "I like you."

Enough to give up his Fool's Gold housing empire?

Enough to tell Nina to go away? Enough to admit a sensible wife was a really stupid idea?

"If you could have anything in the world," she said. "Anything. Money, fame, sixteen children who adored you, what would it be?"

He hesitated. "Can I get back to you?"

"Sure. But if you asked me that question, I would have an answer. I want the ranch. I want to live here for the rest of my life. I want this to be my home."

He dropped his hands to his sides. He didn't back away, but he didn't have to. His actions were enough.

ANNABELLE LAID THE OPEN BOOKS on the dirt floor. Charlie had been by early and set up several powerful portable lights, illuminating the uneven cave walls. Heidi shivered and zipped up her jacket.

This deep in the mountains, caves were a constant fifty degrees. The air had a faint, musty quality to it, as if there wasn't enough circulation.

"You cold?" Annabelle asked.

"No. I've never been this far back in the caves. It's a little creepy." It was also giving her a bit of a headache.

"Don't worry," Annabelle told her. "I have maps and a compass. We won't get lost." She pulled two large plastic bags out of her backpack and opened them. "The paint is a special blend. I found the recipe online. I took what you bought and mixed it with a few ground-up, dried leaves and herbs. Amazingly, my college studies didn't cover how to fake cave paintings. When this dries, it will look old. The trick is to paint in the style of the Máa-zib women."

She pointed to the books she'd brought. "These pictures are samples to give you an idea. We don't want to duplicate them exactly. That's a huge red flag."

"Do you think we're going to fool anyone?" Heidi asked, taking the brush Annabelle offered.

"Not for long, but this is all about buying time. Unless you've changed your mind?"

Heidi shook her head. "I appreciate you helping me with this. If it all goes badly, I'll swear it was my idea alone."

"So only you go to prison?" Annabelle asked. "That's so nice. Thank you. I'm thinking the library board wouldn't approve of my actions right now."

"You don't think they'd be impressed with your skill and ingenuity?" Heidi asked.

"I doubt they'd see it that way."

Annabelle studied the photograph of the drawing. Heidi moved next to her.

"The paintings tell a story," she said. "We don't want to get that elaborate. See this one. It's about surviving a difficult winter, and here's a series about a gathering. Probably to celebrate the harvest."

She flipped the page, and they stared at a stick figure with an obvious erection. "I'm not sure what this one is about, but we'll skip over it."

Heidi grinned. "You have to admire their attitude."

"Use men for sex, then send them on their way? It's a sensible plan. Men are nothing but trouble."

She turned a few more pages. "We'll do best with recreating a nature scene, I think. Less challenging for us, and more confusing for anyone who sees them."

"So, trees on the mountain and maybe a basket?"

"Perfect," Annabelle said, handing her a stick with a fuzzy willow bud at the end.

"This is..."

"Your paintbrush." Annabelle smiled. "The women of the Máa-zib tribe couldn't trot off to a craft store when they felt the need to be creative."

"Good point."

Heidi dipped her stick in the paint. The liquid was thicker than she'd expected and didn't go on evenly, but she supposed that was the point.

"Well, crap." Annabelle tilted her head. "I thought I would do some kind of marriage scene, but these women didn't marry men."

Heidi studied the sticklike figure of a woman. "Could you show the guy leaving? Or being sent away."

"That could work. As long as I don't have to draw the erection." She started on a tree for background. "Men are such a pain in the butt. Why do we want to be with them so much?"

"Biology," Heidi said with a sigh. "We can't escape our DNA destiny. Women are hardwired to bond. Especially after sex."

"That sounds interesting."

Heidi realized she'd said a little too much. "Um, I meant in general. I'm not talking specifically."

"Uh-huh. I'm not sure I believe that." She dabbed more paint on the wall. "Loving people can be the best thing ever, and it can really suck. Where are you on that scale with Rafe?"

Heidi felt her mouth drop open. She carefully closed it, then studied the wall in front of her.

"I don't love Rafe."

"That could be a matter of timing. You're falling for him."

"Maybe a little. But I'm being careful." At least, she hoped she was. Some days it was difficult to tell. "How did you know?"

"You were angry when you found out about the houses, but you were also hurt. It was personal, which means you had a connection."

"You're good," Heidi told her.

Annabelle shrugged. "Those who can, do. Those who can't, talk about it."

Heidi sighed. "I'm confused by him and what's happening between us." She decided not to mention they'd slept together. "I hate having to do this." She pointed to the cave walls.

"Have you talked about compromise? Is that possible?"

"Rafe likes to win. That's going to matter more than anything else."

"He's also a guy who cares about the people in his life. Look how he is with his mother. He still has a heart. Maybe you should appeal to that."

"I could try," she said slowly.

"Tell you what. We'll do the painting, but I won't phone in the tip until you tell me to. How's that?"

"Perfect."

Perhaps when you are next planning to be in the office, you can warn me, so I can go online and view your picture. I want to be sure I remember what you look like.

RAFE STARED AT THE SARCASTIC email from his normally professional assistant, then logged off the internet and closed his laptop.

He was willing to admit that he'd been gone from the office awhile. More than a while. Dante was on his back, too, trying to get him to return to San Francisco and handle the various business deals they had in the works. Rafe was doing what he could from Fool's Gold, but a few things required his presence. Or if he wasn't willing to go in, he had to hand more responsibility over to his partner.

Dante would be more than happy to take over the deals. There was nothing Rafe's lawyer friend liked more than a messy contract or difficult negotiations. But Rafe didn't want to step back from his business. He'd grown it from nothing and usually enjoyed the process as much as his friend. Just not right now.

He couldn't explain what was different. With the barn remodel finished, his mother had him planning a major addition to the house. He enjoyed the manual labor more than he'd thought possible. He'd come to appreciate what it meant to ride the land, losing himself in the quiet broken only by birds and the thundering of his horse's hooves. Hell, he even liked Heidi's goats.

He crossed to the living room window and stared out at the ranch. He had hated the idea of living in Fool's Gold, of being surrounded by the ghosts of his past. Now he knew there weren't any ghosts, and the town wasn't responsible for what he and his family had gone through. If anything, the people around him had done their best to make things better.

He looked past the barn, to where the development would begin, and imagined rows of houses, tree-lined streets and cars parked at the curbs. But it was impossible. All he could see was an old sheep and some llamas, Heidi's goats and a couple of Shane's horses.

Progress demanded change, he reminded himself. With the casino coming in, he could make a killing on those houses. The sheep would have to find somewhere else to live.

He heard a crash from the back of the house and hurried in that direction. He found Heidi leaning against the large table in the mudroom, her face pale and her eyes unfocused. Several stainless-steel bowls had fallen to the floor.

"What's wrong?" he asked, even as he put his hand on her forehead. She was clammy and hot at the same time.

"I feel awful," she admitted. "The room started

swimming for a second." She looked at the bowls. "Did I drop those?"

"You're sick," he told her.

She stared at him. "No, I'm fine." She pressed a hand to her stomach. "Okay, maybe I need to throw up."

"Come on, goat girl. We're going to get you into bed."

"But I have to move the goats to another field this afternoon and get the rest of the cheese to the cave."

"I'll take care of the goats and the cheese." He put his arm around her, helping her to the door.

She stumbled along beside him, but when they reached the stairs, she shook her head. "I don't think so."

"Lightweight," he murmured, as he picked her up in his arms and started up the stairs.

She shrieked and wrapped her arms around his neck. "What are you doing?" Then she moaned. "I really feel sick, Rafe."

"Hang on. We're nearly there."

He got her to the bathroom just in time. She rushed to the toilet and dropped to her knees.

"Get out," she yelled, waving frantically at the door, then turned back to the toilet.

He backed out just in time.

Fifteen minutes later, she emerged, looking pale and shaky. He guided her to her bedroom, quickly stripped off her clothes and pulled her nightgown over her head. He was aware of her soft skin, the shape of her breasts, and his expected reaction to the sight, but ignored it all. He might have flaws, but slobbering over a woman with the flu wasn't one of them.

He helped her into bed.

He'd already pulled the shades and collected extra pillows. Now he sat next to her and stroked a damp washcloth across her face.

"You're going to have a rough couple of days," he told her. "I talked to my mom. She's going into town for supplies. Ginger ale and whatever she needs to make her famous chicken soup." He smiled at her. "She uses rice instead of noodles, so it's easier to keep down."

"I'll be fine," Heidi insisted, her eyes drifting closed. "Once I don't feel like I'm dying."

"You're not going to die. Try to sleep."

"I might need to throw up again."

"I promise not to tie up the bathroom."

Her lips curved into a slight smile. "Thank you."

He pressed a kiss on her cheek. "That's what friends do for each other."

"Are we friends?" Her voice was low, a little sleepy and barely audible.

"I hope so, goat girl."

HEIDI WAS VAGUELY AWARE of the passage of time, mostly because sometimes it was dark outside her window and sometimes it was light. She spent the first twenty-four hours puking her guts out and wishing she were dead, and the next twenty-four fighting a fever and wishing she were dead. Sometime after that, she slept for what felt like three weeks.

She knew people were coming and going, that a person she didn't know examined her and proclaimed that, yes, she had the flu and to keep her hydrated. Then she slept some more.

Through it all, she was aware of Rafe. May and Glen took turns at her bedside, but mostly there was Rafe's strong presence. She felt him wiping her down with a cool cloth and sometimes holding her hand. He'd brought in a TV and tuned it to the Home and Garden channel. One night she woke up to find him next to her in her bed. He was fully dressed, on top of the covers, his arm around her. She'd been surprised but comforted, and had snuggled close before going back to sleep.

Now she opened her eyes and saw light spilling into the room. The brightness suggested it was long past morning. She blinked, not sure what day it was, but feeling more like herself than she had in a long time.

"You're back."

She turned and saw Rafe standing in the doorway of her room. He looked good—tanned and strong, his shirtsleeves rolled up to his elbows. She frowned. Two bruises that looked suspiciously hoof-shaped marred both forearms.

"What happened to you?" she asked.

He crossed toward her and moved the pillows against the headboard so she could sit up. She sagged against them and touched his left arm. The bruise was still swollen, almost a welt.

He sighed. "Athena didn't want to move to another part of the ranch. We had words. Or rather, I had words, and she kicked me."

"Ouch."

"Don't worry. I kicked her back."

Heidi grinned. "You didn't."

"No, but I wanted to."

"Did you get her moved?"

"Do you have to ask?"

"Silly me."

He leaned over and touched her forehead. "Good. The fever's gone. Are you hungry? Could you keep soup down?"

She touched her stomach. "I think so. How long have I been out of it?"

"Nearly four days."

"That's not possible. I've never been sick like that before."

"You had us worried," he admitted. "We called in a doctor. But she said you'd be fine, and she was right." He straightened. "Let me get you some food. Mom will be thrilled to know you're awake. She'll insist on serving about a quart of soup, but only eat as much as you think you can handle. Trust me, there's plenty more waiting."

He left.

Heidi leaned back against the pillows. Four days?

She didn't remember much about what had happened, but it couldn't have been pretty.

She got out of bed and had to pause to steady herself. Her legs felt wobbly, but she made her way to the bathroom. After nearly shrieking at her reflection, she washed her face and brushed her teeth, then ran a comb through her hair. She was desperate for a shower, but based on how weak she felt, that would have to wait.

She managed to make it back to her bed without collapsing, and lay there shaking for a couple of minutes. Less than a minute later, Rafe returned with a tray.

She smelled the soup before she saw it, and her stomach growled.

"It's even better than it looks," he told her. "Mom made this every time one of us was sick. It was the best part of feeling like crap."

Next to the soup was a plate with plain toast and a glass of ice water. She took it all in and realized she was even more thirsty than she was hungry.

The cool water went down easily. Then she started in on the soup. But despite her best intentions, she only managed a half dozen spoonfuls before exhaustion overtook her.

Rafe moved the tray to the top of the dresser. "I'll bring some more in a couple of hours. You should try to rest."

"That's all I have been doing," she said, even as

she felt her eyes closing. "Just give me a second and I'll be perky again."

"Sure you will."

There was humor in his voice.

She was nearly asleep when she felt the soft brush of his mouth against hers. Nice, she thought hazily, already drifting off to sleep.

Rafe had taken care of her, had been there for her when she needed him. As she drifted off, she knew she couldn't go behind his back and pretend the ranch was an important Máa-zib site without talking to him. They needed to find a way to compromise and find their own solution to the problem. Because… Because…

"I love you," she whispered.

When there was no answer, she opened her eyes. Rafe had left and she was alone.

BY THE NEXT AFTERNOON, Heidi was going crazy. May and Rafe had both insisted she stay in bed, but she couldn't stand it anymore. She'd showered that morning, watched hours of HGTV, had bought new sandals and a really cute shirt from QVC, and eaten enough soup to float an armada.

By five o'clock, she'd gotten up and pulled on her jeans, only to find they were loose. The old stomach-flu diet, she thought, pulling on a clean T-shirt. Good for at least five pounds. If she had enough fashion sense to own a pair of skinny jeans, she could now fit into them. Unfortunately, she didn't, she thought happily, so she'd have to eat her way back to her old weight. Oh, darn.

She made her way downstairs and was pleased to find she wasn't dizzy or exhausted. She heard May and Glen in the kitchen and followed the sound.

"You're up," her grandfather announced when he saw her. He crossed to her and hugged her close, then led her to a chair. "I'm too old for you to scare me like that, Heidi."

"Sorry," she said, smiling at him. "I'm better now."

He studied her for a second. "You look good. You up to joining us for dinner?"

"As long as it's real food." She turned to May. "The soup was delicious."

The other woman laughed. "I understand. After a couple of days, it gets old. I was going to make pasta. You think you can eat that?"

"It sounds delicious."

While May puttered around the stove, Glen brought Heidi up to date on what had been happening around the ranch. As he talked, he put another place setting on the table. Heidi realized there were only three.

"What about Rafe?" she asked.

"He's not joining us," May told her. "Nina called and said she'd found the perfect woman for him. Isn't that exciting? He was very eager to go on his date. He left about a half hour ago." She paused. "Didn't he tell you?"

Heidi shook her head because she couldn't possibly speak. Rafe had gone on a date? After all that had happened between them? What about all they'd been through together? The sex, the conversation and laughter? She'd fallen in love with him, and he'd gone on a date?

Fury blended with pain, the combination uncomfortably close to how she'd felt when she'd had the flu. Tears threatened, but she knew she couldn't risk crying. Not in front of May and Glen. They would ask questions, and she didn't have any answers she could share with them.

"How long until dinner?" she asked, hoping her voice sounded normal.

"About fifteen minutes."

"Great. I need to make a call. I want to let Annabelle know I'm all right."

"Of course, dear."

Heidi left the room and got her cell. She stepped outside, then pushed the button to phone her friend.

"Hey, you," Annabelle said when she answered. "I heard you were sick. Everything okay?"

"I'm better now." Better and worse, she thought. "It's time. Can you contact the people you know?"

There was a pause. Heidi had asked Annabelle to wait to announce the cave-painting find, and her friend had agreed. But that had been before. Everything was different now.

"Of course," Annabelle told her. "I'll make the call right now."

CHAPTER FIFTEEN

RAFE PACED THE LENGTH of the living room of his mother's house, holding his cell phone to his ear. "No. I don't know how to make myself more clear. I'm not going on any more dates, Nina."

"You're not being reasonable," his matchmaker told him. "Tell me what was wrong with the last woman. She was everything you said you wanted. Intelligent, reasonable, successful in her job, but interested in being a stay-at-home mom. Do you know how hard it is to find that combination? On top of that, she was pretty. You asked for the moon and I gave you the moon, and now you're telling me you're not interested?"

"This isn't a good time for me," Rafe said.

Lately everything in his life seemed complicated. Dante was bugging him about the business, he knew he couldn't stay here indefinitely, and yet he didn't want to leave. And then there was Heidi. On the surface, everything was fine between them, but sometimes when she looked at him, there was something in her eyes. If he had to put a name to it, he would say it was disappointment.

None of which made sense, but he couldn't escape

the feeling that something was wrong. The last thing he needed right now was to be dating.

"If it's about the money, send me a bill," he said firmly. "I know you've done a good job, Nina. I appreciate the effort. I'm happy to recommend you to anyone you want. But I'm not interested in seeing anyone right now."

"Is there someone else?"

"No," he said quickly, then wondered if he was lying.

"Tell me what went wrong on your date. Because she said it was amazing."

He held in a groan. He didn't want to tell her what was wrong. In truth, the woman had been fine. It was him. No, it wasn't him, dammit. It was Heidi. He didn't want to go out with someone else. He didn't want to talk about music or politics or British castles. He wanted to talk about cheese and goats and the latest gossip from town. He wanted to look into Heidi's green eyes, he wanted to see her smile and hear her laugh. He wanted her in his bed. That single night had done nothing to quench his thirst for her.

"I'm hanging up now, Nina. We can have this conversation when I'm back in San Francisco."

"And when will that be?"

"I have no idea."

With that, he pushed the end button and stuck his cell phone back in his shirt pocket.

Ms. Jennings and Dante both wanted to hear from him, but they were going to have to wait. What he needed was a good, long ride on Mason. That would clear his head and then he could think.

He crossed the living room and opened the front door. He was halfway down the porch stairs when a white van with a satellite dish on the roof pulled onto the property. He didn't recognize the TV station listed, or the pictures of the local-news broadcasters. Seconds later, a second van drove in, this one with the call letters of a San Francisco TV station with a network affiliation.

The doors of the vans opened and several people poured out. Guys went to work on equipment, while a well made-up woman and a guy also wearing makeup walked toward him.

"We're looking for the owner of the ranch," the woman said. She glanced at her smartphone. "Heidi Simpson."

"Right here."

He glanced over his shoulder and saw Heidi had stepped outside. He stared at her, trying to figure out what was different. She still wore jeans and boots, but she was somehow dressed better. She had on a blouse instead of a T-shirt and was wearing makeup—not as much as the TV people, but more than usual. Her hair was loose and wavy. He looked closer. She was wearing earrings. She never wore earrings.

"What's going on?" he demanded. "What are they doing here?"

The female reporter stepped past him. "Is it true?" she asked. "You made another find?"

"I did," Heidi told her with a pleasant smile. "I was looking for more room for my cheese. I make goat cheese and age it in the caves. I thought I'd do a little exploring and I got lost. I ended up deeper in the caves than I've ever been, and that's where I saw them."

Rafe felt as if he'd stepped into the middle of a movie with no idea of where the story was heading. "Saw what?"

Heidi glanced at him. "Cave paintings. They're amazing. I thought maybe they were from the Máa-zib tribe." She turned back to the reporter, her eyes wide. "They're Mayan women who migrated here and lived for hundreds of years. There was that gold discovery last year. I have a friend who has studied the Máa-zib women, and she thinks the cave might have been used in sacred rituals. That would make this an important find."

The reporter nodded. "I was on the story last year. The viewers loved it, especially the women. Can I see the cave paintings?" She glanced back at her truck. "I want to bring one of the guys with me. He'll be able to tell what we need to set up for filming. Light's the main thing. Can we do that? Set up our lights without hurting the paintings?"

"I'm sure we'll be fine," Heidi told her.

"Great."

The reporter hurried back to her van. The second reporter was on his phone, but Rafe was confident he, too, would want to hear the whole story. The amazing story. The unbelievable story.

He looked at Heidi. "Cave paintings? You and I went to that cave together, and there were no paintings on the wall."

She kept her hands in her front pockets and shrugged. "I guess we didn't go in deep enough. There are several wonderful paintings and some artifacts. This could be a very important find for the tribe. Annabelle thinks this is sacred ground."

"I heard that. Who the hell is Annabelle?"

"A friend of mine. She's a librarian."

He was quickly going from disbelieving to annoyed. "Well, if she's a librarian, she must be an expert."

Heidi raised her chin. "As it happens, she has a minor in Máa-zib studies, so she is a kind of expert."

"And when did you make this miraculous find?" he asked.

"Yesterday."

"While you were still recovering from the flu?"

"I wanted to check on my cheese. I guess I got disoriented."

"I'll bet. And you didn't want to mention anything to me?"

"You were gone. On a date."

Guilt muted his anger, but he refused to be distracted by facts. "I'm not sure when Annabelle had the chance to come look at the caves, let alone make an expert assessment of them."

"She's very quick."

"Or the cave paintings are a recent addition to the ranch."

Heidi stared directly into his eyes. "I have no idea what you're talking about."

"Right." He drew in a breath. "So, what's the plan?"

"I'm not sure what you mean. I guess we'll have to have some archaeologists come look over the site. They'll need to find out if there are more cave paintings, and study the artifacts. If this really was sacred ground, then that kind of changes things."

"Sacred, my ass," he muttered. This was nothing more than a trick. What he couldn't understand was why Heidi was doing this. Why now? She shouldn't feel any more threatened today than she had a month ago. Nothing was different.

Unless she had found out about his plans.

Not possible, he told himself. No one knew except Dante. He hadn't even sent an email on the subject. So she couldn't possibly know about the houses. Which left him with the questions, why this and why now?

"We're ready," the female reporter called.

The reporter on the phone looked up. "Hey, I'm coming with you."

The woman rolled her eyes. "Fine. Just stay out of my way. I got here first."

"By about one minute."

Heidi stepped around Rafe. "If you'll excuse me, I need to see to the reporters."

He watched her walk away. When he was alone,

he pulled his cell phone out of his pocket and scrolled until he found Dante's number.

"You won't believe what's happening," he said, when his friend had answered. "We have cave paintings."

He explained about the reporters and the potential issue of "sacred" ground. When he was finished, Dante began to laugh.

"You have to admire her originality," Dante told him.

"The hell I do. We have a problem and it has to be fixed."

MORE MEDIA TRUCKS ARRIVED. Over the next couple of days, reporters swarmed, their cameras and lights littering the yard. Heidi set up a small stand to sell her cheese, while May charged two dollars for bottles of water and soda.

Rafe avoided the women in his life. He decided this was a fine time to go back to San Francisco. He could deal with his pressing business problems, sign some paperwork and figure out his next move.

Now, in his office, he waited for a sense of rightness to fill him. For the calm to take over—*calm* being a relative term. He was in a suit, behind a computer. All should have been right with the world.

"What?" Dante asked, leaning back in his chair, looking almost hurt. "Those are the best terms ever. I worked my ass off for them."

"Sorry, what?" Rafe glanced at the file in front of him. "Oh, right. Great job."

His friend clutched his chest. "Hold on. That was so emotionally meaningful, I think I need a tissue."

Rafe got up, walked to the floor-to-ceiling window and looked out at the bay. It was one of those perfect days, with clear skies and the sun glinting off the water. The city at her best.

"It's not you," he muttered.

Dante chuckled. "We're not dating, Rafe. It's never gonna be me. You still have your head up your ass."

Rafe faced his partner. "I what?"

"You heard me. If not your ass, then it's back in Fool's Gold. You're no good to me like this."

"I'm fine."

"You're distracted. You're pissed because she surprised you, and you don't like that."

"She's cheating."

"She's working outside the box. You should admire that."

Rafe turned back to Dante. "I thought she trusted me. I thought we were..."

Dante raised his eyebrows. "Involved?" He swore. "Do not tell me you're sleeping with her."

"It's not like that."

But it was exactly like that.

Rafe still couldn't pin down what was wrong. He was pissed—that was a given. What he couldn't understand was why Heidi had done it. And why her actions bothered him so much.

"I'm going back," he said, grabbing his suit jacket from the back of his chair.

"Color me surprised."

"I'll call you."

"They all say that, and they never do."

Rafe didn't bother changing. He just got in his car and headed east. When he finally drove onto the ranch, it was to find yet another truck by the barn. Only this one wasn't from any media outlet, and what was slowly backing out of the trailer had him as open-mouthed as any cartoon character.

"What the—"

"You see it, too, then," Heidi said coming up beside him. "I thought maybe I had brain damage from the flu."

He turned to stare at her, taking in the green eyes, the full mouth, the return of the goat girl braids. Pleasure welled up inside him. Pleasure and need. He wanted to grab her and kiss her, then maybe shake some sense into her.

"Are you going to tell me what's happening?" he asked.

"I don't know, either."

He returned his attention to the elephant backing out of the trailer.

"Any chance that's a rental?" he asked.

His mother burst out of the house. "She's here. Look at her. Isn't she beautiful?" She came to a stop beside him.

Rafe watched the incredibly huge creature come to rest beside the barn.

"It's an elephant, Mom."

"I know. I've always wanted one."

Heidi shook her head. "You're impressive, May. You know how to do things in a big way. I'm thinking Dr. McKenzie is going to have to read up on elephants."

"Our vet is a smart man. He'll figure it out."

Rafe wondered if the vet would want to have his mother checked out by local mental health professionals.

"You know where you're going to put her?" he asked.

"Of course. While you were gone, I had a shelter built."

He nodded, feeling as if he was trying to empty the ocean with a teaspoon.

"I'm going to guess elephants are expensive."

"Yes, they are. Even when they're old."

"So there was paperwork and I probably signed it."

His mother leaned her head on his shoulder. "You did."

But he hadn't read it, because, apparently, he was a slow learner.

"Mom?"

"Yes, dear?"

"Where are you getting the money to do all this?"

"I sold my condo."

"The one I bought you?" The one with the perfect

view, in Pacific Heights. The one easily worth over a million. Dollars.

"Uh-huh."

May wandered toward the man holding on to the elephant. Heidi glanced at him.

"You would have had to sign the closing papers on her condo, too."

"Thanks for pointing that out."

HEIDI LAY CURLED UP on her bed, reading. It was late and she should probably be asleep, but she felt she'd slept enough while recovering from the flu. Besides, there were a lot of things on her mind, and reading helped distract her. Getting lost in a juicy romance always made her feel better.

A light knock on her door caused her to look up. The fluttering in her heart told her who she wanted her visitor to be, but a small, sensible part of her brain mentioned having it be May would be much safer.

"Come in."

Rafe opened the door. "Got a minute?"

She nodded and put her book on the nightstand, then shifted so she was sitting cross-legged on her bed. He walked to the chair by the window and sat down.

He looked tired, she thought. As though he hadn't been sleeping well. Maybe his couple of days in San Francisco had consisted of late nights with beautiful women. The thought made her want to work herself up into righteous indignation, but she had a feeling he'd spent his time working. At least, she hoped he had, because she found herself wanting to move close to him and hold him. To tell him that everything would be all right. Crazy, when she remembered he was the cause of her problems.

"Do you think there's something wrong with my mother?" he asked. "Some kind of dementia?"

Heidi's instinctive response was to laugh, but she could tell Rafe was serious.

"May is one of the most lucid people I know. There's nothing wrong with her."

"She bought an elephant." He swore and ran his fingers through his hair. "Name one normal person who doesn't work for the circus who does that."

"She said she wanted the ranch to be a place for old animals to retire. We assumed she meant llamas and sheep. Obviously, she had more in mind."

"What's next?"

"I don't think there's anything else as surprising as an elephant. Seriously, would a zebra shock you now?"

"Not really."

"So, she's peaked. That's good." She tilted her head. "I swear, she's fine. It's not what you would have done with the money, but then, you would never have bought the ranch."

She thought about what May had said that afternoon. "I'm sorry about the condo. Was it nice?"

"I thought so. Two bedrooms, two and a half baths, twenty-five hundred square feet, with a killer view."

"You take good care of her. I'm sure she appreciates that."

He shrugged. "I started early. That kind of thing never goes away."

Meaning, he would be taking care of his mother the rest of her life. That was nice, Heidi thought. Comforting to know Rafe was consistent. In so many ways, he was a good man, so why was he planning to develop her land without even talking to her?

She wanted to ask, to explain that was why she'd done the cave paintings, but what had been done couldn't be undone, and talking about it wouldn't change that.

"I'm sorry," she said instead.

"Me, too."

She doubted they were apologizing for the same thing, but that was okay.

"My mother told me that elephants need companionship."

Heidi winced. "So she's buying another elephant?"

"No. She wants to try some of the animals already here, to see who the elephant bonds with. She wondered if you would mind if she introduced Athena to the elephant."

"Does the elephant have a name?"

He drew in a slow breath, his expression changing to that of a man about to walk the plank. "Priscilla."

Heidi pressed her lips together, trying not to laugh. "Seriously?"

"Do you think I could make that up?"

She felt the laughter building inside her and finally

gave in. She laughed until she had to collapse back on the bed, where she struggled to catch her breath.

"Priscilla, the elephant? I love that. May might have bought her based on the name alone."

"She said she bought her because she looked sad in her pictures."

Heidi wiped away tears. "Sure. Priscilla can meet Athena. Or any of the goats." She chuckled. "Your mom is the best. I really like her."

Rafe moved without warning. One second he was sitting in the chair by the window, the next he was crossing the room and reaching for her.

She wasn't sure who got there first, but then she was in his arms and it didn't matter. His mouth settled on hers as he kissed her deeply.

His lips pressed against hers, claiming her with the hunger of a man who had been without too long. His need fueled hers, and she dove into the liquid desire washing through her. She parted her lips for him, then met his tongue with eager thrusts of her own.

He lowered her to the bed, stretching out next to her. She shifted closer, wanting to feel all of his body. Their hands began to explore. She traced his arm, then shifted to his shoulders. Thick muscles moved under her fingers.

He rolled her onto her back and stared down at her. "You're so beautiful."

"Glen always told me never to believe what a man says when he has an erection."

Rafe gave her a slow, sexy smile. "Then I'll tell you again in the morning."

"Maybe I'll believe you in the morning."

"What do you believe now?"

"That you want me."

"It's a good start," he murmured, before lightly kissing his way down her jaw to her neck.

The warmth of his mouth created mini-explosions of fireworks along her sensitized skin. She felt constricted by her clothing and hungry for what would come next. She wanted more than the delicate dance of arousal. She wanted him in her, riding her, taking her hard and fast until she had no choice but to lose control. She wanted to be swept away.

Deciding that a direct, if nonverbal, message was best, she reached between them and unfastened his belt. He lifted his head and stared at her.

"You're telling me to move it along?"

"I'm suggesting you go get condoms and return to me naked."

"A woman with a plan. I respect that."

He gave her one more quick kiss and left her room. In the time it took her to pull back her covers, fluff the pillows and reach for the hem of her T-shirt, he was back.

He'd removed his boots and socks, and his shirt was open, as were his jeans.

A man who listens, she thought happily, walking toward him. A rare and precious find.

She took the small box of condoms from him and

dropped it on the nightstand, then slowly drew off her T-shirt. With his gaze locked on hers, she stepped out of her jeans. A muscle twitched in his jaw. His hands curled into fists and his erection flexed against his briefs.

Heidi didn't consider herself especially pretty or sexy. She was a fairly average woman. But at this moment, with Rafe's breathing getting more rapid and his eyes dilating, she felt like the most sexual creature on the planet.

She reached behind herself for the hooks on her bra, but was careful to keep her arms tightly at her side, so it didn't fall. When the hooks were undone, she grabbed the center of her bra and gave a little tug, exposing more of her breasts, but not all. His breath hissed.

She didn't have a plan for the rest of her striptease, but it turned out not to matter. Before she could even toss the bra away, he'd reached for her. He ripped the bra from her fingers, lowered his head and drew her left nipple into his mouth. He licked and sucked like a desperate man. He teased her other breast with his fingers, and used his free hand to squeeze her butt. The sensual assault had her arching against him, an act that brought her crotch in contact with his groin.

Soft met hard. Her hunger exploded and she felt herself spiraling out of control. She put her hand on his chin to raise his head, then kissed him. As she plunged her tongue into his mouth, she pressed her hand against his belly. She moved lower, sliding under his briefs, then rubbed the impressive length of him. She circled the tip of him, feeling the soft skin sheathing the flexing strength below.

Touching him like this, intimately, aroused her. She felt her blood pounding with every heartbeat. Between her legs, she was already swollen and aching. Foreplay was all fine and good, but right now she wanted more. She wanted him.

"Rafe," she breathed, and nipped his lower lip.

Apparently it was the signal he'd been waiting for. Without warning, he swept her up in his arms and lowered her onto the mattress. He ripped off her panties, jerked down his jeans, taking his briefs with them, and settled between her thighs on the bed.

He bent down, as if to kiss her intimately. She put her hands on his shoulders to stop him.

"I want you inside me," she pleaded. "Just do that. Please."

Indecision darkened his eyes. She appreciated his concern about getting her over the top. Another excellent quality in a man.

"I'm ready," she whispered. "Trust me."

He straightened and grabbed a condom. When he'd put it on, she reached between them and guided him inside.

He filled her with a slow, steady thrust. She arched toward him, taking all of him, feeling her body shudder with pleasure as nerve endings quivered. This was what she wanted, she thought, as she sucked in air. What she needed.

She opened her eyes and met his gaze. “Don’t hold back.” She wrapped her legs around his hips for emphasis. “Please.”

He braced himself on either side of her. She rested her hands on his shoulders and gave a little pulse to urge him on.

He withdrew, only to push in again. He went deep, moving a little faster than the time before. The action was repeated. She let her eyes sink closed as she lost herself in the sensations of the rhythm of their lovemaking.

With each thrust, she felt an answering throb low in her belly. Muscles tensed. She moved with him, pulling him closer, arching her back as she absorbed all he offered. In and out, their sensual dance continued. Their breathing increased. Her skin grew more sensitized. Every cell in her body focused on that point of contact, on the feel of him. Fiction and fantasy. The primal act of joining.

Faster and faster until she was gasping, straining. Her muscles began to quiver from the tension and then they released.

Her orgasm began in midthrust. Rafe pushed into her all the way, carrying her along. She clamped down on him, massaging him with her release, wanting this to never stop. She shook and cried out, and then his groan joined hers as he shuddered. He moved in her until she was still, then he turned them both and sank onto the bed, facing her.

Slowly she opened her eyes to find him watching

her. She touched his face, feeling the stubble, and then ran her fingers down his arm.

"What am I going to do with you?" he asked softly.

"A question for the ages."

He leaned in and kissed her. "Mind if I stay the night?"

"Not at all."

His mouth curved up in a smile. "You're my kind of girl."

Words that should have made her happy. The problem was, when it came to Rafe, she wanted more. She wanted to be everything to him. She wanted him to love her.

All wishing after the moon got a person was a pain in the neck. She'd heard that a lot when she was growing up. So, maybe tonight she would simply dream about the possibilities and leave the future to sort itself out.

RAFE WOKE SOMETIME BEFORE dawn to the sound of trucks rumbling into the yard. He realized several things at once. He was naked, he was in Heidi's bed and he had an erection. The facts were equally interesting to him, especially if he could take advantage of all of them at the same time. Unfortunately, the noise from outside seemed more pressing.

Heidi sat up and rubbed her eyes. "What is that?"

"I was about to find out."

He got out of bed and pulled on his jeans, then crossed to the window.

The faintest sliver of light glowed in the east. The night was clear and probably would have been still, except for the sound of trucks and a *beep-beep-beep* as one of them backed up to make room for the rest.

Heidi joined him, tightening a robe around herself. She stared at the large truck, then grinned.

"They're here!"

"Who? Or what?"

She gave him a quick hug, then ran to collect her clothes. "The carnival!"

CHAPTER SIXTEEN

HEIDI BURST OUT THE BACK DOOR of the house and down the steps, into the arms of her friends. She was literally squeezed from all sides, hugged and passed on to the next person, not exactly sure who was holding her close, but feeling safe and cared for every second.

"Look at you. Still so pretty."

"Are you taller? Aren't you too old to be getting taller?"

"I've missed you, Heidi."

"How do you like living like a townie? Ready to come back to the carnival?"

The last question came from Glen's friend Harvey, who held on a little longer than everyone else.

"You're good?" she asked the old man.

He nodded. "Got a checkup just last week. The cancer's gone."

News that made her current troubles seem insignificant by comparison.

The back door opened again and Glen came out, trailed by a nervous-looking May.

"My friends and family," Glen said, holding open his arms. He paused, then motioned for May to join him. "You probably won't believe this, but I think I've found the one."

"Took you long enough," Harvey yelled.

Glen chuckled. "Everyone, this is May Stryker. May, my family."

Heidi crossed her arms over her chest and shivered in the cool morning air. Not that she was interested in going inside. Watching the reunion was nearly as fun as being a part of it.

Madam Zoltan, otherwise known as Rita, joined her. "It's good to see you."

Heidi hugged her. "I'm so happy you're here. I've missed you."

"Not enough to come back and join us."

"I like living in one place."

Rita, formerly a natural redhead, arched her penciled, auburn brows. "You've become one of them."

"Not really, but I do like the stability. I always wanted a home that didn't have wheels."

"Now you have it."

Heidi hoped that was true. After all, the case hadn't been decided yet, and the judge could rule against her. But, thanks to her increase in sales, her bank balance was steadily climbing. If the caves could be declared sacred Máa-zib land, that would help, too.

Rita linked arms with her. "So who's the guy?"

Heidi followed her gaze and saw Rafe had come out of the house. He stood on the porch, all tall and sexy in his jeans and shirt. She found herself wanting to walk over to him and introduce him as someone important to her.

"He's May's son. He's staying here for a while." Heidi thought about the circumstances. "It's complicated."

"The best ones usually are." Rita looked at her. "Is it serious?"

"Not for him," Heidi said lightly, and forced a smile. "Wish I could say the same."

Her friend squeezed her arm. "Want me to read his fortune and tell him he's going to wake up as a frog one morning?"

"While I would enjoy that, I'm not sure he would believe you."

Rita smiled at her. "Too bad. I do love the believers."

"How long are you in town? I know the festival runs through the weekend."

"Just four days. This is a short stop for us. We'll be on our way Tuesday morning."

"Then I'd better get my visiting done in a hurry," Heidi teased.

Rita pointed to where the goats had collected by the fence. They were watching everything with interest. "Look at these wonderful girls! Are you going to introduce me?"

"Sure. I'll even let you milk one if you want."

"Don't think I'm doing your chores for you, missy. I got tricked into that enough when you were young." Rita laughed.

"Would I do that?"

"In a heartbeat."

WHAT RAFE KNEW ABOUT the workings of a carnival could fill a teacup and still have room left over for plenty of cream. Given that, he wasn't sure how he'd been roped into assisting with the setup. But here he was, in the middle of town, helping a bunch of guys he didn't know unload equipment and pitch tents.

The rides of the carnival were set up in the park's parking lot. He knew enough about building to have figured out why. The ground was level and the asphalt provided support. There were a dozen or so rides, including an impressive Ferris wheel. The booth games, or whatever they were called, were being placed along the main street of town. Food vendors were setting up on the other side, which meant plenty of foot traffic for everyone.

"Do you even know what you're doing?"

He looked up from connecting bolts to find Heidi watching him. At the sight of her, his gut tightened and heat coiled a little farther south.

"I can tighten a bolt."

"Just make sure you do so with the understanding you're now working in the time-honored tradition of bringing fun to millions of people everywhere."

He stood and moved so close that she had to lean her head back to still meet his gaze. "Is there a secret handshake or a manual I should read? A code of ethics?"

"There's always a code of ethics. I'm not sure you'd follow them."

"I'm a very honorable guy."

She snorted.

"Hey," he protested. "I am."

"We'll see." She tapped the side of the stand. "Do you know what this is going to be?"

"No."

"It's the dart game. Balloons are pinned to a board. You throw a dart and try to puncture a balloon."

"If I win?"

"You get a very fancy stuffed animal and bragging rights."

"Seems like a fair trade."

Her green eyes sparkled with laughter. He liked how she smiled, and she seemed happy and excited to have the carnival in town.

"How come you're not introducing me to your friends?"

She took a step back. "What are you talking about? You've met nearly everyone."

"Sure. Glen showed me around. Are you afraid of what people will think?"

"No. It's not that. The carnival is made up of a very close group of people. There are no secrets. Gossip runs rampant. If I were to introduce you, there would be a lot of questions and even more assumptions. I didn't think you'd be comfortable with that."

"About last night," he said, lowering his voice.

She shook her head. "I'm a big girl, Rafe. I wanted

to. There was no seduction involved. You have nothing to feel bad about."

"I don't feel bad. But I do want to be sure that you're okay."

"I'm fine. Why don't we talk about how you're feeling?"

"I'm a guy. Articulating my feelings isn't in my genetic makeup."

"Rafe? There you are. I've been looking all over for you."

Rafe turned and saw a tall, slender, well-dressed blonde walking toward him. If there'd been a wall nearby, he would've banged his head against it.

"Hello, Nina," he said instead.

His matchmaker put her hands on her hips. "You've been avoiding me."

"I didn't have anything more to say."

"But I did." Nina smiled at Heidi. "I don't think we've met. I'm Nina Blanchard, Rafe's matchmaker."

"Heidi Simpson," Heidi told her. "It's so nice to meet you. I don't think I knew you were coming to Fool's Gold."

"I didn't know, either," Rafe said, not sure why Nina had shown up, but knowing the reason wasn't going to be a good one for him.

"It was an impulsive decision," Nina admitted. She smiled at Heidi. "Rafe is being very difficult."

"I'm not even surprised," Heidi told her. "Rafe is a really stubborn guy. If you want him to pay attention, you're going to have to take charge."

"Hey!" Rafe stepped between them. "Maybe we should all stop talking about me."

Heidi shrugged. "I thought you liked being the center of attention."

"You thought wrong." He took Nina by the arm. "Let's go get coffee." He glanced at Heidi. "I'll deal with you later."

She looked unrepentant and a little smug as she smiled. "If you think you're up to it."

He took Nina to the Starbucks on the corner, bought her a nonfat latte, then they sat outside at a shaded table.

"What the hell are you doing here?" he asked, when she'd added her artificial sweetener and stirred her drink.

"I told you. You've been avoiding me."

"I said I was done with your services. I'll pay you whatever is owed, but I don't want you getting me any more dates."

"Because of Heidi?"

"What? No. Because of a lot of things."

Nina didn't look convinced.

Back in her office, he'd thought she was in her early forties. But out in the bright sunlight, he could see more lines around her eyes and pegged her at a few years older. Not that her age made any difference. She was still a pain in his ass.

"I said I'd find you a wife, and I will."

"I don't want to find a wife right now."

"Because of Heidi."

He sighed. "Didn't I already say no to that?"

"I don't believe you. I saw how you were looking at her." She leaned close. "Have you two had sex?"

"That's none of your business."

"Which means yes. Oh, Rafe, I meet a lot of interesting people in my business. You're not the kind of man who needs a matchmaker, but you wanted one."

"I made a mistake once. I don't want to make another mistake."

"By finding the perfect wife."

"I'm not interested in love." Mostly because he didn't believe in it.

What he'd had with his first wife had faded away. Shane and his first wife had been crazy in love, and she'd cheated on him every chance she got. If love existed, it did so in a world of pain and betrayal. Better to find someone he could be friends with. Someone who wanted what he wanted and shared his goals and values. Maybe that wasn't romantic, but it made sense to him.

"You're afraid," Nina told him firmly. "You're afraid of falling in love for real this time, because you don't know what it will do to you."

"You have no idea what you're talking about," he told her. "You don't know that much about me."

"I know enough. I know you were the one who took care of your family when your dad died, even though you were, what, eight or nine?"

His past had been written about in the press a few times. He supposed Nina was thorough and had done her research. "I'm not driven by something I saw as a kid," he said firmly.

"Maybe not, but you're influenced by it. You saw what happened to your mom, and you filed that information away. When it was your turn, you picked what you thought was the perfect wife. You went through the motions, dated, got married. I would guess you didn't love her, though. You weren't willing to risk those intense feelings."

"Thanks for stopping by," he said, turning away.

She stepped in front of him. "Let me guess. About the time you met your first wife, someone close to you also got involved. But his or her relationship was different. Intense, wild. What they had scared you, so you went in the other direction."

He refused to speak, but he couldn't stop himself from thinking about Shane. Nina was right. Shane had met Rachel about a year before he, Rafe, got married. They'd been passionate lovers from the first day. Shane had talked about being swept away by passion, how Rachel was everything to him. Rafe had tried to warn his brother to be careful, but Shane had refused to listen.

Rafe told himself Nina was guessing. She'd been in the business a long time and had picked up a few tricks. This was one of them. Maybe she had a point. Maybe he had been too cautious the first time around. But that didn't mean he couldn't make a reasonably well thought-out relationship work.

"There's nothing wrong with wanting to be sure," he said at last.

She gave him a sad, knowing smile. "You're wrong. Love isn't about being sure. Love is about risking it all. The only way to be truly in love is to give with your whole heart. To put it out there and be vulnerable. To offer all you have without knowing if it will be enough. Love is standing naked in front of the world and announcing, 'This is who I am,' then waiting to be accepted or not."

"Then I'm not interested."

"It's worth it," Nina told him. "I promise you that. If you find the right person, it's amazing. Notice I'm not saying 'the one.' I don't believe there's just one person for each of us. There are many, and sometimes we can find that magic a second or third time. You never found it at all."

"I don't need that in my life."

"Yes, you do. At least once, Rafe. Risk your heart."

He shook his head. "Are we done here?"

"No, but you can go. I'm now a woman on a mission. I want to see you happily married."

He held in a groan. "This I don't need right now."

"That's okay. I can wait."

BY EARLY AFTERNOON, RAFE was ready to run screaming into the mountains around Fool's Gold. He'd managed to escape from Nina, only to continue setting up for the carnival. The dart game he'd started to put together required him blowing up hundreds of balloons.

The tall, skinny guy who had introduced himself as Ham had shown him three empty, massive cardboard boxes and said they had to be filled with balloons. Then he'd pointed to a box of balloons and an air compressor. He'd slapped Rafe on the back and disappeared. Rafe sensed he'd been had.

Still, he went to work, blowing up the balloons, tying them off, then dropping them into the boxes. Late morning turned into early afternoon. The sun rose higher in the sky, the day warmed and the sidewalks around him grew crowded.

By three, his fingers were cramping from the twisting motion. Give him a ten-foot fence line or a herd of "feral" cattle any day, he thought. At least that was work he enjoyed. And it was solitary. Because along with the bottomless box of balloons, he'd had a long string of visitors.

Harvey of the recently cured cancer had stopped by to talk about his good health and how Glen's generosity had literally saved his life. When Rafe had pointed out that the money had come from his mother and Glen had lied to get it, Harvey had been unimpressed. He'd done ten minutes on the state of health care in this country, recounted two funny stories about Glen and had told him that everyone was watching him, before drifting away.

A pretty, middle-aged redhead appeared next in a flowy, long dress, and stopped in front of him. "You must be Rafe," she said. "I'm Madam Zoltan, but you can call me Rita." Her green eyes swept over him. "Nice. Very nice."

He didn't know what she meant, and he decided it was better not to ask.

"Good to meet you," he said, continuing his balloon work.

"So you're with Heidi."

Rafe's grip on the balloon he was filling with air loosened, and the bit of rubber went flying through the air. It zigged and zagged around them before fluttering to the sidewalk. A little boy ran over and picked it up, then darted away.

"I need a drink," Rafe muttered, and he wasn't talking about the bottle of water Harvey had brought him.

Rita smiled. "She's a wonderful young woman, but then you already know that. May I?"

She reached for his hand. He let her take it, then she bent over his palm. Her fingers were long and cool. They lightly touched his skin, tracing lines before rubbing the base of his thumb.

"I'm going to meet a dark stranger who will change my life forever?" he asked.

"No, nothing that simple. You're a complicated man." She tapped a line. "Very loving, although you try to hide that part of your character. You take care of the people around you."

This was the second time in one day a woman he barely knew was talking about him as if they had exclusive emails delivered from heaven. He pulled back his hand.

"It was nice to meet you," he said firmly, picking up the next balloon.

"You're dismissing me." She seemed more amused than angry. "All right. I'll take the hint. But first, to get your heart's desire, you're going to have to be willing to take a leap of faith. To be vulnerable."

Involuntarily, he remembered what Nina had told him that morning. About being naked in front of the world. Had the women around here had a meeting and decided today was the day they were going to torture him?

"It's worth it," she assured him.

"Good to know."

She smiled and left.

He stared after her for a couple of seconds, then reached for the next balloon. About an hour later, he'd nearly finished when Charlie walked up to him. She was wearing a Fool's Gold firefighter uniform, so it took him a second to place her.

"Charlie."

"That's me. I came to—"

He held up both hands and took a step back. "I'm not talking about my past, who I date or Heidi. You can't read my palm, ask about my mother or discuss any aspect of my life, now or in the future."

Charlie raised her eyebrows. "Are you okay?"

"No. Go away."

Her mouth twitched, as if she were holding in a grin. "If you insist, but at some point I have to check the booth. Fire regulations."

"Not now. Get out. Stop talking about me. Pretend we never met."

Charlie chuckled. "Now I can honestly say I have no idea what Heidi sees in you."

"You were leaving."

She was still laughing when she strolled away.

THE GROUP OF SIX WAS EVENLY split between archaeologists and reporters. Heidi touched the back pocket of her jeans, where she'd shoved the notes Annabelle had given her, and hoped she remembered all the important points. Speaking in public, even to a small group like this, wasn't her idea of a good time. Of course, she only had herself to blame for the situation, something she needed to remember.

She'd come in before the tour and left lanterns in the caves, then given everyone a flashlight. Now, as they stepped into the darkness, light was swallowed up in the darkest corners, and the temperature dropped noticeably with every step.

"The front part of the caves have been used for decades," she explained. "Maybe hundreds of years. When I bought the ranch last year, I knew they would be perfect for aging my cheese. The caves maintain a steady temperature. The farther back you go, the cooler it gets. The lowest temperature is just below fifty degrees."

"Did you find any gold?" one of the reporters asked.

"No. I know there was a large find in the mountains. I guess that was where they stored it. Because of the paintings, we're wondering if this cave is some kind of sacred ground. Maybe a holy place."

"But no gold?" the woman asked again.

One of the archaeologists glared at her. "The intrinsic value of a find isn't determined by whether or not it's shiny."

"My viewers are a whole lot more interested in gold than a few wall paintings."

"Perhaps if they were more educated."

"Perhaps if you lived in the real world."

Heidi cleared her throat. "As I was saying…"

Both women turned to face her.

She forced a smile. "We don't know exactly what we have here. Something valuable, obviously. Important to our history here in Fool's Gold. As most of you know, there has always been a connection between the town and the Máa-zib tribe. They were a matriarchal civilization, and we have strong women here."

Women strong enough to solve their problems without deception, she thought grimly. Women who acted instead of lying. She answered a few questions, then led everyone to the cave paintings. As they took pictures and studied the primitive art, she knew she'd made a mistake.

This wasn't who she was. She'd spent her whole life doing the right thing. This time, when everything she wanted in life was on the line, she'd cheated and lied. Even if Rafe had gone out on a thousand dates, she still should have talked to him and found a point of compromise. She should have talked to May, figured out a way to make it all work. Now she'd set events in motion, and she didn't know how to stop the runaway train. She could only hope everyone got out before there was a hideous crash, and that the aftermath wouldn't destroy everything she cared about.

CHAPTER SEVENTEEN

"I HAVEN'T SEEN NINA in a while," Heidi said.

Rafe came to a stop in the middle of the sidewalk. Crowds flowed around them.

"Let's make a deal," he said. "We won't talk about Nina, and I'll buy you anything you want at the carnival."

"I like to think I have higher standards than that. It would take at least three Ferris wheel rides and cotton candy to buy my silence."

"Done."

A little boy ran into the back of her legs. Rafe pulled her off the sidewalk and into a brightly lit alley by the sporting goods store.

"I didn't ask Nina to come here."

His gaze was steady as he spoke, as if he wanted to be sure she believed him.

"I didn't think you had."

"She just showed up."

"I'm sure that's true." She smiled. "You looked shocked when she walked over."

"You have no idea. I'd already told her we were done. I'm not using her services anymore."

She studied his familiar face, the dark eyes, the

strong line of his jaw. He looked different these days. Tanned, even more muscled. In his cotton shirt and jeans, he was just a guy. Not Rafe Stryker, dangerous tycoon.

But he was as dangerous as he had always been. Not only because of their pending case before the judge, but because of what he could do to her emotionally. His making sure she knew he wasn't going to be dating Nina's picks was both good and bad news. At least she didn't have to think about him out with other women. On the other hand, she could now pretend it was because of her. That he cared and they were involved and she wasn't going to get her heart broken.

"She's determined," he added. "I guess she doesn't believe in letting clients get away. That's why she came."

"It's okay," she told him.

He stared into her eyes. "I wanted to be sure you knew."

He reached for her hand and linked their fingers. His hold was strong and sure. As if he would protect her from danger. They stepped back into the Friday evening crowd.

Fool's Gold was the kind of place that loved festivals. There were year-round events, celebrating everything from summer to harvest to the traditional holidays. For the few weeks when the average calendar didn't provide an excuse to party, the town made up events.

The locals came out to participate, and tourists arrived from all over. Hotel rooms were booked weeks in advance, as friends, couples and families took advantage of the affable atmosphere and easy fun.

"Now about that Ferris wheel ride," he said.

Heidi shook her head. "I was kidding. I don't need to ride the Ferris wheel."

"Who said anything about need?"

"You said you like the Tilt-A-Whirl."

"I did as a kid. I don't think it would be as appealing now."

They stopped and bought churros, because dessert before dinner was important. As they were waiting in a line for drinks, Heidi waved to one of her friends.

"Nevada Hendrix," she said, then laughed. "I mean, Nevada Janack. From the construction site."

"Where we went to get Athena."

She watched him carefully as he spoke, wondering if he would give a hint of his real plans, but he only nodded.

"An impressive project."

Nevada and Tucker joined them.

"I love when the carnival comes to town," Nevada said, after they'd greeted each other. "It's fun. Dakota is taking Hannah on the Ferris wheel for the first time. Finn is trying to juggle a camera and the baby, so we have to get back to help." She hugged Heidi. "I don't see you enough. Let's have lunch this week."

"I'd love that."

When they'd all gotten their drinks and Nevada and Tucker had left, Heidi turned to Rafe.

"Dakota, Nevada and Montana are identical triplets. They all fell in love last year and got married over the holidays. Dakota was concerned she couldn't have children, so she adopted a baby girl. About the same time, she got pregnant, and now they have two kids. Montana is hugely pregnant and due to pop any day now. I guess Nevada will be next."

She heard the wistful tone in her own voice. She'd always loved children and wanted to have her own. When she was younger, that had been her plan. A husband then kids. After Melinda had killed herself, she'd been less sure about taking a chance on falling in love. Probably because Glen had always told her love was for suckers. As her heart had never seemed that interested in any guy, she hadn't worried about the problem.

Now, with Rafe, she was more confused than ever. He said he wanted marriage and children, but without falling in love. His list of requirements didn't sound anything like her. Which meant she wasn't in the running. Had she finally found "the one," only to discover she wasn't "the one" for him?

"I have more respect for carnival rides now that I've worked to put them together," he told her.

A safer topic, she thought. "There's a science to how the rides are grouped together. One has to take traffic flow into account, along with price and how many people can ride in an hour."

"Do the prices vary from venue to venue?"

She nodded. "It's easier to charge the same for everything, but some rides are more popular than others. The popular rides often cost more. But there are other factors. How many people can you get on and off in a certain amount of time."

She pointed to the Ferris wheel. "There are sixteen cars, each holding two people. With a good crew, you're talking four hundred riders an hour."

"That many?"

She nodded, then turned so they were looking at the YoYo. "See those swings?"

"There's only one rider."

"But there are thirty-two swings. They can handle nine hundred people an hour."

"That's a big difference."

"Exactly. Most of the rides fall somewhere in between. It's all about getting people safely on and off. You don't want the rides so short anyone feels cheated, but you can't have lines taking forever. The carnival has to make money, and so does the town."

"Did you work the rides when you were a kid?"

"I did everything. Rides, games, the food carts."

"Took care of goats?"

She smiled. "I did have my first goat when I was a kid, yes."

"You don't miss the life?"

"I miss the people, but I like being settled. Who wouldn't want to live in Fool's Gold?" She shrugged. "Except you."

"It's not so bad," he admitted. "I like it better now

that I'm not dependent on their kindness to survive." He hesitated. "Do you know who Raoul Moreno is?"

"Sure. He's married to Pia. They have twin girls."

Rafe laughed. "Fair enough, but he was also a great quarterback. That's football."

She pushed him with her free hand. "I know what quarterbacks are, and I have more than a passing understanding of the game."

"I wasn't sure. What with you being a girl and all."

"I thought you liked me being a girl."

He pulled her off the sidewalk and between a couple of buildings. There were still a lot of people around, but it was a touch more private. And nice, she thought, when he lowered his head and kissed her.

"I do like you being a girl," he murmured, his mouth against hers.

"Me, too."

She could get lost in him, she thought. But the price would be too high.

"So, about Raoul?"

"Right." He led them back into the crowd. "He started a camp up in the mountains. For inner-city kids who don't have much. He has big plans. It's a great idea and an ambitious program. But there are other kids. Kids in small towns and on farms who need help. What about them?"

"Are you thinking about doing something with them?"

"I don't know. Kind of. I've been fortunate, and being back here has got me thinking. Not every town can take care of its own the way Fool's Gold took care of my mom and the rest of my family. I hated being poor and people giving me stuff, but without those baskets of food and gifts, we wouldn't have had anything for the holidays. Mayor Marsha gave me my first bike. Denise Hendrix brought us clothes. The woman had six kids and she'd already taken in a seventh, and she still thought of us. I wonder how many Denise Hendrixes and Mayor Marshas there are in the world."

"You surprise me."

"I surprise myself. I haven't done anything yet. But I've spent the past couple of weeks playing with the idea."

She wished he hadn't. Of course, she wanted him to help people, but hearing him talk about it made her like him more. She hardly needed help in that department.

"Enough about that," he said, and dropped a kiss on the top of her head. "I'm thinking chili dogs. What about you?"

"That sounds perfect."

LATE SATURDAY NIGHT, HEIDI was curled up in Rita's old trailer. She remembered helping her friend re-cover the sofa with the bright floral fabric. Nelson, Rita's gray-and-white cat, perched on the ottoman, grooming his handsome self.

Rita poured Heidi and herself a brandy, then handed over a glass.

"I remember doing this when you turned twenty-one," Rita told her. "That was a fun night."

"Melinda was with us. Her birthday was four months before mine, and she loved to tease me about being able to drink first."

"Neither of you partied very much. Or got into trouble with boys."

"We were saints," Heidi said lightly, sipping the liquid. "Someone should have given us a plaque."

"You still miss her." Rita set down her glass. "I don't need any psychic powers to figure that out. I can see it in your eyes when you talk about her."

"She was my best friend."

Heidi fought against the sense of betrayal she often felt when she talked about Melinda's death. If there had been an accident, she was pretty sure she could have come to terms. But Melinda had acted deliberately. More than once. She'd taken her own life, leaving friends and family behind.

"Why weren't we enough?" she asked, her eyes filling with tears. "We all loved her. He was just some guy. He wasn't worth it."

"Do any of us have the power to hurt you as much as Rafe does?"

Not a question she wanted to answer. Glen could annoy her and frustrate her. He could make her want to throw something, as when she'd found out about the money he'd taken from May. But, no, he couldn't hurt her. His love was absolute, and she'd relied on it her whole life. No matter what, they would be there for each other.

"I don't want to love him," she admitted.

"You're not like Melinda."

Heidi sucked in a breath. Trust her friend to expose her darkest fear. "You can't know that. What if my heart breaks as much? What if I can't face the pain? Melinda had just as much to live for."

"She was never strong. You were the rock in that relationship."

"I should have gone to college with her. I could have kept those girls from bullying her, or maybe kept it from mattering so much."

"You know that's not true. Melinda had a sadness about her even before her heart was broken. You're not her, and Rafe is nothing like that boy she loved."

"You never met him. You can't know that."

"I know you, and I've watched him. He's a good man. Confused about a few things, reluctant to risk his emotions. But once he does, he's loyal. Kind."

Ridiculously good in bed, but why go there.

"He doesn't want me. He wants a perfect wife. He has a list, and I don't meet any of his criteria."

"He's protecting himself, trying not to get hurt. It's what everyone does." Rita sipped her brandy. "Rafe wants what everyone wants. To belong. Don't let the fear win. Embrace who you are, including your strength."

"I want to, but I'm scared."

"True courage is acting in the face of fear."

"Can't I just run instead?"

Rita smiled. "That was never your style. You'll do what must be done, and you'll survive."

RAFE'S MOTHER SPREAD OUT several large sheets of paper on the kitchen table. As she put them in order, Rafe recognized the basic outline of the ranch. The house and surrounding buildings had been sketched in, along with the fence line. Places for her various animals were marked. He ignored the notations that mentioned a camel and two zebras.

"Here's what we were thinking," May told him, practically bouncing in her chair. "Winter homes for the carnival workers."

She paused expectantly, as if waiting for him to be as excited as she was.

"What do you mean?" he asked, thinking of all the houses he'd planned to build. Houses he could sell for a profit to the future casino and hotel workers.

"Trailers can get cold in the winter," Glen said, absently patting May's butt.

Rafe immediately stared directly at the paper and did his best to shut down his peripheral vision.

"We're not thinking anything too large. A couple of bedrooms, living room, kitchen. Bathroom and laundry. What, twelve hundred square feet? If there were plenty of space between them, there would be room for the trailers. It would be like a little town."

May pointed to several spots on the map. "In the summer, they could be vacation rentals. That would provide income. Imagine how wonderful it would be for families to come to Fool's Gold for a week and be able to rent a place like that. You could even build a couple of them with a third bedroom."

"Lucky me."

"You don't like the idea?" His mother appeared shocked by the concept.

"It's interesting."

Not at all what he'd had in mind. Based on what she'd done, there would still be plenty of unused acres. So maybe he couldn't put in as many houses as he'd first imagined, but he could still do part of the development.

"Want me to draw up some designs?" he asked.

May nodded. "If you wouldn't mind."

Glen stood. "I promised Heidi I'd move her goats. Athena's looking feisty these days, so it may take a while. I'll be back." He kissed May on the cheek, nodded at Rafe and left.

When he was gone, May turned to Rafe. "You hate it."

"I don't. I'm surprised. I didn't think about vacation rentals, but sure. Why not?" Now that she'd thought of it, he doubted his mother would be willing to give up the idea. Better to work with her than against her.

May sagged in her chair. "You think I'm a terrible mother."

"What?"

Tears filled her eyes. "It's because I am. Do you know what today is?"

It took him a second to figure that out. "You're not a terrible mother."

"I haven't called her. I should. But I never know what to say. She's so distant, and I know that's my fault."

"It's not your fault."

"She's my daughter. We should be close. You and I are close."

"That's because you won't let me escape."

He'd hoped to make her smile, but instead, the tears spilled over and ran down her cheeks.

He stood and circled the table, then pulled May to her feet and hugged her.

"Call her," he said. "Wish her happy birthday."

"Shouldn't I want to talk to Evangeline? Shouldn't I miss her? No, that's wrong. I do miss her, but I'm also confused. Does she hate us? You never talk to her, either."

"If I do, I'll yell at her."

His sister was a disappointment. She'd had so much potential. A brilliant dancer, Evangeline had been accepted to Juilliard and had dropped out her second year. Seven years ago, his business had been growing and he'd plowed every penny back into it. The fifty thousand a year in tuition had been a stretch, but he'd been determined she wouldn't have to worry about money. So he'd paid it all, and had given her a generous allowance, so she could hang out with her friends and buy whatever it was eighteen-year-old girls needed.

She'd walked away from it and had never said a word as to why. He'd only found out when the school had returned his tuition money, telling him Evangeline was no longer a student there.

"She's all alone," May whispered. "It's her birthday and she's all alone."

He held his mother while she cried, and didn't know what to do to fix the problem. If Shane were here, his brother would probably tell him it was all his fault. Maybe it was. Maybe he expected too much from his family. But, dammit all to hell, Evangeline could have gone all the way. However, like Clay, she'd chosen what was easy. She'd walked away from her dreams, and he couldn't forgive that.

"You should call her," he repeated. "You'll feel better, and she probably will, too."

She drew back and wiped her face. Her eyes were still sad, though, and she sighed. "We have that in common, you and I. We don't fight for what's important to us. Our pride is easily bruised, and when someone walks away, we let them."

He wasn't comfortable with the assessment. "I don't do that."

"You did with Evangeline and with Clay. Maybe your first wife. I don't know enough about the details to be sure. One day you're going to have to stand up and fight for what you want. I am, too. First, I just have to figure out what that is."

She left the kitchen. Rafe stared after her, not sure what she had meant. He knew how to fight. His business was proof of that. He'd started with nothing and was now worth millions.

But in his gut, he understood his mother didn't mean anything financial. She was talking about risking his heart. Clay had disappointed him, as had Evangeline, and he'd cut both of them out of his life. He'd been disappointed by love and refused to risk his heart again. He wasn't a man who forgave easily.

He'd always thought that was a strength, but maybe he'd been wrong.

HEIDI POINTED TO THE CAVE paintings. Rita held her flashlight high and then burst into laughter.

"They're wonderful. You did a perfect job. I would be completely fooled."

Heidi sighed. "Unfortunately, we don't have to convince you. The experts have already arrived and seen everything. I don't know how long we can string them along."

Rita studied her. "You're not happy about this."

"I know. I made a mistake. I was having second thoughts, and then I was hurt and mad and said we should do it. It's like rolling a rock downhill. Once you give it a push, there's no pulling it back."

She touched the cool, uneven wall of the cave. "I should have talked to Rafe. I should have tried to work things out. Instead, I'm scamming the whole town. When they find out, they may never forgive me."

"I think you're being a little hard on yourself."

"I was wrong."

Rita leaned in and kissed Heidi's forehead. "My sweet girl. You've always had character."

"Not enough, or I would have found another way."

"Deep breaths. It's done now, and you simply have to ride out the storm. It might not be as bad as you think."

"I hope you're right."

"I usually am. Come on. Show me the rest."

Heidi led her deeper into the caves. As they turned the corner, they didn't notice the reporter hovering in the shadows. Nor did they see her hurry out to tell her producer everything she'd just learned.

CHAPTER EIGHTEEN

RAFE STOOD IN THE CENTER of the kitchen, feeling the surge of anger rising through him. He didn't look at Heidi—couldn't look at her. Not after what she'd done. He knew he was too close to saying something he shouldn't. Something they would both regret.

He'd suspected all along, but to have it come out like this… He was furious and couldn't completely say why.

"I'm sure if Heidi explained…" May began, but his mother sounded doubtful.

Glen hovered between the two women, as if unsure of where his loyalties lay.

Heidi pressed against the counter, maybe for support, maybe in an attempt to put more room between them. Rafe wasn't sure and he didn't care.

The morning news had trumpeted the story of the fake cave paintings in Fool's Gold. The reporter had personally overheard Heidi confessing all. The reporter had taken great glee in saying Heidi had betrayed them all.

He realized then that was the source of his anger. Not that she'd tried to win, but that she hadn't trusted him to—

He swore silently. Trusted him to what? Take care of her? He wanted the land for his development. She shouldn't trust him. But he wanted her to. And that was why he was so pissed.

"You lied to me," he said at last.

Her chin came up slightly. "Yes. I lied to you. I tried to get the judge to rule in my favor and make sure you couldn't carry out your plans."

May sank onto a kitchen chair. "Oh, Heidi. I don't understand. I thought we were getting along. I thought you liked having me here."

"I do," Heidi said, glaring at Rafe. "You're not the problem. It's your son. Because I believed the same thing you did, May. That we were coming to terms and working things out. Then I found out Rafe had gone behind my back. He has plans for the land. Plans to build houses for the casino workers."

Heidi's voice turned bitter. "Don't worry. From what I saw, he's leaving you a few acres for your animals, and you get the house. But the rest of the land will be developed, and Glen and I are to be thrown out."

Rafe swore under his breath. He had no idea how she'd found out about his idea or what she'd seen.

His mother stared at him. "Rafe? Is that true? You're building houses and throwing out Heidi? How could you?"

"I haven't done anything," he pointed out. "I made up a few drawings."

Heidi's mouth twisted. "That's not all. You made

calls and found out about zoning. You contacted the city very quietly."

"You can't know that."

"No, I can't," she admitted. "But I know you, and that's the next logical step. Or am I wrong?"

They were all staring at him. Glen and Heidi were pissed, but his mother was hurt, her dark eyes swimming with tears.

"I had Dante make a few calls," he admitted. "I haven't done anything else."

"What about Heidi?" his mother asked. "You were planning on having her leave? And the goats? Where were they supposed to go?"

A question he couldn't answer. "Mom, you were cheated from the start. I was only looking out for you."

"Oh, please," Heidi said, rolling her eyes. "I'm sure she'll appreciate having hundreds of homes just a few feet away. Roads cutting through the ranch she loves. Pristine wilderness turned into a parking lot. You didn't do any of this for her. This is about you and profit and winning."

"That's not true."

"Then what's it about? Why didn't you tell any of us that you were planning this? I didn't know how to stop you, so, yes, I created the cave paintings and planted the artifacts. I was wrong, and I have to tell you, it's a relief to be caught. I'll accept the consequences of my actions." She swallowed. "I was trying to protect my home, to make sure that Glen and I could stay here."

She turned to May. "I should have come to you.

That's my mistake, and I'm sorry. I was so scared when I found out what Rafe wanted to do. And hurt. You've been nothing but gracious and warm since you arrived." She drew in a breath. "I'm so sorry."

May's lower lip trembled. "I understand." She stared at Rafe. "Why didn't you say something to me? You had the perfect opportunity to explain everything when Glen and I talked to you about the vacation homes."

May glanced at Heidi. "Your grandfather and I were thinking of having small vacation homes built on some of the land. Enough for the carnival workers to winter here. They could be rentals in the summer. You know, for families who want to come to Fool's Gold."

A single tear slipped down Heidi's cheek. "I would have liked that."

Rafe felt a growing sense of unease. The situation had slipped out of his control, and he wasn't sure where it was going.

"Heidi still lied," he pointed out. "She tricked us all."

"So did you," his mother snapped. "Rafe, I would never agree to give up the ranch for a housing development. A few acres, maybe. At the far end and closest to the casino. But not much more. And I would never allow you to throw out Heidi and her goats. You took charge, like you always do. You assumed you knew best."

She rose. "I know some of that is my fault. I depended on you too much when you were little. I made you grow up too quickly. Now you steamroll over everyone."

He felt the ground shifting as the attention focused on him.

"Wait a minute," he began.

"No. I don't want to talk about this anymore."

His mother walked out of the kitchen. Glen followed.

Rafe walked to the table and took one of the chairs. "Happy?" he asked as he sat.

"Of course not. This isn't what I wanted."

"What did you want?"

"Not to lose my home. I thought about coming to you, trying to reason with you, but..." She shook her head. "You have to win. Always. I can't believe your mother talked to you about those vacation homes and you didn't tell her what you had planned." Her eyes narrowed. "I'll bet you were figuring out a way to have both. Put in the vacation homes she wanted, and use the extra land to build your development."

He didn't have an answer to that, mostly because it was true.

"I see," she said quietly. "Let me guess. There wasn't any room for me in the new plan, either."

He shifted on the chair, feeling guilty and uncomfortable.

"Heidi," he began.

"No," she told him. "You can't talk your way out of this. As far as you're concerned, I'm someone you slept with. Nothing more. You don't care about me or what happens to me. You would be very content to toss me out."

"That's not true."

"Okay, prove it. Show me where I fit in your plan. Point out one square inch of this ranch you had left for me."

He stood. "I don't have any details," he hedged.

"You don't have anything."

She stared at him for a long time. He waited for her to start yelling, but instead, she was quiet. Her eyes grew sad.

"I was wrong," she said quietly. "I accept that. I did what I did to protect my home, and while that's not good enough, at least it's a reason I can accept without feeling like a jerk. You did what you did for profit. You ignored everyone but yourself. Your mom is right. You force your will on everyone, consequences be damned. The reason you didn't feel anything when your marriage ended is because you don't know how to care about anyone but yourself. Using a matchmaker is a really good idea, Rafe. Just make sure Nina explains to your prospective bride that the man she's marrying was born without a heart."

RAFE HAD ALWAYS THOUGHT he had a pretty good handle on his world. He understood the rules, the consequences, and he played to win. Sometime in the last two days, he'd completely lost control. Heidi had lied to him and his mother, tricked the town and been outed by a reporter. But instead of anyone standing up and asking what the hell she'd been thinking, he had become the bad guy.

His mother had asked him to move out of the ranch and back to the hotel in town. He hadn't seen Heidi, Glen wasn't speaking to him and everywhere he went in Fool's Gold, he was getting angry stares.

"People really hate you," Dante said cheerfully, his long legs stretched out in front of him.

They were sitting in the bar at Ronan's Folly. Rafe had moved back to a suite there, and Dante had joined him to wrap up a few business details. In a couple of days, they would both head to San Francisco. There was no reason to stay in Fool's Gold. It wasn't as if anyone wanted him around.

The situation was too pathetic for him to stand, he thought grimly, as he gripped his Scotch.

"It's an interesting insight into human behavior," his partner continued. "Technically, Heidi is the one who broke the rules. She deceived everyone. All you did was scratch out a few tentative plans for some houses. Yet she's forgiven and you're the devil."

"Thanks for the recap."

Dante looked around. "I like it here."

"You're a sick guy."

"Maybe. But there's a sense of community. Heidi's the pretty, helpless woman done wrong by the big, bad developer."

"I didn't develop shit."

"But you could have. And your sins would be much greater. I respect the sense of loyalty."

"I hope you respect the lack of profits. There's no way we're going to be able to develop any houses around here."

"Not on your mother's land, no. But there might be other places. After all, the casino is still going to need to hire people."

Rafe shook his head. "No, thanks. I'm done with Fool's Gold." His initial instincts had been right. He should never have come back.

"Then I might look around."

"Help yourself."

Rafe started to say more, only to be distracted by angry, stomping footsteps approaching. He looked around and spotted Shane headed toward him. His brother didn't look happy.

"Brace yourself," Rafe muttered.

He and Dante both stood as Shane came to a stop in front of them.

"You're back," Rafe said.

"Obviously."

"This is Dante Jefferson, my business partner."

Dante and Shane shook hands.

"Nice to meet you," Dante said cheerfully.

"Are you as much of a jackass as my brother?" Shane asked.

Dante grinned. "No. Not even close."

"Good." Shane turned to Rafe. "What the hell were you thinking?"

Rafe sank back into the overstuffed chair. He understood his brother well enough to know Shane didn't actually want an answer.

"You knew I wanted to bring my horses here," Shane continued, taking the chair opposite, his dark eyes bright with fury. "I've put a bid on a hundred adjoining acres. I'm breeding horses, Rafe. I can't have a development pushing up against my land. I'd already talked to Mom about leasing some of her land for grazing. We were going to grow hay, maybe some other crops. Where do you get off trying to destroy all of that?"

"Technically, he didn't do anything," Dante pointed out, his tone cheerful. "There were a few drawings, a couple of conversations."

"You should stay out of this," Shane told him.

Dante raised both his hands. "I'm just saying."

"You didn't tell me about your plans," Rafe said, surprised Shane and May had decided so much between them.

"I didn't want to hear why it wouldn't work."

Rafe frowned. "I wouldn't say that. You know what you're doing when it comes to horses."

"Gee, thanks. I appreciate the endorsement, but you'll have to forgive me for not expecting you to be supportive. If I remember correctly, you hounded me about college, even though I had no interest in going. When I was eighteen and took off to work on a ranch, you told me that if I failed, I was on my own. That you didn't agree with my decision and that you wouldn't be there for me."

Rafe winced. "I didn't mean it that way. I wanted the best for you."

"You don't get to decide what that is."

"You're right."

"Too little, too late." Shane leaned toward him. "You do this all the time, Rafe. You butt in, make pronouncements, demand action. You don't ask, you decide. You're not interested in our opinions. I guess you think we're not bright enough to have figured it out for ourselves."

"That's not true." Rafe was once again left wondering when he'd become the bad guy.

"Sure it is. You haven't spoken to Clay or Evie in years. That's not because of them. You think they're wasting their lives. Sure, you worked hard to support all of us, and we appreciate that. But the price is too high. You expect ownership in return for what you did, and no one wants to give you that."

Shane rose. "You're not going to develop the ranch. Mom and Glen's idea for the vacation homes is great, but there won't be anything else. No housing development, no retail. Nothing. We're keeping the rest of it for horses and farming. You got that?"

Rafe nodded.

Shane left.

Rafe leaned back in his chair. "Be grateful you're an only child."

"Oh, I don't know. I wouldn't mind having a family member or two." He sipped on his Scotch. "Now what?"

"Hell if I know. I'm getting out of here in a couple of days. I'll make sure the construction guys are finishing up the barn, and make sure everything else my mom needs is being handled, then I'm coming back to San Francisco."

Dante raised his eyebrows. "No one would be surprised if you left her to deal with the construction on her own."

"I probably should." But he wouldn't. Taking care of her and his siblings was too much a part of him. Even if it was a thankless job.

He thought about what Shane had said. That he pushed his own views and decided for others. While his brother had a point, Rafe wanted to protest that he'd done the best he could, raising all three of them, looking after Mom. He'd sacrificed plenty, had struggled to make sure they got to be kids, while he'd worried about their futures.

Now he would do things differently, but at ten or sixteen or twenty, he hadn't known any better.

He wanted to talk to Heidi. To tell her what Shane had said and listen to her opinion, maybe get her advice. She had a way of seeing both sides of a problem. She would know what he should do next.

Only Heidi was avoiding him, and he doubted she would want anything to do with him, if they did run into each other. She'd been so angry with him.

He missed her. What could have been awkward—living in the same house together with his mother and her grandfather—had been fun. He'd enjoyed getting to know her, discovering her moods, what made her smile. He missed the sound of her voice, her laughter, the way she turned him on just by walking into a room.

She was what he would miss most when he was gone. She had shown him he didn't want a perfect wife anymore. He wanted…

Heidi? Love?

The idea of being with her excited him and terrified him in equal measures. She would never accept a relationship based on shared values and friendship. She would hand over her whole heart and insist he give the same. There would be no safety net, no place to hide. And if she were to leave him, he would never be the same.

The idea of being with her, of having to put so much on the line, was too much. He pushed it away and reminded himself he had to stay in control. That was how he'd survived all these years, how he'd taken care of everyone around him. To give that up was to risk it all.

Something he would never do.

HEIDI PUT CURED AND WRAPPED bars of soap into the boxes in front of her. She was taking her first shipments for China to the post office that afternoon. They would be put on a cargo ship heading east, and in a few months she would know if she'd managed to break into the growing Asian market.

This was a big step for her business, and one that

should make her happy. The problem was, lately she couldn't seem to feel anything but sad. The carnival had moved on to their next stop, leaving the space around the house and barn looking empty. She hadn't seen Rafe for days and hated how much she missed him. She was too embarrassed to go into town and visit with her friends, although she'd gotten several phone messages of support.

The truth was right now her life sucked, and she only had herself to blame.

"Are you all right?" May asked, walking into the mudroom.

"Tired," Heidi admitted, putting down the soap and facing her friend. "It's been a rough couple of days. How about you?"

"I'm working some things through."

Heidi shoved her hands into her jeans, then pulled them out again. She and May had been friendly enough, but they'd continued to dance around the most important topic of all. No offense to Priscilla, but they were ignoring the elephant in the room.

"I'm sorry for what I did," Heidi told her. "And relieved to have been caught. I'm not the type to be very good at a life of crime."

May smiled. "I'm happy to hear that. As for apologizing, you have, and I understand why you did what you did. Rafe didn't leave you much choice."

"He and I have a complicated relationship." No way she was going to admit they'd slept together. May might be lovely and charming, but she was also Rafe's mother. "I didn't know how to talk to him, but I could have come to you. I should have."

"I wish you had," May admitted. "We could have worked something out. A compromise. I never wanted to hurt you or Glen."

Heidi sighed. She was about to say maybe they could figure something out now, when a car pulled up to the house. She recognized it as belonging to the Fool's Gold police department.

"What on earth?" May said, heading for the back door.

Heidi followed, and they found Police Chief Barns walking toward them.

"Mrs. Stryker," Chief Barns said with a nod. "Heidi."

"Hi." Heidi's stomach tightened. Rita would tell her she was experiencing a premonition. But it wasn't that the police chief was going to inform her she'd won the lottery.

"Heidi Simpson, you are ordered to appear before Judge Loomis in the morning." Alice handed her an envelope. Her stern expression turned sympathetic. "Just so you know, she's mad. Don't be late."

Heidi took the envelope and swallowed. "She knows about the cave paintings?"

"She knows everything."

LAST TIME HEIDI HAD SEEN the judge, she'd been in back with the observers, and Glen had been the one seated next to Trisha Wynn. Now Heidi was beside the lawyer and, despite the fact that she was sitting, she felt herself shaking all over.

"I'm not even speaking to you," Trisha said in a low voice, as they waited for Judge Loomis to appear. "Of all the half-brained ideas. Why didn't you come talk to me?"

"I don't know. I just reacted."

"You better hope that old saying about God helping fools is true."

"I thought the saying was more like God didn't suffer fools."

"You really want to correct my English right now?"

"Sorry."

"All rise."

Heidi stood, clutching the table to keep from collapsing. She was more scared than she'd ever been. Last time, she'd been able to focus all her worry on Glen and what would happen to him. Now she was the one the judge wanted to see. Worse, she was in the wrong. When her actions were combined with what her grandfather had done, Judge Loomis was going to assume they were a family of criminals and thieves.

The judge took her place, and they were instructed to sit. Heidi perched on the edge of her chair, her back straight, her hands clasped tightly together.

The courtroom was filled. She tried not to look at who had come to see her publicly humiliated. She knew May and Glen were there. Heidi's friends would show up to offer support. She was less sure about

Rafe. He might have already left for San Francisco. Or maybe he'd come to gloat.

The judge slipped on her glasses and studied the paperwork in front of her. Heidi told herself to keep breathing.

The judge looked up and removed her glasses. "Ms. Simpson."

Heidi rose.

"I am deeply disappointed in you, Ms. Simpson. I believe I made myself very clear when you and your grandfather were last before me. I had hoped you and the Stryker family would come to terms, but I see that is not the case."

Heidi's mouth began to tremble, and she did her best to keep from crying.

The judge paused. "Do you have an explanation?"

"No, Your Honor. I'm disappointed in myself, as well. When I discovered Mr. Stryker planned to use the ranch to build a development, I went a little crazy. I was angry and hurt and felt betrayed. All I've wanted all my life is a home. A place to belong. I thought I'd found that here, in Fool's Gold. I have my grandfather and my friends, my goats, the ranch."

She drew in a breath. "When Harvey got sick, and Glen took the money from Mrs. Stryker, I knew everything I loved was in danger of being lost. You gave me a second chance, and I was very appreciative. I've been saving money to repay Mrs. Stryker. I've expanded my business. May and I have been working well together. She's bought some animals and made improvements. When I found out about what Rafe had planned, I should have gone to her."

"But you didn't."

Heidi shook her head.

"While I can sympathize with your distress upon discovering what Mr. Stryker planned to do, there is a big difference between a plan and an action. You chose to act, Ms. Simpson. You deliberately deceived this town you claim to love. You defrauded the people you care about. Once again, our town is being mocked in the media, something those of us who have lived here all our lives do not appreciate."

A tear slipped down Heidi's cheek. She brushed it away.

"There is no excuse for your behavior. You have disrespected yourself, your community and this court."

"Your Honor?" May rose and waved her hand.

"Yes, Mrs. Stryker."

"Please don't be angry with Heidi. I'm not, and don't I have the most reason? She and I can work something out. We'll share the ranch. I don't want Heidi to lose her home."

More tears fell. Heidi couldn't believe May was defending her, offering to help her.

"I'm afraid it's not your decision," the judge said. "Ms. Simpson must suffer the consequences of her actions." She turned to Heidi. "The D.A. has discussed bringing charges, but at this time, she would prefer not to. So you will not be going to jail."

Heidi's knees nearly gave way. She hadn't considered jail an option.

"However, with the exception of the caves where you age your cheese, Ms. Simpson, and one acre surrounding the caves, I'm awarding the Castle Ranch to Mrs. Stryker."

Judge Loomis banged her gavel. "This court is adjourned."

CHAPTER NINETEEN

HEIDI SAT IN THE BOOTH at Jo's Bar, her hands wrapped around her diet soda. Charlie and Annabelle were with her, making sympathetic noises. Actually, that was mostly Annabelle. Charlie was more into action and thought they should go find Rafe and punish him. She was a little vague on the details of the punishment.

"It's not his fault," Heidi said firmly, determined to not complain. She'd made a choice, and now, as the judge had pointed out, she would deal with the consequences.

The sound of the banging gavel still echoed in her head. She'd heard the news and run. Run from Glen, run from May, who called after her to wait. Run from them all, because she couldn't face them or what she'd done.

"Rafe didn't do anything," she continued. "He had some ideas, made plans, but he didn't act."

"Only because he didn't have time," Charlie grumbled. "I could take him."

Heidi was less sure of that. Charlie might be strong, but Rafe's muscles were honed through hard, physical labor. And he was a guy—which meant he started with an excess of upper body strength.

Annabelle's delicate features were sharp with anguish. "It's my fault. I encouraged you to fake the find. I helped with the cave paintings. If I hadn't gotten in the way, you would have talked to Rafe, and none of this would have happened."

"Even I know it wasn't all because of you," Charlie muttered.

"She's right," Heidi said. "I don't blame anyone but myself. I didn't like what I was doing, but I did it, anyway. I asked you to put the word out because I was hurt. Rafe had gone on a date without telling me."

Both her friends stared at her.

"What does that..." Annabelle caught her breath. "You were sleeping with him."

Charlie's blue eyes widened. "No way."

"Way," Heidi told them. "I couldn't help myself."

"He is hunky," Annabelle said with a sigh. "I miss hunky. Honest to God, I can't remember the last time I slept with a hunky guy. Or a not-so-hunky one. Sex is a distant memory. I think it was a Tuesday."

Charlie leaned toward her. "Not about you."

Annabelle blinked. "Oh, right. Sorry." She put her hand on top of Heidi's. "Putting the pieces together, you didn't just lose your home, you lost the man you love."

Charlie straightened. "You love him? When did that happen? Why didn't I know this?"

Heidi started to say she didn't, but there had already been too many lies. "I'm not sure when it started, but yes, I love him. I've been so scared to trust myself and my heart. I worried about getting lost, about not being strong enough." She drew in a breath. "I lost everything this morning. My home, my plans for the future, my pride. I've learned a lesson about who I am, and here's what I know. I'm strong and I'll survive this. I have my goats and my business."

Ironically, her business was in better shape than ever, thanks to Rafe. She had product going overseas; she'd started selling in specialty stores in L.A. and San Francisco.

"It'll take me a few years to save the money for a down payment, but I'll buy other land eventually."

"So you're not leaving?" Annabelle asked anxiously.

"No. I belong here."

Fool's Gold was where she wanted to be. This town had become her home.

"What about him?" Charlie asked.

Heidi assumed her friend meant Rafe. "I don't know. He's leaving, if he's not already gone."

"He was in court this morning. He didn't look happy."

"I can't imagine why not. He's getting everything he wanted." Heidi fought against hopelessness. "May will be upset. She's not the type who revels in winning, but Rafe doesn't believe in taking prisoners. He'll get over any guilt he might feel."

Along with any other emotions, she thought sadly. Because she honestly didn't know what their relationship had been to him. What he wanted, she couldn't be. And even if she could, she wouldn't do that to herself, wouldn't try to change to fit some preconceived mold of the perfect wife and mother.

Jo walked over and slapped a piece of paper on the table. "I'm not sure why everyone thinks I like taking messages." She slid the paper toward Heidi. "Take it."

Heidi looked at the sheet. There were notes about different rental houses. The number of bedrooms, the locations, the cost per month. Beside each listing were notes.

Tell Heidi no deposit required. She's family.

There are two master suites. Perfect for Heidi and her grandfather.

Big yard. Pets okay, and I wouldn't mind if she used the goats to mow the lawn.

Heidi looked at Jo. "I don't understand."

"Word spread. Everyone knows what happened in court this morning. You need a place to stay, and we take care of our own." Jo shrugged. "It's pretty simple."

Heidi opened her mouth, then closed it. Whatever shame lingered in her body was pushed out by gratitude.

Jo tapped the list. "The house with the big yard is great. Updated kitchen on a quiet street. It's the closest to the ranch. Oh, and these just came."

She put three large, disklike campaign buttons on the table, then walked away.

Annabelle and Charlie each reached for a button. Heidi picked up the third one and stared. In big block letters it read: Team Heidi.

For the second time in as many minutes, she felt confused. "What is this?"

Charlie was already pinning hers on. "We're taking sides. Team Heidi, Team Rafe. My guess is no one is going to be stupid enough to wear a Team Rafe button."

Annabelle held hers up to the front of her dress, moving it from her right side to her left. "Where do people look first?" she asked.

"If you want women to see it, put it on the left. If you want guys to see it, put it on your boobs."

"Very funny." Annabelle secured it to the left side and patted the button. "I like it."

Heidi blinked as the ramifications of the pin crashed into her. Someone had taken the time and trouble to make sure she knew she was loved. Maybe only a few people would wear the buttons, but seeing even one would be amazing.

"I don't deserve you guys," she whispered, pinning the button to the left side of her T-shirt.

"That's true," Charlie said cheerfully. "But you're stuck with us. We're like weeds in the lawn. You might think you've gotten rid of us, but we just bounce right back."

HEIDI SAT IN HER TRUCK, staring at the small house. It was pretty, with a new roof and fresh paint. Flowers grew alongside the walkway, and the bushes were neatly trimmed. It was a charming home. She would guess there was plenty of hot water and that all the appliances were in working condition. As far as rentals went, it was perfect.

And nothing she wanted.

She wanted to be back on the ranch, hoping she could finish washing her hair before the water went cold. She wanted to fight with the washer, wince at the faded and slightly peeling paint, and listen to the porch creak when she walked on it. She wanted to see May's menagerie of old, unwanted animals, ride Shane's horses and watch the sun set over the gentle hump of Priscilla's silhouette.

Despite her promises to be strong, she felt like a failure. Consequences sucked. She supposed the sooner she accepted that, the better.

She glanced at her watch. She was a few minutes early for her appointment to see the house. Maybe she would walk around and look at the backyard while she was waiting.

As she climbed out, a bigger, older truck pulled up

behind hers. She watched her grandfather park and then walk toward her.

"What are you doing here?" she asked.

Glen reached her and wrapped his arms around her. "I got a call that you were here, and I came to look at the house."

"Who called?"

"One of your friends."

She hugged him back, inhaling the familiar scent of him, and the memories that came with the man who had been her only family nearly her entire life.

"But you're not moving in with me," she said. "You're staying with May." She stepped back. "I've seen you two together, Glen. You've known a lot of women, more than I want to ever imagine."

He smiled. "I always promised, no details."

"I appreciate that. But I have to admit, you've got something special with May. You really care about her."

"Yes, but you're my granddaughter. I'm not going to stay with her when you've lost everything and it's all because of me."

She hugged him again, holding on tight. "It wasn't you. It was me. I think if I hadn't screwed up, the judge would have given me a better deal. Or I could have worked something out with May. You were helping Harvey. I would rather have things work out the way they did, with him alive, than the alternative."

He kissed her forehead. "You're a good girl. I love you, Heidi. I'm not leaving you."

She felt his caring, his support, and it gave her strength. She stepped back and smiled. "Maybe it's time for me to be on my own. I'm twenty-eight. We should probably risk it."

He touched her cheek. "You've been taking care of me for years. You just think I haven't noticed. This isn't about you being on your own—it's about you being alone."

"Maybe it's time for that, too." She took his hand in hers. "Glen, don't lose May because of me. I don't want that. She's a wonderful woman. It's taken you decades to fall in love. Why would you walk away from that?"

"There was your grandmother," he began.

"Oh, please. You got her pregnant and had to marry her. It wasn't a love match. You never admitted it, but I always knew the truth. You got lucky and she left you. Otherwise, you would have been miserable."

He smiled. "You've always been a smart girl."

"So listen to me. I'm renting this house on my own. You're going back to May. I insist. Even if you don't, I'm not letting you move in here. So you'll have to find your own place."

"You're a tough negotiator."

"Tell me about it."

RAFE WANDERED THROUGH Fool's Gold. It was the weekend and there was yet another festival going on. This one didn't include a carnival, although there were plenty of booths selling things. He saw jewelry, wind chimes and organic honey. He didn't get the latter. Wasn't honey made by bees? Weren't bees inherently organic?

He kept moving, taking in the sights and sounds. The smells of barbecue and burgers. He was surrounded by crowds and he'd never felt more alone.

For days now, he'd been dodging calls from Dante. His friend wanted to know when he would be back in the office. A reasonable question, considering Rafe had promised to be there nearly a week ago. But for reasons he couldn't explain, he hadn't been able to take the final step of packing and driving away.

He knew he was waiting for something, but couldn't figure out what. His mother wasn't speaking to him, and he hadn't seen Heidi in days. The closest he'd come to contact with her was the damned Team Heidi buttons he saw dozens of women wearing. So far he'd seen only one Team Rafe button. It had been on a beer-bellied guy, who'd given him a thumbs-up and said to keep up the good work. As if Rafe had something to be proud of.

He slipped into Morgan's Books and looked at the thrillers on the front table. There were also a few mysteries, including one by Liz Sutton, with a big Local Author sticker on the front.

"She's very good," Mayor Marsha said, coming up to Rafe. "Liz has a series set in San Francisco. You'd enjoy that. In her first few books, one of the victims always looked like your friend Ethan."

"Why Ethan?"

"They had a troubled past. Ethan can give you the details. It all worked out."

"Isn't Ethan now married to Liz?"

The older woman smiled. "As I said, it worked itself out. Love has a way of doing that."

A woman in her thirties wearing a Team Heidi button greeted the mayor, glared at Rafe and left the store.

Mayor Marsha motioned to a seating area off to the side in the store.

"I would imagine you're getting a lot of that sort of thing these days," she said, when he'd seated himself on a plush sofa and she'd taken the chair opposite. "People assuming the worst about you."

"I didn't have anything to do with the judge's decision. I didn't want Heidi to lose her house."

"Were you going to build those houses for the casino?"

He shrugged. "Probably. If my mother had agreed. The land is in both our names, but it's her property. Everyone is pissed because they think I stole Heidi's home. I didn't, and regardless of their opinion of me, the town is going to need extra housing."

"Yes, and sooner than we're willing to admit." Her blue gaze was steady. "I think your heart was in the right place, but your actions were a little ahead of where they should have been."

"Is that why you're not wearing a Team Heidi button?"

"I've found it's better for everyone if I don't take sides." She studied him. "I've learned not to interfere.

It was a hard-won lesson, as the most important ones are." She paused. "My daughter died a few years ago."

"I'm sorry," he said automatically, not sure why she was telling him.

"The tragedy is so much more than her death at a relatively young age. Because that's not when I lost her. I lost her years before, when she was a teenager. I demanded too much, expected more than was reasonable. I might be a relatively benign mayor, but I was a difficult mother. I held on too tight. Maybe I was afraid, maybe I thought that's what love was. Rather than fight me, she ran away. She was still a teenager."

"Did you ever reconcile?"

"No. I finally found her, but she wanted nothing to do with me. She had a daughter, my only grandchild, who I didn't meet for years. I learned a harsh lesson."

"If you love something, set it free?"

She smiled. "In part. But I also learned that who we love and who loves us truly defines us as people. Who do you love, Rafe?"

The question surprised him and caused him to shift on the too-soft sofa. "My family."

"Including the brother and sister you never speak to?"

"How do you know about them?"

"I have a network that puts the CIA to shame. People talk, I listen. It's not too late for you. With them, or with..." She paused. "This can all be fixed. You can belong here again."

"This isn't my home."

"Of course it is. Home is where there's love. We would like you to be part of the community that is Fool's Gold." She smiled. "If you'll have us. As for those homes that need to be built, I have some land I think you'd be interested in."

"A bribe?"

"A mutually beneficial business deal. You should respect that."

"I'll call your office and set up an appointment." He waited. "Aren't you going to ask me about Heidi?"

"No. You're not ready. When you are, I won't have to ask."

He chuckled. "You like being cryptic."

"At my age, I need to find my simple pleasures wherever I can."

RAFE LOADED UP HIS CAR. He should have left town days ago, but until a few minutes ago, he hadn't known where to go. Now that he had an address, he was ready. Dante had already sent over the paperwork releasing Rafe from title on the ranch.

He got into his Mercedes, but before he could start the engine, a very large fire truck pulled in behind him, effectively blocking him from backing out. A tall woman climbed down and slowly walked toward his car.

Rafe recognized Heidi's friend Charlie and knew immediately she'd come to remind him of his promise. That he wouldn't hurt her friend.

He got out of his car and prepared for her to take him on.

Charlie was only a couple of inches shorter than him. She was large boned. There was plenty of muscle and lots of attitude. He had no idea how to win a fight when she had all the advantages. After all, it didn't matter if she took a punch. No way he could ever lay a hand on a girl.

"Leaving?" she asked, the truck's engine still rumbling.

He nodded.

"You haven't said goodbye."

"Heidi doesn't want to see me."

"About the only time she's shown any sense where you're concerned," Charlie told him, then crossed her arms over her chest. "Why isn't she good enough for you? What do you need that she doesn't have?"

"Nothing," he said honestly. "Nothing at all."

"Don't make me hurt you, jerkwad," Charlie growled.

"I'm not playing. I'm telling you the truth. This isn't about Heidi—it's about me. There's something I have to do, and then I'll come back."

Charlie's lip curled. "And I should believe you, why?"

"You shouldn't. Take Heidi's side. If I'm wrong, then hunt me down and do your worst."

"That's a very interesting invitation. Why should I wait?"

"Because I might be telling the truth."

She muttered something under her breath. "Why couldn't all women be lesbians? Life would be a whole lot easier. At least, mine would."

"Less fun for us guys that way."

"You're not my main concern."

He stepped toward her, put his hands on her shoulders and kissed her cheek. "Trust me."

"You're trying to piss me off, aren't you?" she asked, pulling away.

For a second Rafe would have sworn Charlie flinched when he kissed her, but then he told himself he was imagining the reaction.

She glared at him, then returned to the fire truck. After moving it back far enough for him to get out, she waited, as if prepared to follow him, to make sure he made good on his word.

Rafe was fine with that. He no longer had anything to hide.

CHAPTER TWENTY

WHEN PEOPLE THOUGHT about Los Angeles, they generally pictured theme parks, the beach or Beverly Hills. There were a lot of other parts to the sprawling city, many of them comfortably middle class. Some neighborhoods were remembered more for what they had been, years ago. Slowly, they lost their way, declining year by year, until the buildings were more than a little ragged around the edges.

Rafe pulled up in front of the two-story apartment building and studied the parched lawn, the leaning palm trees by the sidewalk. A couple of windows had aluminum foil as a stand-in for curtains, and there was a car up on blocks in the carport. He looked at the address on his cell phone, then back at the building and knew he'd found the right place.

It wasn't supposed to be like this, he thought grimly. He should have done a better job of protecting those he was responsible for. He wondered if Evangeline would agree.

He got out of his car, then locked it. The Mercedes stood out on the quiet street, a flashy and unwelcome reminder of his wealth. He crossed the lawn, climbed the steps to the second floor and knocked on the door of apartment 220.

A busty blonde opened the door and smiled up at him.

"Hi. You must be lost, because we don't get guys like you in the neighborhood. Not that I'm complaining."

She wore tiny shorts and a cropped T-shirt, makeup for five and her toenails were covered with orange polish that glittered.

"I'm here to see Evangeline."

The blonde gave him an exaggerated pout. "Can I get you to take me out instead? I'm much more fun."

"No, thanks."

The blonde motioned for him to step inside, then turned toward a closed bedroom door.

"Evie, there's some guy here to see you. If you don't want him, can I have him?" She gave Rafe a sassy eyebrow wiggle as she posed the question.

The bedroom door opened. "A guy. I'm not expecting—"

Rafe hadn't seen his sister in nearly seven years. She was tall and slender, with a dancer's build. Unlike May's other children, she had green eyes and honey-blond hair. But he could see May in the shape of her face.

Her expression was more resigned than excited—not a surprise, considering their last conversation. But it hadn't been a conversation, he remembered. He'd yelled, and she hadn't said a word. Then she'd walked out, and he hadn't seen her again until now.

"What are you doing here?" she asked.

"You know him?"

"He's my big brother."

The blonde started toward him.

Rafe shook his head. "Still not interested."

"Why not?"

"I'm with somebody." At least he hoped to be. Very soon. But first he had some fences to mend.

"Can I buy you a cup of coffee?" he asked Evangeline.

He suspected she wanted to say no, but also didn't want to risk his talking in front of her roommate. She nodded once and disappeared into the bedroom. Seconds later, she reappeared, a small handbag with a long strap slung over her body. Unlike the blonde, she wore jeans, and her T-shirt actually covered her waist. She'd stepped into loafers.

"I won't be long," she said, as she followed him to the door.

They didn't speak as they got in the car. He'd already located a Starbucks nearby and drove directly there. They went into the shop, ordered, picked up their drinks and a couple of scones, then settled in a table in the corner.

Rafe studied his sister, taking in the defined lines of her face. Evangeline had always been thin. It was her natural build, and her dancing had only emphasized the leanness of her body. But now she was almost gaunt, and there was something in her eyes. Wariness? Or desperation?

"Are you getting enough to eat?" he asked, before he could stop himself.

She looked at him, her eyebrows rising. "Really? That's where you want to start this conversation?"

"Sorry. No." He sipped his coffee. "It's good to see you."

She leaned back in her chair. "Why are you here?"

"I've been thinking about you and wanted to know how you were doing."

"You could have called."

"I wanted to see you."

"Why? We don't stay in touch."

He wanted to point out that she'd been the one to walk away, to disappear. He'd gone after her.… Okay, technically, he'd sent an assistant to talk to her. Evangeline had said to stay the hell out of her life. That was a direct quote. So he had. He'd told himself she would come around when she was ready. That she knew how to find him. Or their mother or Shane or Clay.

What he'd chosen to ignore was that she'd been all of eighteen. She'd walked away from Juilliard with no skills, no experience in the world, and he'd let her. Because it was easier than dealing with her directly. He'd dumped a few thousand dollars into a checking account and, through the assistant, had told her to come see him when she wanted more. She'd taken the money and closed the account the next day.

"How are you?" he asked.

"Fine."

"Are you dancing?"

She glared at him. "Why are you here? What do you want?"

"To talk. To reconnect. We're family."

"No, we're related. A family is a collection of people who care about each other. Who look out for each other. I have a mother who has ignored me from the time I was born, and an oldest brother who's spent my life disapproving of every decision I've ever made. I guess Shane and Clay are my family."

She stood. "Thanks for stopping by."

"Wait," he said, coming to his feet. "Please."

She stared at him. "Please? Can you say that word without turning to dust? I wouldn't have thought it was possible."

He felt her anger and understood it, but what bothered him more was the sadness lurking underneath. The profound sense that she was completely alone in the world.

"I'm sorry," he said. "Please stay for a few more minutes."

She reluctantly sank back into the chair. He settled across from her.

"I'm sorry," he began slowly. "I was wrong to walk away from you. I was wrong not to listen or try to understand. You were a kid, and I turned my back on you."

"So did Mom."

He nodded. "So did Mom."

He'd always thought about his sister in terms of the trouble she caused, and how her dancing consumed her. He'd never considered what it must have been like from her point of view. Growing up an obvious afterthought, the result of a single night spent with a stranger. He and his brothers had been born to a couple very much in love. They'd been the family Evangeline had talked about. But she was a constant reminder of the pain they'd felt after their father had died. Odd man out.

May had been uncomfortable with Evangeline from the beginning. The woman who loved her children unrepentantly had kept her only daughter at a distance. Rafe had been too busy being the man of the house to worry about a little girl. It had fallen on Shane and Clay to parent her, and they'd only been kids themselves.

"It was your birthday a few weeks ago," he said. "I thought of you then."

"Did you? You thought of me?" Her eyes widened. "Oh, Rafe, that makes everything so much better. Knowing you took the trouble to think of me. I don't know how to thank you."

"Dammit, Evie."

She stood again. "Go to hell. I don't want you around, and I sure don't need you. Maybe I did once. But you weren't there. Not you or Mom. I had to figure it out on my own." She narrowed her gaze. "Whatever you want, you're too late. I'm not interested."

"I don't want anything."

"Then why are you here?"

"Because I was wrong before. Because I want us to be a family again."

"We were never a family."

"Then let's be one now."

She turned to leave.

He stood. "I need you."

She stopped, but didn't look at him.

He circled around the small table and stepped in front of her. "I need you," he repeated. "I was such a jerk. I never asked why you left school. I never asked what went so wrong. I never bothered to find out where you went or what you did. Hell, I didn't even teach you to ride a bike."

"Shane did," she whispered.

"I'm glad. Please. You're right. I do want something. I want to get to know you. Just give me your phone number and take mine. We'll talk every couple of weeks. I'll come back, and we'll go to dinner. We'll start slow."

"I don't trust you," she admitted.

"Fair enough. I wouldn't trust me, either."

She stared at him for a long time. Her gaze seemed to see inside of him, down to his soul. He hoped she would be generous in her assessment, because he doubted he would earn many points based on merit.

She turned back to the table and sat down. "I'll take your number. You can't have mine."

He chuckled. "Okay."

"You can't date Opal."

"Who's Opal?"

"My roommate."

He thought about the busty blonde and held up both hands as he sat across from his sister. "Not a problem. I have no interest in Opal."

"Also, no questions. I'll tell you what I want you to know. You don't get to dig around in my life or pass judgments."

"Forget it," he told her, picking up his latte. "I'll ask all the questions I want."

One corner of her mouth turned up, even as she was careful to look bored. "I won't answer them."

"Fine. You always were stubborn."

"You don't know enough about me to say what I was."

He ignored that. "So, Evangeline, what are you doing these days?"

"I'm a neurosurgeon. In my free time, I fly fighter jets and solve crimes."

"Ambitious. I like that. Is there a guy in your life?"

She rolled her eyes. "No. What about you, Rafe? Still married? Any little mini-tycoons running around?"

"I'm not married."

Her distancing facade fell as she leaned toward him. "What went wrong?"

He saw the moment she remembered she wasn't supposed to care. The slightly bored mask slipped back in place.

He took advantage of her interest and told her the

truth. "We got divorced years ago. But now there's this woman. She's making me crazy."

"I like her already."

"You would like her. She raises goats and makes cheese, and when she smiles, it's like the sun has come out."

His sister stared at him. "You're in serious trouble."

"I'm starting to figure that out."

HEIDI RETURNED TO THE MUDROOM with the fresh milk to find May waiting for her. Heidi had done her best to avoid the other woman for days, slinking in and out of the ranch, dumping some of the milk so she didn't have to face May. But orders were piling up and she had cheese to make, so she'd braved the house, only to come face-to-face with Rafe's mother.

"Good morning," she said, setting the milk on the long table.

May put her hands on her hips. "You'll finish there and come into the kitchen. You're not leaving this ranch without talking to me. Is that clear?"

Glen had been a loving grandparent. He'd preferred to leave the discipline to others. Even so, Heidi recognized the steely tone, the promise that she didn't want to know the consequences of disobeying.

"Yes, ma'am," she murmured before she could stop herself.

"Good."

May disappeared back into the kitchen.

Heidi poured the milk into bottles and stuck them

in the refrigerator, then washed out her buckets and the funnel. Sanitizing could wait, she told herself. Better to get the conversation over with.

She already had a plan. Although she'd been unable to bring herself to sign the lease on the rental, she vowed she would take care of that as soon as she was done here. The kitchen was big enough for her to work in, and the second bedroom would be a perfect office and shipping area.

The rental payments were so much less than the mortgage on the ranch that she would be able to save a fair amount each month. In two, maybe three years, depending on how her business went, she could buy another piece of land. Start over.

She paused at the door to the kitchen. Rafe was gone. She didn't have to brace herself to see him. And although it would be difficult to face May, once that was done, she could move on. Start healing. Rita had been right—she was strong. Unlike Melinda, taking her life wasn't anything she would consider. However much it hurt to be in love with Rafe and know that he didn't want to love her back, she got through the day. In time, she would heal.

She stepped into the familiar kitchen.

"I'm done," she said.

"Good." May motioned for her to join her at the table. There were several stacks of papers there.

Heidi supposed she had things to sign. The judge's decision had meant May would now be responsible for the mortgage and everything else that went along with the ranch.

She took a seat. "I want to say I'm sorry for what I did. Faking the paintings and artifacts. I should have come to talk to you, May."

The older woman sighed. "I'm sorry, too. I was so busy falling in love with your grandfather that I didn't stop to think about anyone else. Here you were, having your own crisis right under my nose. I feel horrible about that."

"Falling in love takes a lot out of a person."

May's dark eyes were knowing. "You've been dealing with that yourself, haven't you?"

Heidi really didn't want to talk about that, but couldn't figure out a good way to distract May. Pointing out the window and saying, "Oh, look. An elephant," probably wouldn't work.

That left her in the less-than-mature place of ignoring the obvious.

"I told Glen that he would be an idiot to lose you over this," Heidi said. "I hope you're going to tell me he listened."

May smiled, then held out her left hand. A small diamond sparkled from a simple band. "He proposed and I said yes. I'm thrilled."

Heidi was stunned. "Congratulations. I'm happy for you." Surprised, but still happy. "I guess Glen's been waiting for you for a long time."

"That's what he said. Oh, Heidi, I'm so happy. I loved my first husband, and when I lost him, I vowed

I would never love that way again. For years, I didn't. What a fool I was. Love is a treasure, a gift. And I'm talking like a greeting card because I'm incredibly happy."

Heidi squeezed her hand. "I'm happy for you, too. When's the big day?"

"We're going to elope. Probably just drive up to Lake Tahoe and get married there. I don't want anything fancy." She patted the stacks of paper. "But that's not why I wanted to talk to you. We need to discuss the ranch."

"There's not much to discuss."

"That's where you're wrong. There's plenty." May handed Heidi a very long, densely written document. "We'll need to go to a notary later, to get all this finalized."

"What is it?"

May smiled. "As you know, Rafe has cosigned every document for the past couple of years. Which means he owns half this ranch." She tapped the form she'd handed Heidi. "This gives his share to you."

Heidi was glad she was sitting, because she felt a distinct shift in her equilibrium. "I don't understand."

"He wants you to have his half of the ranch, and so do I." Happy tears filled May's eyes. "Wait until you see."

The other woman reached for more papers and spread them across the table. "There's so much to be done." She smoothed out a drawing of the ranch, including boundaries and the roads that surrounded the land.

"The vacation rentals will go here."

Heidi leaned forward and saw the small, neat drawings.

"You're still doing that?" she asked.

May nodded. "Winter homes for the carnival workers and rental housing for summer. I've worked up some preliminary numbers, and the income stream is impressive. Rafe will front the building cost of the houses as a loan to us, and we'll pay him back with the proceeds." She beamed. "It helps to have an in with a rich man."

"Apparently," Heidi murmured.

May laughed, then returned her attention to the map. "Here's where my animals will go. Here's where Shane is buying adjoining land for his horses. Glen and I will build a small house here, because I think we're going to be one of those annoying, cheerful couples, and who needs to see that first thing in the morning?"

She looked at Heidi. "Which means this house is yours, my dear. Along with the rest of the ranch. Plenty of room for your goats. I do hope you'll let me use the barn. I've heard the cold can be challenging for zebras. Obviously, we'll have to build a special enclosure for sweet Priscilla."

Heidi sat in her chair, too hopeful to even draw breath. To have what had been hers returned was unbelievable, but to have it come from Rafe? She desperately wanted to think it was because he cared, but she couldn't be sure.

"Glen and I are planning a series of cruises starting in the fall," May continued. "Through Europe, mostly. Did you know your grandfather is the most divine dancer? I can't wait to get him out on the dance floor. We'll cha-cha the night away. We'll miss most of the construction on our new place, but I'm hoping that, until it's done, you'll let us stay here when we're in town."

"Ah, sure." Her head spun, and she couldn't read the words on the contract she held. Everything blurred. "May, why are you doing this? You could have had it all."

"I never wanted it all, Heidi. I wanted a home. Coming back here has been wonderful. I've found so much more than I had ever hoped. As for giving you his half of the ranch, that was Rafe's idea."

Rafe, who had never been what he seemed, she realized. Underneath that exterior of cool confidence, lay a warm and giving heart.

"Is he back in San Francisco?" she asked.

"Yes. I'm not sure when he plans to return, though." May's tone was concerned, as if she were worried about Heidi being upset by the news.

"Can you tell me where his office is?" she asked.

"Yes. Of course. You're going to see him?"

Heidi nodded.

Like May, she'd been given her heart's desire. Fear

and the need to protect herself had nearly robbed her of the perfect ending. But everything was clear now.

She and Rafe were so much alike. They both took care of the people around them. They urged others to do better, to achieve. But under all the words was fear. Fear of losing. Fear of being rejected. Fear of being hurt.

She'd lost her parents when she was a toddler, and although Glen had loved her, she'd felt a gaping emptiness. She'd been afraid to love and lose again. Not consciously, but underneath. Then Melinda had taken her own life, cementing Heidi's belief that loving meant losing in the most destructive way.

Rafe, too, had seen the consequences of love and loss. His father hadn't just died—his passing had ripped away Rafe's childhood. He'd grown up too quickly, and parts of him had never healed.

When his first marriage had failed, he'd had his fears confirmed. The dissolution was worse, because he didn't feel devastated. Not realizing he'd deliberately avoided love, he took the absence of pain as proof love didn't exist.

They probably all needed years of therapy. Maybe they could get a group rate somewhere. But until then, they had each other. Because she knew what had gone wrong. Neither of them had been willing to risk it all. Neither of them had put their hearts on the line, exposing their souls. Neither had taken the chance.

"I'm going right now," Heidi said. "Just as soon as I find one thing I'll need to take with me."

HEIDI DIDN'T LIKE CITY DRIVING in the best of times, and making her way through the downtown part of San Francisco turned into a disaster. She got lost three times before finally spotting the building that housed Rafe's office. She parked in an underground lot that had what felt like six hundred levels. She expected to have to pick her way over molten rivers from the earth's core when she finally climbed out of her truck.

She consoled herself with the hope that she would never have to come here again—at least not by herself. If things went well, then next time Rafe would be with her. If they went badly, she was going to let Athena loose in his lobby.

Comforted by her plan, she took the elevator up a dizzying forty-something floors and was deposited in an elegant lobby with stunning views of the bay.

The receptionist glanced at the pin on her blazer. Finding a Team Rafe button had been a challenge, but May had finally located one of only a half dozen made, and Heidi had collected it before leaving town.

"I'm here to see Rafe Stryker," Heidi told the well-dressed woman at the reception desk.

"Do you have an appointment?"

"No."

"Mr. Stryker requires all visitors to have an appointment."

"Why am I not surprised?" she muttered. "Please tell him Heidi Simpson would like to see him."

A stern-looking woman in a black suit paused by the reception desk. She turned to Heidi.

"You are Ms. Simpson of Fool's Gold?" she asked.

Heidi felt as if she'd been called before the principal for mooning the school board. "Um, yes?"

The gray-haired woman actually flashed a smile. "I'll take care of this, Charlotte."

"Of course, Ms. Jennings."

"Follow me, please," Ms. Jennings said.

Heidi fell into step behind her.

Minutes later she was walking past a big desk guarding double doors. Ms. Jennings opened the one to the right.

"He's in a meeting, but I'm sure he won't mind the interruption." There was another unexpected smile. "Well done, Ms. Simpson. Well done."

Heidi had no idea what she was talking about, but nodded, anyway, and stepped inside. Rafe sat on a sofa next to a stunning blonde. They were very close together, bent over some papers. Heidi was pretty sure she saw the blonde's hand edging toward Rafe's thigh.

"I don't think so," she snapped, heading toward the couple.

They both looked up. Rafe jumped to his feet.

"Heidi? What are you doing here?"

"I want to talk to you, but first, I need to take care of some business." She stalked over to the blonde, put her hands on her hips and raised her chin. "No. You can't have him. I don't care what Nina told you and how compatible you think you are. The answer is no. He's mine. He may not realize it just yet, but he will. He's the kind of guy who accepts the fact that his mother bought an elephant. He takes care of my goats when I have the flu and… and I love him."

The woman stared at her for several seconds. "I'm the decorator."

Heidi blinked. "What?"

The blonde smiled. "It's okay. I can see you two have some things you need to work out. I'll be in touch with you later, Rafe." She collected sketches and fabric samples, slipped them into her briefcase, then stood. "I like your button," she said, then left.

Heidi felt heat on her cheeks. If they were closer to being on actual ground, she would wish for it to open up and swallow her whole. Or half. Half a swallowing would be a distraction.

Rafe leaned against his desk. "You know how to make an entrance."

"I thought…" She swallowed. "You probably know what I thought."

"I told you I was done with Nina."

"You told me a lot of things."

"You should listen better."

"You should…" She sighed. "I can't think of anything good to say."

He moved toward her. "You were doing fine a few minutes ago." He touched the button on her shirt. "You mean that?"

Here it was, the moment she'd been anticipating the whole drive over. She'd rehearsed speeches in her head, not able to get the words right. Which meant she was probably going to get this all wrong, but she had to try.

"I'm sorry about the cave paintings, and the artifacts."

"I'm sorry I even thought about putting up those houses. It was a mistake. The town needs them, but not on the ranch."

She drew in a breath. This was going better than she'd hoped. "I'm sorry I didn't talk to you. That I just acted. I should have trusted you."

"I should have trusted you, too." He stroked the side of her face, then bent down and kissed her. "We're both pretty bad at this, huh?"

"At what?" she whispered.

"Being in love. You did say you loved me."

"I meant it."

His dark gaze locked with hers. "I love you, too, goat girl. That decorator you attacked? She's helping design the vacation homes we're building. Later, she's going to handle the remodel of the building I bought in Fool's Gold."

She was still caught up in the magical phrase "I love you, too," and couldn't make sense of the rest of it.

"What are you doing in Fool's Gold?"

"Moving my company. Dante swears he's not leaving the Giants, but I think he can be convinced."

Her mind seemed to shut off. She heard the words, but they had no meaning.

Rafe chuckled, then kissed her again. "If we're going to be together, it'll help if we're in the same city, don't you think?"

She nodded.

"You were planning to marry me, weren't you?" he asked.

She nodded again.

She wasn't sure if she reached for him or he reached for her. Either way she ended up in his arms, which was just where she wanted to be.

"I'm never letting go of you," he promised. "I've let go of too many of the people I love. It's taken me a while, but I've learned my lesson."

She wasn't sure exactly what he was talking about, but they would have plenty of time for him to explain.

"You know, your mom and Glen are getting married."

"Yeah. He asked my permission to propose. That was a comfortable conversation."

She laughed, still hanging on, so safe and happy in his arms.

"She really has bought some zebras," Heidi told him. "I saw their stalls on the plans."

"You know anything about zebras?"

"No."

"Then we'll figure out that together, too." His

mouth brushed against the top of her head. "Ready to go home?"

"As long as I'm with you."

"You're never getting rid of me, goat girl."

"That's a promise I can live with."

* * * * *

A new tale of love under the vast Montana sky from #1 *New York Times* bestselling author

LINDA LAEL MILLER

The illegitimate son of a wealthy rancher, Sheriff Slade Barlow's father never acknowledged him. But now, Slade has inherited half of his father's prosperous ranch in Parable, Montana. That doesn't sit well with his half brother, Hutch, and it stuns his onetime crush—the beautiful Joslyn Kirk.

Scan the code with your smartphone or visit
http://www.LindaLaelMiller.com
to view the behind-the-scenes video!

PHLLM643QR